WHERE THE DISTANCE ENDS

WHERE THE DISTANCE ENDS

BOOK ONE

THE LIVES WE CHOOSE

LIZ BROWN

TREASURE STONE PRESS

🤍 *In memory of those I have lost,*
but will forever have a place in my heart. 🤍

Car, vois-tu, chaque jour je t'aime davantage, Adjourn 'hui plus qu'hier et bien moins que demain.

— ROSEMONDE GÉRARD

CHAPTER 1

Melanie

The kettle clicked off, and Melanie Brooks poured the water over a single teabag, watching the color bloom in the cup. The kitchen was quiet except for the tick of the clock above the sink, a sound she sometimes found too loud in the evenings. The television murmured faintly from the living room, left on more for company than interest.

She opened her laptop, the monitor lighting up her face. Another evening, another scroll through the headlines she'd already read twice. Somewhere between habit and hope, she clicked on the pen pal site link she'd bookmarked weeks ago.

For friendship and conversation across the miles.

She'd almost laughed when she first saw it as it sounded like something from another decade but using email instead of handwritten letters. But tonight, the idea felt strangely comforting.

The profile page blinked open. "Tell them a bit about yourself," the text box said. Melanie hesitated.

What was there to tell? She loved books and baked pies that were always slightly burned around the edges. She volunteered at the library part-time now that her daughter Emily's children were in school. She had a cat, Haiku, but she was into naps, not appearing unless it was dinner time or she wanted a treat. Maybe there was someone out there that needed a friend as much as she did. She smiled at the thought, half shy, half brave, and began to type.

Her profile was cautious:

Book lover. Baker of imperfect pies. East Coast of the US. Looking for friendly conversation.

She uploaded no photo, just a little image of a teacup clipart the site offered. It felt safe, impersonal. She doubted anyone would notice it.

Andrew

The rain against the windows of his flat had a rhythm Andrew Collins knew by heart. It had been raining most of the week. He sat at his desk with a cup of cooling tea and an unfinished crossword. He'd stopped midway through, distracted by the quiet. He'd once liked the quiet, prized it, even. But lately it felt heavier. Too much time alone meant too much time listening to his own thoughts. He'd been meaning to call his friend Nigel for days, but he knew how that would go: *Come down to the pub, man, stop brooding.*

He wasn't brooding. Not exactly. Just... still. His path had been different, though it left him somewhat solitary. He'd spent his career as a history teacher at a local secondary school in Yorkshire. He'd been good at it. His former students remembered his dry humor, his habit of carrying chalk on his jacket even after whiteboards had replaced blackboards. He retired with polite speeches and a gift card, and then... silence.

He'd never married. There had been a few near misses: a college sweetheart who wanted to move abroad, a colleague who married someone else while he hesitated. Over the years, he'd grown comfortable with solitude, filling his time with books, the occasional pub night, walks through town. His sister Margaret checked on him, fussed over his health, but most evenings were spent in his flat with the television or a stack of papers to read. He hadn't thought himself lonely, not really.

When the email from a book club newsletter mentioned a site for "international correspondence," he'd clicked it on impulse. He told himself it was curiosity as he liked words, after all, and letters had always seemed the purest form of them. He filled out the profile:

Retired teacher, Yorkshire. Fond of history and tea, reading, walking by the river, always curious about new places and would like to make a good friend.

He realized he was writing less for the faceless strangers who might read it, and more as if someone specific already could. Someone who might understand quietness. Someone who might even answer.

He sat back, reread what he'd written, and allowed himself the smallest of smiles before pressing *send*.

Andrew had joined the site with no grand intentions. Margaret had called his evenings "too quiet," and in a fit of annoyance he'd signed up just to prove her wrong, not that letter writing was at all noisy. Most profiles he skimmed over as they were full of quotes, emojis, and flashy photos.

But he stopped when he read something on Melanie's profile that made him smile: *"Baker of imperfect pies."*

He tapped out a message before he could overthink:

> We don't have pie quite the way you do in the States. Here we muddle along with puddings and custards. Still, I admire your honesty, most people would leave out the 'imperfect' part. Perhaps that makes yours more genuine. ~Andrew, England.

Melanie

When Melanie opened her inbox and saw a message from "Andrew, England," she almost deleted it unread. She wasn't sure she was ready to make small talk with strangers. But the word *puddings* caught her eye, and curiosity tugged her forward.

She read his brief message twice, then found herself chuckling aloud. *More genuine pies,* indeed. The sound startled her. She couldn't remember the last time she'd laughed at something from a stranger.

Her fingers hovered over the keyboard. Then she typed:

> Hello Andrew. You're right, imperfect pies are honest pies, and mine usually sag to one side or have slightly singed crusts. But they taste all right, and that's what matters, isn't it? You'll have to tell me more about these puddings of yours. Do they all involve custard? ~Melanie

She considered deleting the whole thing, but she pressed *send* and sat back, her hand shaking a little.

Andrew

The next morning, Andrew was surprised to see a new message waiting. He opened it quickly, and as he read, a grin spread across his face. She'd written back. She hadn't been put off by his clumsy attempt at humor.

He tapped out an answer almost at once, a little longer this time:

> Melanie, I must tell you about two of my favorites, treacle sponge and jam roly-poly. They're the sort of puddings that feel like childhood wrapped in steam and sugar, the kind my mum used to make on Sundays. Treacle sponge is golden and sticky and smells like warm syrup, and jam roly-poly is exactly what it sounds like, rolled and sweet. ~Andrew

> Andrew, I've never had either one of those, but the names themselves make them sound delicious. I saw in your profile that you live in York. I visited England once, many years ago, but only London. I've always wanted to see the north with all its winding streets and old stone walls. ~Melanie

Melanie, yes, York does have its share of winding streets, though they're usually crowded with tourists or pigeons. I hope I don't sound too forward, but the site seems clunky for longer messages. If you're comfortable, perhaps we might continue by email? Entirely up to you, of course.
~Andrew

Melanie

Melanie hesitated and stared at the screen for a long time. Giving her email address to a man she'd never met felt reckless. But she was enjoying their friendship so far. He hadn't pushed or demanded, only offered.

So, she typed back:

Andrew, your profile said you like books and rivers, also two of my favorite things. I volunteer part-time in a library, so I suppose you could say I live among stories, though the dust often outnumbers the readers at times. I'll send my email address in a separate message. If you spam me with pudding recipes, I'll know my trust was misplaced. Though I might forgive you if they're good ones. ~Melanie

She hit *send* with a nervous smile, wondering if she'd regret it.

CHAPTER 2

Andrew

When her email address arrived, Andrew exhaled as though he'd been holding his breath for weeks. He copied it carefully into his contacts, typing his first "proper" letter to her that same evening.

From: A.Collins

To: MelanieT55

Subject: Re: Just saying hello

Hello Melanie,

"Hello" is an excellent start. Far better than "Greetings from a drizzly city," which was my first attempt at wit.

I do love to read. I'm not sure I'll ever finish my stack of "to be read" books as somehow it keeps growing. I don't think one can ever have too many books.

I volunteer in archives, so I also spend most of my time

with things that smell faintly of dust and history. It sounds as if we share a fondness for old stories that insist on being kept.

Best,

Andrew

He reread it twice, deleting a line about the weather that felt too gloomy. When he finally pressed *Send*, he found himself oddly reluctant to close the tab.

From: MelanieT55

To: A.Collins

Subject: Re: Just saying hello

Andrew,

I laughed out loud at "drizzly city." We've had snow here all week, and I'm beginning to think there's no pleasing either of us with weather.

Archives! That sounds fascinating. I imagine you surrounded by leather-bound books and mysterious letters no one's read in centuries. Do you ever come across something unexpected?

At the library, I sometimes find notes people leave inside books like shopping lists, little sketches, once even a pressed flower. They feel like whispers from strangers. I can never quite bring myself to throw them away. I have a special box I keep them in.

I agree with you that one can never have too many books. In my case I think I don't have enough book-shelves!

Melanie

When she sent it, she realized she was smiling. Haiku gave her a dubious look from the armchair, as if questioning her newfound cheer.

From: A.Collins
To: MelanieT55
Subject: Re: Just saying hello
Melanie,
You might be disappointed to learn that our archives are more dust than leather, though occasionally a surprise turns up. Once, I opened a box marked "City Council, 1892" and found a love letter tucked inside a tax ledger. The handwriting was exquisite.
I like your thought about whispers from strangers. Perhaps you and I are doing something similar, slipping notes into the pages of each other's lives.
Andrew

From: MelanieT55
To: A.Collins
Subject: Re: Just saying hello
Andrew,
That's the most romantic thing I've read in a long time, "slipping notes into the pages of each other's lives." You're a poet disguised as an archivist, Andrew.
I'm glad I wrote to you. It's been a while since I've had someone to exchange words with simply for the joy of it.
Melanie

When she closed her laptop that night, the house didn't feel quite so quiet.

Andrew

It was Melanie who sent the first photo, almost by accident. Attached at the end of an email about her garden was a snapshot of her tomato plants. He opened it, expecting greenery, and there she was in the corner of the frame, squinting at the sun, holding a basket.

Andrew leaned back in his chair, staring longer than he should. She looked… real. Not polished, not posed, but warm and human. Light brown hair with hints of silver just above her shoulders, and her eyes looked as if they were blue. It was hard to tell though. He felt suddenly shy, like a schoolboy caught staring.

He typed quickly: *"The tomatoes are impressive. And the gardener isn't bad either."* Then he deleted it, embarrassed, and replaced it with: *"You've got quite the crop there. I'm assuming that is you with the basket? If so, you look nice."*

He smiled every time he looked at the photo.

Melanie

She hadn't meant to send herself along with the tomatoes, but when Andrew asked if it was her, it gave her a warm feeling inside, and she felt a little silly for sending it as he hadn't asked for one. She considered never sending another photo, but something about his kind reply made her bold. A week later, she sent another: a lopsided pie, with herself in the background, making a face of mock despair.

When Andrew responded with a picture of himself at a windswept cliff, cap pulled low over gray hair, Melanie studied it far too long. His eyes had small lines at the corners. He looked exactly as she'd imagined, and yet, not at all. Both things, somehow, at once.

CHAPTER 3

They both found themselves anticipating a new email notification in their Inbox; usually Andrew in the mornings and Melanie in the evenings, due to the time difference.

From: A.Collins

To: MelanieT55

Subject: Odd comfort

Melanie,

Do you ever find comfort in small, unnecessary things? This morning, I brewed tea before I realized there was no milk. I drank it anyway, far too strong, and it reminded me of my grandmother. She used to say the bitterness built character. I'm not sure that's true, but it made me smile.

I think perhaps that's what writing to you does as well, it brings a small, unnecessary comfort that brightens the day.

Andrew

He hesitated before sending it, aware that it revealed more than he meant to. Then he thought of her pressed flowers, her little found notes, and decided it was safe to be a little human.

From: MelanieT55
To: A.Collins
Subject: Re: Odd comfort
Andrew,
Yes. Every day. There's comfort in the ordinary. Folding laundry while the kettle hums, the smell of paper when a new book arrives, the way the light hits the kitchen table in late afternoon.
I sometimes think we overlook the very things that keep us stitched together.
Your story about the tea made me smile. My grandmother used to keep an old tin of loose leaf just for "proper" occasions. I never quite learned how to make it her way, though. It always seemed to be perfect when she made me a cup and never quite the same when I made it myself.
Melanie

She didn't mention that the quiet of her evenings had begun to feel a little less hollow since his first message. Some things were best left between the lines.

From: A.Collins
To: MelanieT55
Subject: On the subject of stories
Melanie,
I was thinking about what you said, about being stitched together by ordinary things.
It reminded me of an essay I once read that said we are "the sum of our kept moments." I like that.
May I ask what moments you've kept?
Andrew

He typed it quickly, then sat back, realizing the question was more intimate than he'd intended. But curiosity won over caution because he wanted to know what filled her days.

From: MelanieT55
To: A.Collins
Subject: Re: On the subject of stories
Andrew,
Moments I've kept... hmm. The smell of my daughter's hair when she was small. Baking cookies with my grandchildren, Jack and Sophie. the hush of the library just before opening. The way fall looks when it begins to gather itself into gold.
There's another, too. After my divorce, I started walking every morning before work. I thought it might make me feel less lost. One day, I saw a robin perched on a fence, singing as though it had never known

disappointment. It seemed so carefree. I've never forgotten it.

What about you?

Melanie

Her finger hovered over *Send*. Opening up like this to him felt like stepping onto a bridge she wasn't sure could hold her weight. But she sent it anyway.

From: A.Collins

To: MelanieT55

Subject: Re: On the subject of stories

Melanie,

A robin's song is no small thing. Thank you for sharing that.

I had to think for a minute when you used the word "fall" as we are more likely to say "autumn" here.

Let's see. Moments I've kept: the smell of books too old to open without care. A walk home from work in the rain where the city felt somehow new again. My father teaching me to tie a bow tie when I was seventeen, his hands steady on mine.

And once, years ago, a conversation that I didn't have the courage to finish.

I've thought about that one a great deal lately.

Andrew

He stared at the blinking cursor. He almost deleted that last line but didn't. There was something about writing to Melanie that made honesty feel less like exposure and more like *relief*.

From: MelanieT55
To: A.Collins
Subject: Re: On the subject of stories
Andrew,
I think I understand.
Some conversations stay with us because of what wasn't said. Maybe ours, can be a way of saying some of the things we couldn't before.
Also, you tie bow ties? I'm impressed. I think a lot of men today would only use a clip-on if they wore one. Myself, I've never mastered scarves, but I'd like to.
Melanie

She laughed when she sent it. Not the hollow kind she used to, but something real.

From: A.Collins
To: MelanieT55
Subject: Re: On the subject of stories
Melanie,
I'll teach you bow ties in case your grandson ever needs to know how. That way you can show him how it's done.
Though it might have to be by written instruction, unless fate conspires otherwise.
Andrew

He didn't know it yet, but that small teasing line, *unless fate conspires otherwise*, would be the first spark of an idea neither could stop thinking about.

CHAPTER 4

Melanie

$\mathcal{M}$elanie had meant to write him that evening. The cursor blinked patiently on her laptop, Andrew's last warm, thoughtful email still open on the screen. She could almost hear his voice in the gentle humor threaded through it.

But then the phone rang. Daniel was away on business and Emily needed help picking up Jack from school; Sophie had a fever and the grocery order hadn't come.

"Could Melanie possibly stay a little longer?" Emily had papers to finish grading and needed to get them finished and it would be easier if she had help with the kids.

Melanie closed the laptop. She told herself she'd write later. Later became tomorrow. Tomorrow became two days. By the third evening, Andrew's words still waited for her, but her energy did not.

She sat at the small kitchen table, hands wrapped around a cup of tea gone cold, listening to the low hum of the dishwasher in Emily's apartment. Jack was finally asleep. Sophie, too. Emily was grading papers at the counter.

"You're quiet," Emily said, glancing up. "Are you all right?"

"I'm fine," Melanie replied automatically.

Emily studied her. "You always say that."

Melanie smiled faintly. "I am fine."

But even as she said it, she felt the familiar tightening in her chest, the old, unspoken understanding that her own wants were always something to fit in *after* everyone else's.

Emily went back to her papers. Melanie picked up her phone, thumb hovering over the email notifications on the screen. Andrew's email was there: unread, unanswered. She set the phone down again.

From the doorway, her cousin Tom watched her. He had stopped by to drop off something for Emily, but he'd seen that look on Melanie's face before.

He had been watching Melanie move between small tasks—rinsing cups, answering questions and wiping down the countertops. Every so often, she would stop, pick up her phone and look at it for a few minutes, and then set it back down.

"You haven't sat down yet," he said.

Melanie smiled faintly. "I'm fine."

Tom nodded once. "You've said that three times."

She paused, then picked up her phone from the counter, glanced at the screen, and set it back down without responding.

Tom's eyes followed the movement.

"You're postponing something," he said.

Melanie looked at him, surprised. "What?"

"Not a task," Tom clarified. "A person."

She hesitated, then sighed. "I've been corresponding with someone. Just emails. He's in England."

Tom absorbed this, nodding once. "And you haven't replied."

"I will," she said quickly. "I just haven't had a minute."

Tom tilted his head slightly. "You've had minutes. You've been reallocating them."

Melanie leaned against the counter, her expression shifting.

"You're giving everyone else priority access to your time," Tom continued, his tone calm, observational. "What's left gets deferred."

"That doesn't mean I don't care," she said quietly.

"I didn't say that," Tom replied. "I said the pattern is consistent."

He hesitated, and then added, more carefully, "You don't seem unhappy doing this. But you do seem... smaller."

The word settled between them.

"I thought you should be aware," Tom said. "In case you weren't."

The words stayed with her after he left.

That night, she sat alone in her own quiet house, the ticking clock loud in the stillness. She opened Andrew's email at last, reading it slowly, carefully.

And guilt washed through her, not because she owed him, but because she wanted to be there, and somehow always forgot to give herself permission. She owed *herself.*

The cursor blinked. She began to type but at that moment a new email arrived. It was Andrew.

From: A.Collins
To: MelanieT55

Subject: Just checking in
Melanie,
I hope this note finds you well.
I don't mean to intrude. I simply realized I haven't heard from you in a few days, and it felt strange enough to make me wonder.
I hope you're not unwell or buried under too many things that need doing.
If you are, please don't worry, I know how life has a way of crowding in.
I only wanted to say that I've been thinking of you.
And that if you feel like writing, I'd very much like to hear from you.
Warmly,
Andrew

Marion swallowed hard and tears rolled down her cheeks; her fingers moving over the keyboard typing out her reply.

From: MelanieT55

To: A.Collins

Subject: Re: Just checking in

Andrew,

Thank you for writing.

I didn't realize how much I needed to hear from you until I saw your name on the screen.

I'm not ill, just a little overwhelmed. My daughter and the children have needed me more than usual, and somehow, I let everything else slip, including something I didn't want to let go of.

I have a habit, I'm afraid, of putting myself at the end of the list. It's an old one. I don't even notice I'm doing it half the time, until someone kind reminds me that I exist too.

I'm sorry I went quiet. Not because I owe you an explanation, but because I didn't want you to think you had been forgotten. You haven't.

I'm very glad you checked in.

Melanie

She sat back in her chair, let out a breath and pressed the Send button.

Andrew

He'd worried, of course. Worried she'd grown tired of him, or worse, that something had happened. When her reply finally came, full of life again, he felt a rush of something he didn't dare name. It wasn't just relief. It was the realization that her absence had left a space in his days he hadn't known could exist. *Was it strange to miss someone so acutely that you've never met?*

From then on, their emails became as steady as morning tea. They traded recipes, inside jokes, photos of half-finished crafts and lopsided bakes. Melanie told him about her book club's squabbles; Andrew told her about the pub quiz team he occasionally joined (always losing, but spectacularly).

Bit by bit, they slipped into each other's routines. Melanie checked her inbox before bed, knowing Andrew's email would be there from across the sea. Andrew brewed his morning tea with her latest story fresh in his mind.

They didn't call it friendship, or anything more. But both knew that what they had was unlike anything they'd expected when they first clicked the "sign up" button.

From: MelanieT55
To: A.Collins
Subject: On fate conspiring
Andrew,
I keep thinking how odd it is that I've never audibly heard your voice, but yet, I imagine it's calm, with a British accent that I hear in my mind whenever I read your words.
Melanie

She hesitated before sending. That last line, was it too much? She nearly deleted it, then thought, *oh, let him think me foolish if he must. I need to be me.*

From: A.Collins

To: MelanieT55

Subject: Re: On fate conspiring

Melanie,

I smiled at the thought of you imagining my voice; I fear it's disappointingly ordinary. But I like knowing you've imagined it.

You might be surprised to know I've often tried to picture you too, usually with a book in hand and Haiku claiming most of the chair. I wonder, like you, what your voice sounds like and often I wish I could hear the sound of your laugh and see the expressions on your face in response to my terrible jokes.

Yours in friendship,

Andrew

From: MelanieT55

To: A.Collins

Subject: Re: On fate conspiring

Andrew,

You're nearly correct about Haiku; he insists on at least half the chair, sometimes more.

I've been thinking lately how strange it is that people separated by an ocean can know each other so well through words alone. I'm not sure geography should be allowed to get away with that sort of arrogance.

Melanie

She hadn't planned to write that line. It simply slipped out, but once written, it felt right.

From: A.Collins
To: MelanieT55
Subject: Re: On fate conspiring
Melanie,
Ah, geography. Always so strict about its boundaries.
I'd gladly argue with it on your behalf.
Yours in friendship,
Andrew

When he sent it, his heart gave a small, uncharacteristic leap.

Melanie

Melanie had been rehearsing the words in her head all week, yet the blank email window still managed to stare her down like a challenge. It seemed ridiculous, after months of daily correspondence with Andrew, trading book recommendations, laughing over absurd news headlines, even confessing small private disappointments, basically talking about everything and anything, that she should feel shy about asking him one simple thing.

She was going to England. Not just England, but to York, the place he so often described with affectionate sarcasm: the crooked lanes, the pub with the uneven floorboards, the sound of the church bells, and the river Ouse where he liked to walk the towpaths.

And yet, now that the chance had arrived, Melanie

found herself hesitating. At fifty-eight, she had long ago assumed the age of blushing uncertainties was behind her. Still, she caught herself worrying whether meeting face-to-face might unravel the easy rhythm they'd built across oceans. Maybe he'd be different in person.

Melanie tapped the keys, then deleted, then typed again. The cursor blinked, waiting. She toyed with the phrasing, aware of how silly it felt to fuss over words to a man who had once confessed, without hesitation, that he still sometimes put his shirts through the wash twice because he forgot the detergent the first time. And yet, this felt different. She wasn't just sharing another article about American politics or a photo of her cluttered kitchen counter and the pie that turned out lopsided.

She was asking if he wanted to see her in person, not just the filtered pieces of herself she chose to send. And what if he saw her and thought…too much? Too much woman, too many years, too many lines carved by laughter and worry. Maybe too much everything? She sighed, back-spaced again, and started once more.

From: MelanieT55

To: A.Collins

Subject: Tea?

Andrew,

This might sound a little ridiculous, but here it is: I have the chance to come to England towards the end of May. It's just a thought for now, an idea, really. I thought perhaps I might see York.

And perhaps, if you didn't mind terribly, see you…and maybe meet for tea?

There. I've said it.

Now I'll go and hide behind my teapot.
Melanie

Her hands trembled slightly when she sent it. She told herself it was just caffeine.

Simple. Honest. She read it three times before pressing *send*, then immediately wondered if she should have said more. Or less. Or nothing at all? Truth be told, she was afraid of being rejected and of not being enough once again.

CHAPTER 5

Andrew

*A*cross the Atlantic, Andrew was making tea when the notification chimed. He carried his cup to the worn armchair by the window, settling into the cushions before opening her message. The words were brief, and his hand trembled as he scrolled back to the beginning and read it again a second time, and then a third, as though the letters might shift into something else if he wasn't careful. He set the cup down, half-forgotten, and let out a long breath that turned into a laugh. *Melanie wanted to meet.*

His first reaction was excitement, he could already imagine pointing out the crooked lanes, ordering her the fish and chips he'd teased her about. But then, like an unwelcome echo, came the old self-consciousness. He imagined her stepping off the train, looking around for him, only to be met by a man whose hair had thinned, whose middle had softened, whose body had long ago ceased to be the sort admired. He adjusted his glasses, grimaced at his reflection in the window, and muttered, "Well, old boy, at least she'll know you're not a catfish."

But beneath the nerves, there was something steadier, an affection that had grown too real to be undone by waistlines or crow's feet. She wanted to meet him. And suddenly, that was enough.

Melanie

It was only an hour before his reply came back. She saw the notification pop up while she looked for new dessert recipes on her laptop.

From: A.Collins
To: MelanieT55
Subject: Re: (no subject)
Melanie,
Ridiculous? Not in the least.
York would be delighted to meet you, though I suspect I'd be even more so. Just say when and where, and I'll be there with my most dazzling smile. (It's a bit crooked these days, but still serviceable.)
Yours in friendship,
Andrew

He smiled as he pressed *Send,* though his pulse was oddly quick. The flat felt brighter somehow, as if the grey day outside had decided to soften.

Melanie laughed aloud, a quick, nervous burst. She typed a response with trembling fingers.

From: MelanieT55

To: A.Collins

Subject: Re: (no subject)

Andrew,

Well then, I'll fly into London, then take the train to York. I'll be there for ten days. Maybe you could choose a spot to have tea after I arrive? Perhaps one of those tea rooms you've sworn make my American teabags look criminal.

And truly... thank you.

For saying yes.

Melanie

She closed the laptop and sat very still for a long time, the corners of her mouth trembling upward before she could stop them.

She hovered over the *send* button, anxiety prickling at the edges of her confidence. He was so quick to agree; was it politeness, or genuine delight? And would he be disappointed to find her in person? The camera never quite showed the way her chin doubled when she laughed, or how her knees ached when she walked more than a block.

Well, she thought, *he'll see all of me, the good, bad, and extra pounds. And maybe that's the truest kind of meeting.* With that, she sent it off.

Andrew

Andrew opened her reply that evening, just after his supper of beans on toast, and smiled so broadly he nearly dropped a bean onto his jumper.

A tearoom, was it? That he could manage. He reached for the keyboard.

> From: A.Collins
> To: MelanieT55
> Subject: Re: (no subject)
> Melanie,
> Tea, certainly.
> Or, if I may be bold, cream tea. I know a place that serves scones large enough to frighten small children. There's a little place here in York, not too grand, but charming. It's not far from the train station. I promise they don't serve teabags, only loose leaves, steeped properly.
> Yours in friendship,
> Andrew

He hesitated before sending, his fingers resting on the keys. What he didn't type: *I'm nervous too. I've grown round in the middle, and my hair's more memory than substance. But I hope when you see me, you'll see the man who's been here in your inbox every morning, steady and real.*

Instead, he signed off as he always did.

Melanie

The following morning, Melanie woke to find Andrew's message waiting. She read it twice before her feet even touched the floor. York. She had to look it up on a map, tracing the route as though the name itself were a promise.

Her reply was lighthearted on the surface:

From: MelanieT55

To: A.Collins

Subject: Re: (no subject)

Andrew,

The tearoom in York sounds perfect. Cream tea sounds perfect. I'll begin practicing my pronunciation of "scone" now to avoid international incident.

The train ride from London will give me time to practice not staring at you like you're a hologram that's come to life. Please tell me you'll wear something special, so I'll recognize you. Perhaps that cap you wore in the photo from the castle ruins?

Melanie

She pressed *send* before she could lose her nerve, then leaned back against the pillows, heart thumping like she'd just agreed to a blind date. Which, in a way, she had. She told herself not to be ridiculous, but the thought remained: *What if I walk in and he thinks, 'Good heavens, she's bigger than her pictures'?* She sighed, tugged the covers up to her chin, and reminded herself he already knew about the important parts: her sense of humor, her stubborn streak, her tendency to burn toast. Surely those counted for more than waistlines.

Andrew

Andrew's reply came late that night.

> From: A.Collins
> To: MelanieT55
> Subject: Re: (no subject)
> Melanie,
> The cap may be retired; I'm told it makes me look like a retired detective, but I'll bring it along if it spares you any trouble. As for staring, I'll be doing the same. I'm not certain I'll believe you're real until I hear your voice without the echo of distance.
> Yours in friendship,
> Andrew

He closed the message with a joke about rehearsing his table manners, but after hitting *send*, he sat just staring at his words on the screen. His mind whispered the same old doubts: the rounded cheeks, the belly that resisted every half-hearted attempt at walking off, the way his trousers no longer fit quite right. He imagined her stepping into the tearoom and then spotting him, and the possibility of disappointment gnawed at him.

Still, the thought of her voice, of the warmth that came through even her shortest messages, was enough to steady him. *If she's half as kind in person as she is in her words,* he thought, *I'll be a fortunate man indeed.*

CHAPTER 6

Melanie

*L*ater that week, she mentioned her trip to her daughter Emily over lunch. "I'll be meeting Andrew...you know...my friend from England."

Her daughter raised an eyebrow. "Meeting someone from the internet? Mom, you can't be serious. What if he's not who he says he is?"

Melanie bristled. "We've been writing for months. He's more real to me than half the people I volunteer with at the library."

But still, the words lingered after the meal, buzzing at the back of her mind. What if she was being foolish? What if Andrew was not the same in-person and Emily was right? What if she traveled all the way to York to meet him, only to have him not be there? That didn't seem like the Andrew she had come to know through their letters though.

That night she drafted another email.

From: MelanieT55
To: A.Collins
Subject: Re: (no subject)
Andrew,
You've no idea how many times I've rehearsed our conversation already. I've decided you'll say something witty within five minutes, and I'll laugh too loudly, and everyone will stare.
My daughter thinks I'm crazy. I told her you're the least dangerous thing on the internet, but still, promise me you're not secretly a criminal mastermind?
Melanie

She meant it as a joke, but she couldn't quite keep the vulnerability from her words.

Andrew

He confided in his mate Nigel over a pint. "Melanie's coming here, to York."

Nigel leaned back, unimpressed. "At your age? What's the point, Andrew? Internet friends, they're just... fluff. Either that or they are out to scam you. You'll both be disappointed, you'll see. I hope she doesn't raise your hopes like this and not show up."

Andrew forced a laugh, but the comment sank into him like a stone. Was it absurd, this whole thing? Two aging pen pals playing at being young again? He did feel almost as though he was a teenager again. He told himself it wasn't absurd, but later that night, as he stared at his reflection while brushing his teeth, the doubt gnawed.

From: A.Collins
To: MelanieT55
Subject: Re: (no subject)
Melanie,

If I were a criminal mastermind, surely, I'd have the sense to choose a younger accomplice? You're safe, Melanie. At worst, I may bore you with local history until you doze off into your teacup.

I admit, one of my mates scoffed at the idea of our meeting. Said we'd both be disappointed. Personally, I'd rather find out than wonder forever. And for what it's worth, Melanie, you've never disappointed me yet. Bring your loudest laugh. It'll do the tearoom good.
Yours in friendship,
Andrew

Melanie

When his note arrived, Melanie felt her throat tighten. *You've never disappointed me yet.* It was such a simple sentence, and yet it steadied her, giving her a feeling of hope.

She carried her laptop into the kitchen and whispered aloud, as if practicing for York, "Hello you." Her voice wobbled with nerves and something else she didn't quite want to name.

She sat down at her kitchen table, opened her laptop, and her fingers hovered over the keyboard for a long time before she typed:

From: MelanieT55
To: A.Collins
Subject: Re: (no subject)
Andrew,
I think I'll pack three different outfits and still feel like none of them are right. Do you suppose York is ready for an American woman who can't walk past a bakery without stopping?
I'm nervous, Andrew. Excited, but nervous. I hope that's allowed.
Melanie

That afternoon she mentioned the trip to her friend Ruth over their usual Saturday coffee. Ruth listened with a skeptical tilt of her head.

"Meeting some man from England? Melanie, honestly. You don't know how these things turn out. What if he doesn't look like his photos? What if it's awkward? What if he's just looking for sex? At our age, who needs that kind of trouble?"

Melanie stirred her coffee slowly. She wanted to defend Andrew; to say he was kind and witty and real in ways that mattered far more than a jawline. Instead, she just said, "It isn't about needing trouble. It's about wanting... connection."

Ruth sighed. "Just don't get your hopes up."

But that night, Melanie's hopes were precisely what she held on to.

Andrew's reply was waiting when she arrived home:

From: A.Collins
To: MelanieT55
Subject: Re: (no subject)
Melanie,
York is always ready for Americans, especially those with an eye for bakeries. I'll even save you the best seat near the window. And nerves are perfectly legal; I've got a fair few myself.
Yours in friendship,
Andrew

What he didn't write: *I've already imagined you walking in, and I worry you'll find me too soft around the edges, too ordinary. But I'd rather face that moment than never know you beyond our words.*

Later, Andrew brought up the trip with his sister, Margaret, while they were on the phone.

"She's coming all the way from the States, is she? To meet you?" Margaret's voice was laced with disbelief. "Andrew, you've barely kept your garden alive this year, and now you're entertaining an American woman? She'll take one look and wonder why she bothered. I'm not trying to discourage you, but I just don't want you hurt."

He laughed it off on the outside, but after the call he sat by the window, gazing at the empty street. Margaret's words stung more than he cared to admit. He rubbed his chin, muttering, "I know I'm not a young man anymore... but I'm still me. And that will have to be enough."

Melanie wrote again later:

From: MelanieT55
To: A.Collins
Subject: Nervousness
Andrew,
If you're nervous too, then perhaps we'll just sit there
in silence until the teapot scolds us into speaking. Do
you think we can manage that?
Melanie

Andrew's answer came within hours:

From: A.Collins
To: MelanieT55
Subject: Re: Nervousness
Marion,
If silence comes, we'll let it. But I think we'll be too
busy talking over one another to notice. Besides, if all
else fails, I'll distract you with scones. No one can be
awkward with a mouth full of clotted cream and jam.
Yours in friendship,
Andrew

Melanie laughed out loud at that, startling herself. She
leaned back in her chair, and thought, *He already knows how
to rescue me, even from my own nerves.*

From: MelanieT55
To: A.Collins

Subject: The practical side of adventure
Andrew,
Well, it's not just a plan anymore. I booked my flight.
Boston to Heathrow, an overnight flight, arriving there
early in your morning. I keep rereading the confirma-
tion email as if it might vanish if I blink.
The idea of traveling alone that far is both exhilarating
and terrifying in equal measure. I haven't been over-
seas in years, or even out of the country, unless you
count a day trip to Canada a few years ago, and I'm not
sure that qualifies. I've never actually traveled by
myself either.
I'll need to learn how to navigate trains, time zones,
and (most challenging of all) suitcases with wheels
that never seem to obey.
Melanie

She reread her message twice before sending, hoping it
sounded more cheerful than nervous. Haiku yawned in
approval, or indifference, before settling down in her lap for
a nap.

From: A.Collins
To: MelanieT55
Subject: Re: (no subject)
Melanie,
I'm grinning like an idiot, though I shall claim compo-
sure if anyone asks.
You'll do splendidly. Heathrow can be intimidating,
yes, but I promise the rest of England is considerably
more polite. There's a direct train from London to York

with comfortable seats, a tea trolley, and the landscape growing greener by the mile.

And, of course, I'll be at the other end of the journey, attempting to appear calm while probably pacing the platform like an overanxious tour guide.

Do you know your arrival date yet? I'll make sure the scones are warned in advance.

Yours in friendship,

Andrew

He typed that last line with a small laugh, but beneath the humor was a quiet pulse of disbelief: *She's really coming.*

From: MelanieT55

To: A.Collins

Subject: Re: The practical side of adventure

Andrew,

Silly me. I was so excited I forgot to tell you the date. The twenty-first of May! I've already marked it in bold letters on the calendar.

I would very much appreciate directions for the train. I looked at a map online and felt as though I'd fallen into an elaborate puzzle. There seem to be several terminals, and I half expect to end up in Scotland by mistake. Also, would it be strange if I confessed that I'm starting to feel... shy? I'm looking forward to meeting you, of course, more than I can say, but part of me wonders what if the "real" me doesn't live up to the one who writes these messages.

Melanie

She pressed *Send* and immediately regretted being so honest, but honesty had begun to feel like the only language they spoke.

From: A.Collins
To: MelanieT55
Subject: Re: The practical side of adventure
Melanie,
I know that feeling all too well.
But for what it's worth, I suspect the "real" you will be exactly as you've seemed here, thoughtful, wry, and entirely yourself.
We'll both be nervous, I imagine. I've already debated whether to bring flowers to the station or if that feels too forward. Perhaps I'll compromise and bring a smile, it's low-maintenance and travel-safe.
And if you do somehow end up in Scotland, I'll come find you. It's only fair.
Yours in friendship,
Andrew

He leaned back, exhaling a laugh. The words *I'm looking forward to meeting you too* hovered on the tip of his tongue, but he decided the smile would say it for him.

From: MelanieT55
To: A.Collins
Subject: Almost time

Andrew,
One week from today, I'll be on my way.
I've made a list so long it could circle the Atlantic. Passport, plug adaptor, sensible shoes, and a small gift for you (but that's a secret).
I keep imagining that moment in York station, trying to guess what it will feel like to finally see you standing there.
Every time I think about it, my heart does this ridiculous fluttering thing I thought it had long since forgotten how to do.
Melanie

Her hands trembled slightly as she hit *Send*.

From: A.Collins
To: MelanieT55
Subject: Re: Almost time
Melanie,
I don't know what I'll say first when you arrive, but I do know I'll be grateful beyond words to see you.
And you needn't worry about the flutter, it's mutual.
Yours in friendship,
Andrew

He stared at the sent message for a long time, a smile tugging at the corners of his mouth, the ache of anticipation already blooming quietly in his chest.

CHAPTER 7

As the final days before her flight drew near, Melanie began making lists of what to pack, which trains to take, and who would take care of her house and cat while she was gone. She asked her cousin Oliver if he would stay in the apartment above her garage and tend to things, which he agreed to do.

She found herself rehearsing again, not just what she'd say, but how she'd smile, how she might stand so her stomach didn't push against her blouse.

Across the ocean, Andrew took to trying on shirts in front of the mirror, discarding one after another. Too tight. Too shabby. Too much belly. He settled on the least objectionable and chuckled at himself. "Ridiculous," he muttered, but his pulse quickened all the same.

Each night, they traded short notes through email: cheerful, teasing, ordinary. But behind every word, unspoken, was the thrum of anticipation.

Two Days Before

Melanie wrote in the evening, suitcase open on her bed, half-filled with clothes:

From: MelanieT55
To: A.Collins
Subject: Re: (no subject)
Andrew,
Packing is an adventure in itself. Every outfit looks suddenly too bright or too dull, and my shoes have staged a rebellion. Do you suppose the tearoom has a dress code for visiting Americans?
I can't quite believe this is really happening. Months of words on screens, and soon, your voice across a table.
Melanie

She reread it twice before pressing *send*, then sat on the edge of her bed. The words *I'm terrified you won't like me* hovered unsent in the back of her mind.

From: A.Collins
To: MelanieT55
Subject: Re: (no subject)
Melanie,
York welcomes all shoes, rebellious or otherwise. And as for bright or dull outfits—you'll outshine them either way. I've already warned the tearoom staff to expect laughter and to have scones ready!
Yours in friendship,
Andrew

. . .

After sending, he poured himself a cup of tea, though his hand trembled slightly. He didn't write: *What if you look at me and wish you'd stayed in London?* Instead, he set down the teacup and whispered into the quiet flat, "She already knows me. That has to count."

The Night Before

As Melanie folded and refolded the same sweater three times, uncertain whether England in late May meant sweaters or umbrellas or both, she felt that old voice stir in her mind. *You never get it quite right, Melanie.* Her ex-husband's tone, mild, almost weary, still had the power to bruise, even as a memory years later.

He'd never shouted, never been cruel in ways that would make outsiders cluck their tongues. But he'd chipped at her slowly, measuring her against some imagined ideal she never managed to reach. Her pies were too messy, her garden too wild, her laughter too loud. *Not enough here, too much there.* It had been death by degrees, until one day she realized she had given up even trying to please him.

Now, tucking a small package into her suitcase, the hand-bound journal, a fountain pen tucked in beside it, she wondered what Andrew would see when they met. Would he notice the laugh lines, her overly soft middle, the awkward way she sometimes tripped over her own words? Would he think her laughter too loud? Or would he, as she dared to hope, see her the way he always had in his letters: enough.

She zipped her suitcase shut and whispered to herself,

"This is me. Take it or leave it." And for the first time in years, she felt the words as a quiet kind of freedom.

Melanie typed a final email; travel documents spread across the table:

From: MelanieT55
To: A.Collins
Subject: Re: (no subject)
Andrew,
This will be my last email before I board the plane. I'll wave at the clouds and think of you on the other side.
If I get lost at King's Cross, you have permission to laugh at me, but only gently.
Melanie

Her finger hovered over *send*. *It's not too late to back out,* a small, doubting voice whispered. But the other voice in her head reminded her of his kindness, his humor, the way he never made her feel foolish. She hit *send*.

Andrew saw the message just before heading to bed. He typed his reply slowly, carefully:

From: A.Collins
To: MelanieT55
Subject: Re: (no subject)
Melanie,
Safe travels. I'll be the man in York at the train station, probably pacing too much, wearing the cap you requested and trying not to spill tea before you arrive. For once, I'm glad the miles are only hours now. Until tomorrow.
Andrew

. . .

He sat for a long time afterward. Tomorrow, the wait would be over. And whether it brought joy or disappointment, he felt oddly certain: meeting her was worth the risk.

CHAPTER 8

Melanie

At Logan Airport, she clutched her boarding pass like a passport to another life. The hum of the terminal was both exhilarating and intimidating: the flow of people walking past her in both directions, the click-clack sound of rolling suitcases, loudspeaker announcements, the scent of coffee and jet fuel.

When she finally found her seat, window over the wing, she fastened the belt with trembling fingers. You're doing it, she told herself. You're really doing it.

Outside the window, the runway lights blurred as the plane began to move and soon the night lights of Boston fell away beneath the clouds. She thought of Andrew's last message, "You needn't worry about the flutter, it's mutual." She smiled at the memory, closed her eyes, and whispered, "Here goes."

The cabin lights dimmed and the hum of the engines

lulled her to sleep for a while. She woke, wondering at first where she was, and then her mind wandered where it always seemed to when she was nervous—backwards. She leaned her head against the window, watching the stars, and thought of the life she'd left behind as she fell asleep once again.

Hours later, somewhere over the Atlantic, she woke to a soft cabin light and the quiet clink of breakfast trays. The sky beyond the window was pale rose, the horizon slowly unfurling before her eyes.

She glanced around at the other passengers and wondered if anyone else was flying toward something as uncertain as she was. She imagined Andrew in York, pacing, perhaps checking his watch, perhaps wondering if he'd made a mistake in agreeing to this.

Her marriage had ended quietly, without shouting or slammed doors. Just years of small corrections— "Not that dress, Melanie, it makes you look bigger. Why don't you keep the garden tidier, like the neighbors? Couldn't you laugh a little less loudly?"

By the time he said he wanted out, she almost felt relieved. Almost. Except for the hollow ache that whispered she hadn't been enough.

She had carried that whisper for years. Even now, packed neatly in her suitcase beside the blouses she'd fretted over, was the question: *What if Andrew thinks the same?*

Melanie closed her eyes, trying to push the thought away. He'd never once hinted at disappointment in his letters. If anything, he'd welcomed her imperfections, teased her gently, laughed with her instead of at her. Still, the old doubts clung stubbornly.

This is different, she told herself, tightening her grip on the armrest. *He's different. And maybe this time, I get to be just... me.*

When the plane dipped low over the quilt of green fields, her heart fluttered so hard she pressed a hand to her chest. *England*, she thought, *I'm really here.*

England. It still felt like a word from a storybook.

Terminal Five at Heathrow was a blur of glass and steel, polished voices echoing overhead and people everywhere. Melanie wheeled her suitcase along, blinking against jet lag and nerves. Heathrow was a labyrinth of escalators, signs, and accents that made her want to stop and listen.

She made it through customs and then it was onward to find the train. The signs were helpful enough, but every choice of direction felt like a test. She pulled out the little notebook where she had scribbled instructions: *Heathrow Express? Or Underground to King's Cross? Then train to York.*

At the ticket counter, she stammered slightly over her destination. "York, please."

The attendant smiled. "You'll take the train from Terminal Five. Easy enough."

Easy for him, perhaps.

By the time she reached the right platform, her pulse had settled somewhere between exhilaration and fatigue. The train doors slid open with a hiss. She found a window seat, stowed her suitcase, and exhaled for what felt like the first time in hours.

Five hours ahead, she reminded herself. Back home it was still dark, her daughter probably asleep, her friend Ruth unaware that Melanie was living out the very thing they'd warned her against. She smiled wryly. *If only they could feel what I feel right now.*

At King's Cross, she followed the arrows, dragging her suitcase over the concourse tiles, the famous arched roof soaring above her. For one anxious moment she thought she'd lost her way, but then she spotted the departures board: York – Platform 5 – On Time. Relief washed over her so powerfully she laughed aloud, startling a man beside her. She didn't even care.

On the train north, she finally exhaled. The countryside unrolled outside her window, patchwork fields and stone cottages flashing past. The rhythmic sway of the carriage soothed her, and she rested her forehead lightly against the glass. *This is real. He's waiting. And in a little while, I'll step off this train, and everything will change.*

Andrew

Andrew was awake before dawn, though he hadn't slept well to begin with. He'd dozed in fits, waking every hour to glance at the clock, as if sheer vigilance could speed her across the Atlantic. By six o'clock he gave up and shuffled into the kitchen, setting the kettle to boil.

He opened the airline's app on his phone, something he'd downloaded weeks ago in a moment of both curiosity and anxiety, and there it was: Arrivals: Boston to Heathrow Terminal 5. On time.

"You're here," he murmured to the little dot on the screen, as though Melanie herself might hear. He carried his tea to the table, hoping it would help calm him. She was in England. Right now, probably navigating the great beast of Heathrow, suitcase in tow, notebook in hand. He could almost see her there.

Still, a nagging worry gnawed at him. What if she'd landed, looked around at the strange country, and thought better of it? What if she decided York was too far, or he wasn't worth the trouble? He tried to shake it off, but the thought lingered.

Then came the doubts. Would she find him disappointing? He wasn't the slim, confident man he might once have been. Years of quiet living had settled around his middle like an uninvited guest, and though he walked the city most days, the mirror was rarely kind.

You've shown her your mind, he thought, buttoning his shirt. But what if she prefers it to the rest of you?

He chose his blue button-down, the one Nigel had once said made him look "almost respectable." He trimmed his beard, brushed his shoes, then made tea again, forgetting he already had a cup sitting on the table.

At half past eight, he checked her train time again. Estimated arrival 3:31 p.m.

To distract himself, he busied about the flat, fussing with his shirt collars until three of them lay rejected on the bed. He went back to the same blue button-down one in the end, loose enough to hide the soft curve of his middle and gave it a stern tug in the mirror. Then he eyed the cap she'd teased him about. "All right then," he muttered, perching it on his head. "If she doesn't recognize me by this, she never will."

By one o'clock, he was restless. He checked the train schedule on his phone, tapping his foot. If her flight was on time, she'd have made it to King's Cross by now. Surely, she was on the train north. Unless...unless she'd changed her mind.

He paced the small sitting room, muttering options aloud. "A handshake? No, too stiff. A hug? Too forward. Perhaps wait, let her make the first move." He groaned and sat heavily in the armchair, burying his face in his hands.

"Blast it, Andrew, she's a friend, not the Queen. Stop rehearsing like a fool."

Yet when he peeked again at the app, noting her flight time, his heart gave another lurch of hope. She was here, somewhere between London and York on the train. And in just a few hours, the blur of typed words and glowing screens would become flesh-and-blood reality.

CHAPTER 9

Melanie

The hum of the train was steady now, almost hypnotic, but Melanie couldn't relax. Each stop announced over the speakers felt like a countdown. She smoothed her blouse for the tenth time, tugged at the hem, shifted her suitcase from one side to the other. Outside, the countryside unfurled in shades of green she hadn't expected, threaded with stone walls, hedges, and a lot of sheep.

She caught her reflection in the window: tired eyes from the overnight flight, cheeks flushed, hair refusing to sit neatly. This is me, Andrew, she thought, testing the words silently. All of me. I hope that's enough.

She imagined stepping off the train and seeing him. *Would she know him instantly?* His photos had been candid, a little grainy, more real than polished. Still, she fretted. *What if she walked past him? What if she saw him and her smile faltered, betraying nerves as disappointment?* She pressed her palms together in her lap, whispering, "Don't be foolish, Melanie. He's your friend. Just your friend." But her pulse raced anyway.

Andrew

Andrew had not meant to stop.

The market was simply on his way, the familiar path between the river and the narrow streets he had walked for years. The morning air was cool, and he kept his hands in his coat pockets as he crossed the square.

The small wooden stall with a handwritten sign, *The Second Cup*, stood near the edge of the market.

Andrew hesitated, then stepped forward.

"Morning," said the man behind the stall.

Andrew smiled, remembering him from the post office years ago. "Good morning...Michael...and Abbie, right?"

Michael nodded, "Exactly. You have a good memory for faces."

"What can I get you?" asked Abbie, arranging cups into neat rows. Andrew had seen her before along the river path, always walking with a steady, unhurried pace.

"Coffee, please," Andrew said.

Michael poured while she reached for a cup and handed it to Michael to fill.

The small sounds of the market filled the space between them.

"Cold morning," Abbie said.

"Yes," Andrew replied.

Michael handed him the cup.

"Here you go."

Andrew turned it slightly in his hands.

A word was written along the side in careful block letters.

Courage.

He stared at it longer than he intended.

Something in his memory shifted, the faint recollection of another morning at The Second Cup, another cup with words he had not expected to matter.

Still time.

He had believed it then without understanding why.

Michael watched him read the word.

Andrew nodded, "Thank you."

"You're welcome," Michael replied.

Andrew stepped away from the stall and crossed the square slowly, coffee warming his hands.

The word remained visible as he walked.

Courage.

He took a sip and found himself looking toward the river without meaning to.

Life did not change all at once, he thought.

Sometimes it began with small things like a cup of coffee, a familiar face, or a word written where you did not expect it.

Andrew continued on, sipping on his coffee as he walked, the morning unfolding quietly around him.

By 3:30, he was standing at the train station, hands in his coat pockets, trying to look casual while feeling anything but. He lingered near the arrivals board, cap in hand, then fidgeted with it until he finally shoved it onto his head.

The station's high arched roof echoed with the sound of

arrivals, a violin busker, suitcase wheels, and announce-ments he barely heard.

He rehearsed a dozen versions of their first words.

"Hello, Melanie." Too formal.

"Welcome to York." Too much like a tour guide.

"Cream tea?" Ridiculous.

Perhaps he should just smile. Let it be simple.

He checked the clock again, fifteen minutes to go, and then caught sight of his reflection in the glass. *I hope she's not disappointed with what she sees.*

He pictured her on the train, perhaps looking out the window, that same half-smile he'd glimpsed in her photo. The thought softened something in him.

For the first time in years, he felt that odd, electric mixture of fear and hope, the sensation of standing at the edge of something that might change his life.

People hurried around him: tourists with cameras, families with prams, businessmen with briefcases. He shifted from foot to foot, scanning each train listed. London to York – On Time. His stomach gave a queasy lurch.

He pictured her stepping onto the platform, suitcase trailing behind, scanning the crowd. *Would she look past him? Would she search for someone taller, slimmer, younger?* He tugged at his shirt, wishing it hung better, and muttered, "At least try not to look like you've been waiting since dawn."

Then came the agonizing question again: *What do I do when she appears?* A handshake felt absurd, distant. A hug? He longed for it, but what if she recoiled? He rehearsed a middle ground: a warm smile, a hesitant lean, let her decide. And then he laughed at himself for overthinking. Yet the worry clung to him, even as he tried to steady his breath.

The Meeting

The announcement came that her train had arrived. His pulse stuttered. He wiped his palms discreetly on his coat.

When the train glided in, the doors slid open, and passengers began to step out onto the platform. He scanned each face, the world narrowing to the simple, urgent act of looking.

Then, through the crowd, he saw her. She was smaller than he'd imagined, her hair slightly mussed from travel, her eyes bright and searching. She gripped the handle of her suitcase with both hands, turning this way and that, and then their eyes met.

The moment stopped. For just an instant, it was utterly quiet, no other passengers, no footsteps, just that hum that began months ago finally taking shape in the air between them.

And Andrew, who had always been a man of words, found that all of them had fled.

He took a step forward, cap awkward in his hands now, suddenly useless.

He was exactly as she'd imagined, and not at all. Taller, broader in the shoulders, with kind hazel eyes that seemed at once uncertain and full of quiet warmth. He stood just beyond the flow of passengers, holding his cap awkwardly in one hand, as if unsure whether to wear it.

For half a second, they simply looked at one another, strangers and yet not, months of words suddenly condensed into this single, wordless instant.

Then he smiled. It was the sort of smile that starts in the eyes and takes its time reaching the mouth.

"Melanie," he said, and the sound of her name in his voice was enough to undo every nervous knot she'd tied inside herself.

She laughed, soft, shaky, but real. "Hello you," she said, voice trembling but warm. "You're real."

"So are you." Andrew's answering smile was crooked, exactly as promised.

"I, um, should I give you a hug?" he asked, half sheepish, half hopeful.

She tilted her head, smiling, "I think a hug would be lovely."

He opened his arms slightly, tentative, offering rather than assuming. Melanie stepped into them with relief so strong it made her eyes sting.

And in that fragile, ordinary hug, distance collapsed.

CHAPTER 10

They pulled back from the hug, both a little startled at their own boldness, but neither letting go fully until the pause stretched too long. Andrew cleared his throat, tugging at the brim of his cap.

"Well," he said, voice a bit rough, "you're real, then."

Melanie laughed, though her eyes were still damp. "So are you. I was beginning to wonder if I'd made you up."

He reached for her suitcase handle automatically, as though it were the most natural thing in the world, and she let him take it. Together they began weaving through the lines of people at the station.

"It's... odd, isn't it?" Melanie said after a moment, her voice soft and a little uncertain. "We've talked for months and now I don't know what to say."

Andrew chuckled. "I suppose we'll have to start again. 'Hello, I'm Andrew, from Yorkshire. Fond of tea, and self-deprecating remarks.'"

She grinned. "Melanie, from Massachusetts. Fond of pie, when it lands on the plate instead of the floor."

Their laughter came easier then, loosening the tight coil of nerves between them.

Outside, the cool air met them, and Andrew gestured toward the car park. "I've brought the car. I know you probably are tired of riding, but it isn't far to your hotel."

"How thoughtful," she said, her relief plain. "Though I should warn you, I don't know if I trust myself on British roads."

"No need," he said. "You'll only be a passenger."

When they reached his small, well-kept car, Melanie set her hand on the right-side door handle. Andrew froze, then broke into a wide grin.

"Unless you mean to drive us, you might want the other side," he said, laughter bubbling out before he could stop it.

Melanie gasped, her face flushing, and then she laughed too, full and unguarded. "Oh heavens, I forgot! You're all backward here. First day in England and I'm already stealing your seat."

"Backward?" he said, laughing.

She grinned back, still slightly flustered.

He hurried round to the proper side and opened the left door for her, with an old-fashioned flourish. "Your chariot, madam."

She raised an eyebrow but smiled as she slid into the seat. "You do realize you've just ruined me for American men. They never open doors anymore."

Andrew shut the door gently, his grin softening into something steadier.

"Are you hungry?" he asked. "I thought we might go for tea, cream tea, if you're not too tired."

"I would love that. I'm more excited than tired!"

He smiled. "Good. There's a place just by the Minster.

The scones aren't as big as I promised, but they make up for it in flavor."

The drive into the heart of York was a blur of winding roads and snippets of conversation. Melanie kept sneaking glances at Andrew, reassured by the sound of his voice beside her, warmer, deeper than she would have guessed it would be. He, in turn, stole quick looks at her, noting how the morning light caught the shimmers of silver in her hair, how she laughed softly at the crooked street signs he pointed out.

When they reached the stone-fronted tearoom tucked along a cobbled lane, Andrew parked in a nearby carpark and hurried around once more to open her door, and Melanie teased him again, "Careful, Andrew, you're setting a dangerous precedent."

Inside, the tearoom was everything Melanie had secretly hoped for: lace curtains framing narrow windows, small wood tables, the quiet clatter of teaspoons against saucers. The air smelled of warm scones and something faintly floral.

They were shown to a small table by the window. Melanie slipped into her chair and Andrew opened his menu, but his eyes kept straying back to her face.

"Well," she said at last, "I believe the tradition is that you have to order for me. As the local expert."

He grinned, setting down the menu. "In that case, it must be a proper cream tea. Scones, jam, clotted cream, and a pot of the strongest Yorkshire tea they can manage."

"Clotted cream," she repeated, rolling the words on her tongue. "I've read about it. Sounds positively sinful."

The tray arrived soon after: golden scones still warm from the oven, tiny pots of strawberry jam, thick cream so rich it looked more like butter. The teapot steamed between them, filling the air with the earthy fragrance of leaves steeped properly, not bagged.

Melanie reached for a scone, then paused. "I've heard there's debate," she said. "Jam first or cream first?"

Andrew's eyes twinkled. "That depends if you're Cornish or Devonian. But since we're in Yorkshire, we're free to be rebels. I'll say cream first, then jam. More stable that way."

"Practical and delicious," Melanie said, spreading a thick layer of cream and then the jam, across her scone. She bit into it, closing her eyes. "Oh my. This might be the best decision I've ever made."

Andrew chuckled, his shoulders easing for the first time all day. "I'll try not to be insulted you're talking about the scone, not me."

Her eyes opened, amused, and she tilted her head. "Who says I wasn't talking about both?"

The words slipped out before she could stop them, and a flush rose on her cheeks. But Andrew only smiled and reached for his own scone.

The clatter and murmur of the tearoom faded for a moment, as though the world itself had stepped back to give them space. And in the quiet between sips of tea and laughter over crumbly scones, they began the gentle work of turning words into presence, friendship into something real.

They lingered long after the scones were gone, the teapot nearly empty. Conversation came easily now.

"So," Melanie said, tracing the rim of her cup, "I have to confess... I nearly lost my nerve. At the airport I thought, what if he takes one look at me and wishes I'd stayed home?"

Andrew blinked, startled. "Melanie." His voice was soft

but firm. "You're here. That's all that matters. And for the record, I'm the one who worried you'd take one look at me and take the next train back to London."

She laughed, relieved, though her eyes shimmered. "Two middle-aged cowards, then."

"Perhaps," he said with a smile. "But cowards with excellent taste in scones."

Their laughter rippled into a silence that wasn't uncomfortable, but thoughtful. For a moment, Melanie felt the truth of it: they'd both risked something in the decision to meet, and somehow, that risk had already begun to feel worth it.

When they finally stepped back outside, Andrew offered his arm, hesitated, then let it drop again, only for Melanie to loop hers through his, laughing up at him.

"Will you show me the famous Shambles?" she asked.

He brightened. "Only if you promise not to trip over the cobbles. They've been lying in wait for centuries."

The narrow medieval street twisted ahead of them, shopfronts leaning and timber beams shadowing the cobblestones. Tourists crowded the street, snapping photos, but somehow Andrew and Melanie moved within their own small bubble.

She stopped at a shop window filled with books, her reflection caught in the glass. "This looks like something from a fairy tale," she murmured.

"York is full of them," Andrew said. "Though most end with someone being chased by Vikings."

She laughed, and as they walked on, she stumbled slightly on a crooked stone. Andrew caught her elbow instinctively, steadying her. The contact was brief, but it left her skin tingling. "I told you they were dangerous," he said, voice light but eyes a little more serious.

"And you saved me. Twice in one day," she teased. "First from the wrong side of the car, now from York's ancient paving. You're earning a hero's record, Andrew."

His answering smile was quiet, almost shy. "I'll try to keep it up."

They walked on, words trailing into comfortable pauses, the city unfolding around them. And beneath it all ran a current neither dared name yet, a sense that something long nurtured in letters and laughter was beginning, at last, to take root in the air between them.

By the time the last of the daylight faded, they wandered slowly toward Melanie's hotel, conversation weaving between little stories and laughter.

Outside the hotel, they paused. Neither moved to go in, as though standing on the pavement a few minutes longer might hold the day open.

"Well," Melanie said at last. "I'd say this was worth the flight. And the wrong side of the car."

Andrew chuckled, but his voice was softer than before. "I'm glad you came, Melanie. More than I can quite put into words."

A small silence followed. He cleared his throat. "Perhaps tomorrow we could take a walk along the city walls. They're a bit drafty, but the view's worth it."

Her smile warmed him all the way through. "I'd like that. Very much."

He opened the hotel door for her, an old-fashioned gesture that made her heart twist, and lingered in the doorway as she stepped inside. "Rest well, then," he said, as he set her suitcase down next to her. "I'll see you tomorrow."

"And Andrew?" she said, turning back, her eyes bright. "Thank you for today."

He tipped his cap, crooked smile in place, and then, reluctantly, let the door swing closed between them.

Reflections—Andrew

Walking back to his car, Andrew felt both lighter and heavier at once. Lighter, because imagining her had finally given way to the reality of her laughter and her presence at his side. Heavier, because now he knew the stakes. This wasn't just an online friendship with convenient distance. She was here, in his world, and every choice he made would matter.

He replayed the day in fragments: her voice saying, "Hello you," her eyes closing over the first bite of scone and the feel of her arm linked with his. He caught himself smiling like a fool in the dark street. "Tomorrow," he murmured. "Tomorrow, and the day after that, if I'm lucky."

Reflections—Melanie

Upstairs in her hotel room, Melanie set her suitcase against the wall and sank onto the bed without even turning on the lights. The day played itself back to her in vivid detail: the creak of his laugh, the steady way he caught her elbow, and the shy pride in his smile.

She pressed a hand over her heart, still racing, and let out a breath she hadn't realized she was holding. She'd been so afraid of disappointment, his or hers. But instead, she felt only relief, threaded with something dangerous: hope.

I don't know what this is yet, she thought. *But I want to find out.*

She smiled into the dark, already imagining the city walls, the view, and Andrew walking beside her. And for the first time in a long while, sleep came easily.

CHAPTER 11

Marion

Melanie woke early, nerves thrumming again at the thought of their walk. She dressed slowly, then reached into her suitcase for the small package she'd tucked away days ago, wrapped in simple brown paper and tied with a ribbon. She'd debated endlessly about whether to give it to him on the first day or wait, but now, before they set out, felt right.

She greeted Andrew with a smile in the hotel lobby, holding the bundle behind her back.

"Good morning," he said, his voice still carrying that gravelly warmth. "Ready for the walls?"

"In a minute," she replied, shifting from one foot to the other. "I... actually have something for you first. I made it before I came, but I wasn't sure if I should..." She trailed off, cheeks warming. "Anyway. I thought now might be the right time."

She held it out.

Andrew blinked, surprised, then carefully undid the ribbon and peeled back the paper. Inside lay a small journal, bound in soft brown leather. The edges were imperfect, but beautifully so; the pages were the work of careful hands, not machines. When he opened the cover, the first page bore her handwriting:

Andrew,
For your thoughts, your stories, your crooked smiles.
May they always have a place to land.
Melanie

He swallowed hard, fingertips brushing the page as if it might vanish. "Melanie... you made this?"

She nodded, nervous. "It's nothing fancy. But I thought... well, you've given me so many words. It seemed right to give you a place to put yours."

From her bag she produced a small case, opening it to reveal a fountain pen with a simple silver clip. "And I couldn't very well give you an empty journal without a proper pen, could I?"

Andrew laughed softly, though his eyes had gone suspiciously bright. He lifted the pen, weighing it in his hand, then looked at her. "You realize this is the finest gift I've ever been given?"

"Oh, I doubt that," she said, embarrassed but secretly glowing.

"No, Melanie," he said, voice steady. "I don't doubt it at all."

For a moment they stood in the quiet hotel lobby, the air thick with things neither of them had yet found the courage to say. Then Andrew slipped the journal carefully back into its wrapping, tucked it into his leather satchel along with the fountain pen, and offered her his hand with a smile.

"Shall we go walk the walls?"

And with her fingers sliding into his, they stepped out into the morning together.

The morning was brisk but clear, sunlight glinting off the old stone of the city walls. From their height, rooftops spread out in uneven rows, the Minster's great spires rising proudly above them. Tourists moved here and there with cameras, but the wall's narrow path lent a sense of intimacy, as though time itself had slowed to let them walk side by side.

Andrew kept glancing down at Melanie, as though making sure she was still real. She walked beside him, her hand trailing along the cool stone parapet, her hair lifting slightly in the breeze.

"So, this is York from above," she said, her voice hushed, reverent. "It feels... older than anything I've ever known."

"It's got a few centuries on Massachusetts," Andrew teased, though his tone was gentle. He gestured ahead. "They built these walls to keep people out. Funny, isn't it, that now we walk them just to feel closer to what's inside."

Melanie turned her head, studying him. "That sounds like something you should write in your new journal."

He smiled, the expression a little shy. "Maybe I will."

They walked in companionable silence for a stretch. The city stretched beneath them: chimneys, gardens, winding streets. A gull flew above their heads, its cry sharp against the hush.

At last, Melanie spoke, her words softer than the breeze. "I was afraid, you know. Not just of the flight, or the trains, but... afraid you'd see me, and think I wasn't the person you'd come to know. That all the words would crumble when faced with... well, me."

Andrew stopped, leaning lightly against the wall, and turned to her. "Melanie, I've seen you all along. The lopsided pies, the laughter in your letters, the way you care about people who don't always deserve it. That's you. And nothing I've seen since you stepped off that train has changed a bit of it."

Her throat tightened. "Were you worried?"

"Yes," he admitted. "I thought you might take one look at me and wonder why you'd bothered. But I'd rather face that than never know."

They stood in the stillness of the wall, the world below them moving on: footsteps, double-decker buses, voices, the ring of a bicycle bell. Between them hung a quiet more meaningful than words. Melanie reached out, touched his sleeve briefly, then let her hand fall.

"Thank you," she said simply.

Andrew nodded, but his eyes lingered on hers, warm and steady.

They resumed their walk, slower now, as if savoring each step. And though neither spoke of it aloud, both knew that something had shifted, something fragile but certain, like a seed finding soil.

By the time they completed the circuit of the walls, Melanie's legs were protesting and Andrew admitted his own knees weren't quite the allies they used to be. They exchanged rueful grins, both a little breathless, and Andrew suggested, "Lunch, before we collapse in front of some cathedral tourists?"

Melanie laughed. "As long as it involves chairs. Preferably padded ones."

He led her down a winding lane to a snug little pub

with a low ceiling and ancient beams. The place smelled of roasting meat and fresh bread, and the small fire in the hearth chased away the chill from the walls.

They found a table tucked in the corner, away from the midday crowd. Andrew insisted she try a proper Yorkshire pudding, and when the plate arrived, Melanie blinked at the golden, puffy creation dominating half her dish.

"Oh my," she said, picking up her fork. "I thought this was dessert."

Andrew chuckled. "Blasphemy. It's the soul of a roast dinner."

She cut into it, tasted, then set down her fork with mock solemnity. "Andrew, I think I'm going to need you to roll me back to the hotel later."

He grinned. "We'll put it in the journal under 'British culinary triumphs.'"

They swapped bites across the table, her roast potatoes for his braised beef, and Melanie teased him for being stingy with the gravy. He feigned offense, wagging his fork at her, and the sight of his expression sent her into a fit of laughter loud enough to earn a few glances from nearby tables.

When the laughter subsided, Melanie dabbed at her eyes with her napkin. "It's been a long time since I laughed like that," she admitted quietly.

Andrew leaned back, his smile gentler now. "Then I'll count it a victory. And I'll do my best to make sure it's not the last time, either."

The words hung between them, carrying more than just humor. Melanie felt the weight of them, and the warmth.

They lingered over their meal, ordering tea after, unwilling to give up the ease they'd found in each other's company. For a while, it felt almost ordinary, two friends sharing lunch, but beneath the chatter, the current of something more was unmistakable.

After lunch, neither seemed ready to retreat indoors. The city had brightened again, the brief rain leaving everything fresh and glistening. Andrew suggested a walk, and Melanie agreed, glad for a chance to stretch her legs at an easier pace.

They meandered through the narrow streets, pausing often at shop windows: a tiny bookshop with its display stacked high in teetering piles, a sweet shop with trays of chocolate truffles, even a window filled with porcelain teapots shaped like cottages.

"You need one of those," Melanie teased, pointing at a teapot whose spout emerged from a roof shaped like a chimney.

Andrew shook his head gravely. "Far too whimsical for me. My tea tastes better out of a battered pot with a missing lid."

She laughed, and the sound mingled with the chatter of shoppers and the clip-clop of a horse-drawn carriage that rattled past.

After a while, Andrew ducked into a small café and emerged with two takeaway cups. "Yorkshire coffee," he announced. "Don't ask how it compares to American."

They found an empty bench in a quiet square shaded by trees, the Minster's spires peeking above the rooftops nearby. They sipped in companionable silence for a moment, watching children chase pigeons across the paving stones.

Melanie leaned back, cradling her cup. "I don't think I've sat still like this in ages. At home I'm always rushing, picking up my grandchildren, errands, cooking, or volunteering. Here, I feel like the world has slowed down just enough to let me breathe."

Andrew studied her profile. "Perhaps that's what holidays are for. Though, selfishly, I'm glad you chose mine for yours."

She turned her head, catching his gaze, and smiled. "Me too."

The pause stretched comfortably between them, the kind that said words weren't needed. Around them, people were walking by, but the bench felt like its own little island.

When their cups were empty and the shadows grew longer, they rose to go back toward her hotel. This time, their steps were slower still, as though parting too soon might undo the fragile magic of the day.

Melanie touched his arm lightly. "Thank you for the afternoon. I think this will be one of those days I remember for a very long time."

Andrew's smile was tender. "Then I'll count it the best day I've had in years."

CHAPTER 12

*A*s they wandered back toward the hotel, Andrew slowed outside a restaurant with a chalkboard sign.

"Hungry again?" Melanie teased, glancing at him.

"Not for a meal," he admitted, scratching at the brim of his cap. "But there's a certain dessert that ought to be considered a national treasure. I'd be remiss not to introduce you before your first full day ends."

Her eyebrows lifted in amusement. "A dessert? Well, Andrew, you know the way to my heart."

They slipped inside and found a small table by the window. When the server arrived, Andrew ordered without hesitation: "Two sticky toffee puddings, please. Extra custard."

Melanie leaned across the table, conspiratorial. "I've heard whispers of this pudding. Dangerous whispers. Will I ever recover?"

"Not if it's done right," Andrew replied, and when the dish arrived, warm sponge cake soaked in caramel sauce, crowned with melting custard, Melanie's eyes widened.

"This is indecent," she declared, scooping her first bite. Then she closed her eyes and sighed. "Oh my. I may never go home."

Andrew chuckled, taking his own forkful. "Then York gains an American, and I gain a partner in pudding. Sounds like a fair trade."

They ate slowly, savoring how rich the dessert was, teasing each other over who scraped their dish cleaner.

As they lingered over the last bites, Andrew cleared his throat. "Tomorrow, if you're willing, we could visit the Minster. It's... well, it speaks for itself. After that, perhaps a wander by the river."

Melanie smiled warmly. "That sounds perfect. I'll follow your lead."

Outside her hotel, they paused once more, the air cool and tinged with woodsmoke. The city had quieted, and the moment felt suspended.

"Thank you, Andrew," Melanie said softly. "For today. For pudding. For everything."

He tipped his cap, though his smile was a touch shy. "I should be thanking you, Melanie. You've turned an ordinary day into something I'll remember."

For a heartbeat, it seemed they might linger forever there on the pavement. Then Melanie touched his arm briefly, before stepping back toward the door.

"Tomorrow then?" she asked.

"Tomorrow," he promised.

She slipped inside, glancing back once to see him still standing there, cap in hand, before the door closed.

Melanie

Back in her room, Melanie sat on the bed, shoes kicked off, the hum of York drifting through the window. She should have been exhausted, but her mind was replaying the day like a favorite film.

She thought of Andrew waiting in the hotel lobby. Of the way he'd caught her elbow on the wall walk. Of his smile over sticky toffee pudding.

And yet, beneath the warmth and happiness, echoes of her old fears lingered. She remembered how her ex-husband used to sigh when she laughed too hard, as though she'd embarrassed him. Today, Andrew had laughed with her, loudly enough that people had stared, and neither of them had cared.

She pressed a hand over her chest, steadying herself. *This is different*, she told herself again. *He sees the real me.*

Andrew

York was quiet as Andrew walked back from Melanie's hotel. His cap was tucked under his arm, forgotten. His mind replayed her laugh, and how wonderful it was just to be with her.

Back in his flat, the silence greeted him as it always did. He stood there for a minute listening to the little clock on the mantel and then sat in his worn armchair.

For years, he'd been "Mr. Collins," the history teacher, or just "Andrew," the quiet man who drank tea at the pub. Rarely more. But tonight, for the first time in a long while, he felt seen, simply as himself.

Andrew rubbed a hand over his face. "Careful, old boy,"

he murmured aloud. "Don't go losing your head." But the truth was, he already felt the ground shifting under his feet.

Later, Andrew sat on the edge of his bed. He should have been winding down with his usual book, but instead he found himself grinning like a schoolboy.

He placed the journal gently on his nightstand and placed the fountain pen beside it. He thought of the way Melanie's eyes sparkled when she teased him and how her laughter had filled the tearoom.

He leaned back in bed, grinning into the dark like a boy half his age. *Tomorrow,* he thought. *I get to see her tomorrow.*

For the first time in years, tomorrow felt like something worth rushing toward. He leaned back against the pillows, folded his hands across his middle, and whispered into the quiet, "Tomorrow."

And with that word, simple and certain, he drifted into sleep.

CHAPTER 13

The morning dawned cool and clear and Melanie met Andrew in the hotel lobby, where he stood waiting.

"Ready for something spectacular?" he asked, his smile making her chest feel oddly light.

"As long as it doesn't involve another wall walk," she teased. "My knees are still holding a grudge."

He chuckled. "No climbing today, I promise. Only looking up."

They set out through the winding streets and the Minster's spires loomed higher with each turn until they stood before it, towering and magnificent, with all its carved stonework.

Melanie stopped, breath caught. "It's... breathtaking."

Andrew's eyes grew tender as he looked at her rather than the cathedral. "It is."

Inside, cool air and quiet reverence wrapped around them. Sunlight passing through the many stained-glass windows created colored light prisms across the Minster's vast church floor.

Melanie tilted her head, studying the play of color across the floor. "I used to come to church every Sunday," she murmured. "When I was married. After the divorce, I stopped. It felt... hollow without someone beside me."

"I used to bring my students here on field trips," he said softly. "Most of them yawned and didn't really want to be here, but a few would stand right where you are now and whisper wow. That always stayed with me."

They lingered in the choir stalls, reading the inscriptions on worn wooden plaques. Melanie traced one with her fingertip. "There's so much history here. I feel small, but in a good way. Like all the things that weighed me down don't matter as much under this roof."

Andrew nodded. "That's exactly it. We spend so much time measuring ourselves, what we should have been, what we should look like. But here..." He gestured up at the stained glass. "Here, we're just people trying to make sense of our little corner of time."

She looked at him then, her eyes shimmering with unshed tears. "Andrew, do you always say things that go straight to the heart?"

He smiled, a little self-conscious. "Only when I forget to guard my tongue."

They stepped back into the sunlight after leaving the Minster, blinking at the brightness. Melanie drew in a long breath, as though the air itself was clearer after the stillness inside.

"Where to now?" she asked.

Andrew adjusted his cap, that familiar crooked smile tugging at his mouth. "I thought we might wander along the river. It's not as grand as the Minster, but it has charms of its own."

"I'll trust your judgment," Melanie replied. "You've not led me wrong yet, though I reserve the right to complain if it involves more cobblestones to trip over."

"Fair warning," he said with mock gravity, "there are a few of those, but they're gentler than yesterday's."

Before heading to the riverside, Andrew steered her toward a side street. Melanie frowned slightly, curious, but said nothing until he stopped beside his car and unlocked the boot.

"I just need to fetch something," he said casually, rummaging.

Melanie tilted her head, then caught sight of a wicker basket, a folded tartan blanket balanced on top. Her brows lifted, a smile breaking across her face. "Andrew... is that what I think it is?"

He cleared his throat, suddenly sheepish. "Well. I thought a picnic might be a touch more pleasant than over-priced sandwiches by the riverside cafés. If you don't mind, that is."

Her laughter bubbled out, bright and surprised. "Mind? Andrew, that's the sweetest surprise."

He lifted the basket with a small flourish. "Then allow me to lead the way."

They found a quiet patch of grass by the Ouse, shaded by a tree whose branches stretched lazily over the water. Andrew spread the blanket with exaggerated care, and Melanie sank onto it, smiling as she smoothed her skirt.

From the basket emerged treasures: small sandwiches wrapped in paper, fruit, a flask of tea, and, at Melanie's delighted gasp, two little pastries from the bakery in the tearoom she'd admired yesterday.

"You planned this," she accused lightly, taking one.

"Just a reconnaissance mission yesterday while you were admiring the teapots," he admitted. "A man has to do his research."

They ate slowly, watching the river traffic glide past: a tourist boat with waving families, a pair of ducks squabbling near the bank. Melanie laughed when Andrew tossed a grape in their direction and missed by a wide margin.

"Hopeless," she teased. "Remind me never to rely on you in a food fight."

"Unfair conditions," he protested. "The ducks were moving targets."

When Andrew began packing away the basket, Melanie sighed softly.

"Already finished spoiling me?" she teased.

"I'd hardly call a few sandwiches spoiling," he said, though his smile betrayed him. He folded the blanket as a breeze lifted off the Ouse, carrying the smell of river and wildflowers.

<hr>

A few yards ahead, a man stood at the railing, leaning slightly on the worn wooden rail as he looked upward. He was maybe early sixties, tall, weathered in the gentle way of someone who spent a lot of time outdoors. He held a small sketchbook open in one hand, a pencil poised but idle.

"What's he looking at?" Melanie asked, softly so as not to intrude.

Andrew followed her gaze. "Ah...that's Eric," he said. "Friend of mine from the walking group."

Eric didn't turn; he simply studied the sky with a quiet, thoughtful intensity.

Andrew smiled faintly. "He's always watching the clouds."

"Clouds?" Melanie asked.

"Aye," Andrew said. "Says they're never the same shape twice. Finds peace in that, I think."

Melanie looked up. The clouds drifted in soft tiers, cream against blue, forming shapes in the afternoon sun.

She found she understood immediately.

"That's... lovely," she murmured.

Andrew nodded. "Eric is a good man. Keeps to himself. He lost his wife some years ago."

"That is sad."

"Mm." Andrew's voice softened. "Sometimes he sketches the clouds. Sometimes he just looks."

Eric lowered the sketchbook, glanced down the path as if sensing them, and lifted a hand in greeting, small, understated.

Andrew returned the gesture. Melanie did too.

A polite smile. A quiet nod. Then Eric continued his slow walk along the water, his pencil marking something gentle and unseen on the page.

Melanie watched him go. There was something about him, something quiet and unfinished, like a story the river was still writing.

"Interesting man," she said softly.

"You'd like him," Andrew replied. "Most people do. Once they get past the silences."

The air was filled with the warmth of the sunlight, laughter, and the gentle murmur of water. For a while, they didn't speak, just stood together on the riverbank, shoulder to shoulder. Melanie tilted her face to the breeze and thought, *This. This is what I've been missing. Not grand gestures. Just this. Someone to share a quiet afternoon with.*

Andrew glanced at her profile, the way her hair lifted in the wind, and thought, *if every day were like this, I'd have no complaints at all.*

They lingered by the river until the colors of sunset filled the sky.

As they headed back to his car, Andrew cleared his throat. "I was wondering... if you'd like to do something this evening. There's a little theatre not far from here, nothing grand, just a local playhouse. Or, if you'd rather, we could hear some live music at one of the pubs. They do a good folk set on Tuesdays."

Melanie's eyes lit. "Oh, music, please. I've not been out to hear live music in years."

So, they walked together into the evening, the streets humming with life. The pub Andrew chose was old and timbered, alive with chatter and the scent of ale and good food. A trio of musicians played in the corner, fiddle, guitar, and bodhrán, filling the air with quick, lilting rhythms.

They found a small table near the hearth. Andrew ordered pints, and Melanie, though more of a tea drinker, took hers with a grin, clinking glasses with him.

"To pudding and picnics," she toasted.

"To laughter," he returned.

The music wound around them, lively and bright, tugging Melanie's foot into a tap she couldn't stop. When the fiddler launched into a particularly upbeat tune, Andrew leaned close and murmured, "Careful, or I'll be dragged into dancing."

She raised a brow. "And that would be so terrible?"

"For you, yes," he said, eyes glinting. "I've two left feet and knees to match."

Her laughter joined the music, and Andrew thought the room could have emptied and he'd hardly notice.

When the music finally quieted and the crowd thinned, they walked back through York's winding streets. The city felt softer at night, the Minster lit like a lantern against the dark.

Outside Melanie's hotel, they paused again, neither eager to part.

"Thank you," she said, her voice warm. "For the music. For today. For… everything."

Andrew tipped his cap, though the gesture was slower, more thoughtful than before. "It's me who should be thanking you, Melanie. You've made this city new again."

The pause lingered, thick with something unsaid. Then Melanie touched his sleeve gently, smiling up at him. "Tomorrow?"

He nodded. "Tomorrow."

This time, as she slipped inside, her smile lingered even after the door closed. And Andrew, standing alone on the pavement, felt the quiet of the city settle around him with a softness he hadn't known in years.

Reflections—Melanie

Back in her room, Melanie set her shoes by the door and dropped onto the bed with a little sigh. Her cheeks still felt warm from laughing at Andrew's grumbling about his "two left knees," and the music still thrummed faintly in her bones.

She thought of how easily he had turned an ordinary day into something rich: the Minster's stained glass, the quiet picnic by the river, the pub's warmth. Each piece was simple, but together they felt like a tapestry, woven with care, with presence, with him.

Her ex-husband's voice tried to rise in her memory. "You're too much, Melanie. Too loud, too sentimental." She pushed it firmly away. Tonight, Andrew had laughed with her, not at her. He had leaned in so close during the music that she'd caught the faint scent of soap and tea, and not once had he looked like a man enduring, but like one enjoying.

For the first time in years, she didn't feel like she had to measure herself against someone else's expectations. She felt seen. She felt enough.

She drew the curtains against the night, heart lighter than she could remember, and whispered aloud, almost shyly, "Tomorrow."

Reflections—Andrew

Andrew let himself into his flat, the hush greeting him as always, but tonight it felt different. The quiet wasn't heavy, it was companionable, because Melanie's laughter still echoed in his mind.

He set the folded blanket and empty basket aside, washed the cups, then settled into his armchair. He thought of her face tilted toward the stained glass, the light in her eyes as she tapped her foot to the music, and the smile on her face as she said, "Tomorrow?"

He was no fool, he knew the dangers of hope. He'd lived long enough to guard his heart, to remind himself that connections sometimes fade, and that good things can slip away. But tonight, he found himself whispering the truth: "I don't want this to fade. I want more."

For years, he'd accepted solitude as the shape of his life. But now, with Melanie across the city, her presence still lingering, he wondered if the shape of things might change.

He carried the journal she had given him to his bedside and opened it for the first time. On the very first page, beneath her inscription, he wrote only one line:

Today was not ordinary. Today was Melanie.

He closed the book, placed it carefully on the table, and turned out the light with a smile.

CHAPTER 14

$\mathcal{M}$elanie found herself awake earlier than she expected, the faint chime of bells drifting through the city streets. She lingered a moment at the window, looking down at the narrow lanes coming to life with shopkeepers and early walkers. Her heart did a little skip at the thought: Andrew would be here soon.

When she came down to the hotel lobby, there he was, waiting with his cap in hand. His smile was a little shy, as though the sight of her still unsettled him in the best way.

"Good morning," he said. "I thought perhaps we might try a proper breakfast today. Something hearty, to balance yesterday's pudding indulgence."

Melanie laughed. "I don't think anything could balance that pudding, but I'm willing to let you try."

They walked together to a nearby café, one of Andrew's favorites, tucked into a side street with ivy curling over its sign. Inside, the scent of bacon and coffee greeted them, and they found a small table by the window.

Andrew ordered the full English breakfast of eggs, black pudding sausage, bacon tomatoes, beans, and toast.

Melanie opted for simply scrambled eggs, sausages and toast, but she insisted she would try "a bit of everything" from *his* plate.

When the food arrived, she laughed at the mountain before him. "Good heavens, Andrew, do you plan to eat again this week?"

"It's tradition," he said solemnly, though his eyes twinkled. "Besides, I promised you balance."

They shared bites, Melanie wrinkling her nose at the black pudding sausage but declaring the beans on toast oddly comforting. Andrew teased her mercilessly about needing photographic evidence to prove she'd tried it.

Melanie

As she buttered her toast, Melanie's mind flickered back, unexpectedly, to Sunday mornings years ago. Sitting in church beside her ex-husband, carefully modulating her laugh, folding herself smaller to avoid drawing his sighs. She remembered how heavy those mornings felt, a performance she could never quite manage.

She glanced at Andrew now, reaching across the table to steal one of her sausages with mock innocence, and thought: This is different. This is easy.

The contrast filled her chest with a warm ache.

Andrew

Andrew sipped his tea and found himself remembering the staffroom during his teaching days: the stale coffee and the hum of tired voices. He used to sit at the edge, marking papers, half-listening to the chatter of colleagues about their weekends with partners or families. He'd told himself he was content with his solitude.

But here he was, across the table from Melanie, trading bites and banter, and realizing how much he'd missed this, the ordinary comfort of a shared breakfast and the way small talk could feel like belonging.

He set down his cup and said lightly, "You know, you've officially passed your first full English breakfast. I think that makes you an honorary Yorkshirewoman."

Melanie grinned, raising her fork in mock salute. "High praise. Do I get a certificate?"

"Only if you promise not to frame it over your lopsided pies," he said.

Her laughter rang bright, and Andrew thought, *This is what I've been waiting for without knowing it.*

After breakfast, Andrew suggested they take the long way through the winding lanes toward the Shambles. Melanie agreed, happy to stretch her legs and take in the sights and sounds of York as it shook off the morning chill.

When they reached the Shambles, she stopped short, tilting her head back to take in the leaning timbered buildings. "Oh my," she murmured. "It looks like something out of a storybook."

Andrew chuckled. "A slightly crooked storybook. They say some of these buildings are so close, you could reach across and shake hands with your neighbor from the upper floors."

Melanie leaned into the street, pretending to measure the distance. "I think you could pass a teacup back and forth. Imagine—no need for kettles, just borrow your neighbor's."

He gave her a mock stern look. "That might work until the neighbor drinks the last of the milk."

They ambled along, peering into shop windows. Melanie lingered over a confectioner's display; the rows of fudge stacked like treasure. Andrew bought her a small packet, though he teased, "You'll have to share or I'll confiscate it under local law."

"Show me the statute," she countered, as she tucked the packet safely into her bag.

At a tiny bookshop, she insisted they duck inside. The scent of old paper and binding glue wrapped around them. Melanie wandered down the narrow aisle, running her fingers along spines. Andrew followed, watching the way she lit up when she found a collection of English folk tales.

"I think you have a soft spot for stories," he said gently.

She glanced back at him, eyes shining. "They're how I made sense of the world when I was a girl. Still are, really."

Outside again, Andrew bought them each a coffee from a small stall. They found a bench tucked against the wall of an old shop. Melanie cupped her drink between her hands, savoring the warmth against the crisp spring air.

"Do you come here often?" she asked.

"Not as often as I should," he admitted. "When you live somewhere, you forget to be a tourist. You forget to notice."

She nodded slowly. "I suppose that's true. Back home, I hardly ever visit the harbor anymore, though I love it. Life just... fills the spaces."

Their eyes met briefly, an understanding passing between them, two people who had filled years with duty, routine, and solitude, forgetting the small joys.

Melanie broke the silence with a teasing smile. "Well, today you're a tourist. And you're buying me more fudge before the day is through."

Andrew laughed. "You're a dangerous influence, Melanie Brooks."

"And you're far too serious, Andrew Collins," she shot back, pleased at how natural teasing him felt.

As they walked further, Melanie thought of her pen pal letters and how she'd once written Andrew that she wished she could "step into a postcard" of England. She hadn't really expected to ever do it. Yet here she was, living out her wish in a lane older than her whole country, sipping coffee with him as though it were the most natural thing in the world.

Andrew, meanwhile, thought of the journal she had given him and how he wanted to write about this exact moment: the crooked houses, the fudge packet crinkling in her bag, the way she laughed with her whole face. He'd forgotten what it was like to have someone to record days for.

CHAPTER 15

The sun had shifted overhead, slanting light into the crooked alleyways, when Melanie stopped in front of a narrow shop wedged between two leaning buildings. Its sign was hand-painted, the words nearly lost under decades of fading: Curiosities & Oddments.

"Oh, we absolutely have to go in there," she declared, her eyes bright.

Andrew raised a brow. "That's where tourists disappear, you know…never to be seen again."

She grinned. "Then you'll just have to come rescue me."

Inside, the air smelled faintly of cedar and old velvet. Shelves bowed under the weight of mismatched treasures: glass bottles with cloudy stoppers, tin soldiers, thimbles, brass candlesticks, and a porcelain clock. A ginger cat dozed on the counter, flicking its tail when they entered.

Melanie leaned close to Andrew and whispered, "I think the cat runs the place."

The shopkeeper, an elderly woman with spectacles perched precariously on her nose, looked up from a magazine. "She does, really. I'm just the assistant."

Melanie laughed, and Andrew felt an odd tug in his chest at the sound, like discovering a favorite song on the radio.

Melanie wandered down an aisle and held up a porcelain figurine of a stern-looking knight. "He looks like he'd tell me off for buying too much fudge."

Andrew smirked. "That's his job description, yes." He picked up a lopsided teacup, the glaze cracked. "This one looks like it's judging me for having plain tea instead of Earl Grey."

"Funny," Melanie said, her lips twitching. "I'd have thought you were the Earl Grey type."

He leaned in conspiratorially. "Only if you're the Lady Chamomile."

She burst into laughter, nearly dropping the knight.

At the back of the shop, Melanie paused before a small display of pressed flowers framed under glass. She traced her finger over one labeled Yorkshire Rose, 1910.

"They remind me of my grandmother," she said softly. "She pressed flowers in her Bible. I used to sneak it off the shelf when I was little and pretend they were treasures she'd hidden there."

Andrew stood beside her, his voice gentler now. "Not a bad definition of treasure, really...something ordinary turned precious because someone loved it enough to keep it."

Their eyes met, the air between them thick with something unspoken. Melanie looked away first, breaking the spell by pointing to another frame.

They left the shop with nothing more than a postcard

Melanie couldn't resist, an illustration of a crooked lane that looked suspiciously like the one outside. Back on the cobbles, Andrew suggested coffee and Melanie thought a mocha latte sounded wonderful.

Soon they sat on a park bench, takeaway cups in hand once again, watching children chase pigeons while a busker strummed a guitar nearby.

Melanie sipped her latte and sighed contentedly. "I'm enjoying wandering around and talking with you; it feels wonderful."

Andrew nodded. "We certainly haven't run out of things to talk about. I'm enjoying this as well."

The words hung between them, tender but not yet too much. Melanie looked away, cheeks warming, and took another sip of her latte.

CHAPTER 16

The narrow lane spilled into a square alive with color and sound, with vendors selling items like wheels of cheese, fish, fresh fruits, bolts of fabric, jars of honey. The Shambles Market was crowded with shoppers.

Melanie inhaled deeply. "Oh, I love places like this. Everything feels like it has a story."

Andrew walked at her side, hands tucked in his coat pockets, smiling at her delight. "And half the fun is inventing the stories if no one tells you."

She gave him a playful glance. "Alright then, what's the story of that one?" She pointed to a stall stacked high with mismatched teapots, their patterns clashing wildly.

Andrew leaned in as though confiding a great secret. "That is the lost collection of Her Majesty's rogue cousin, Lord Geoffrey the Impractical. He believed no two cups should ever match, on principle. Scandalized the entire peerage."

Melanie laughed, shaking her head. "You're ridiculous."

"True," he said gravely, "but at least consistently so."

They meandered further until Melanie stopped abruptly, her hand on Andrew's arm. "Oh, look at this one!"

A small wooden stall was draped with rich fabrics, its table laid out with rows of fountain pens, each gleaming under the canopy's shade. Bottles of ink in jewel-like colors, sapphire, emerald, and garnet, were arranged like a painter's palette.

The vendor, a man with ink-stained fingers, looked up with a smile. "Good afternoon. Feel free to try any of them but careful with the nibs."

Melanie's eyes lit up as she picked up a slim pen with a marbled blue barrel. "They're beautiful," she whispered, almost reverently. "I've always loved fountain pens, ever since I was a girl. My father used to sign letters with one, and I thought it looked like magic, the way the ink flowed so smoothly."

Andrew watched her, struck by the way her face softened. He picked up a pen himself, heavier, black with silver trim, turning it carefully in his hand. "I love using them even though I seem to manage to blot the page sometimes."

Melanie glanced up at him, her voice warm. "You'd be surprised. Sometimes the imperfect marks are the ones that give a page character."

Something in the way she said it settled into him. He looked at her a moment longer before setting the pen gently down.

At the corner of the stall, Melanie spotted a small box, half-hidden. Inside lay a scattering of tiny glass bottles filled with unusual inks of assorted colours. She picked one up, the label hand-written: Midnight Rose. When she tipped it, the ink shimmered faintly between black and crimson.

"Oh, Andrew," she breathed, holding it up for him. "This one looks like it was made for stories. Don't you think?"

He took the bottle from her carefully, turning it in his hand. As the ink caught the light. He thought of her journal gift, of her laughter at the river, of her words about ordinary treasures. "Yes," he said at last, his voice low. "It does."

For a long moment, neither moved. The busy market surrounded them, but the two of them stood as though the world had slowed.

Then Melanie cleared her throat and set the bottle back, a faint flush on her cheeks. "Well. We'd better not dawdle. You still owe me more local fudge."

Andrew smiled. "Dawdling, I'll remind you, is half the point of markets. But yes, fudge."

Not far from the fountain pens, a stall stretched wide with wheels of cheese in every shade of cream and gold. A hand-painted sign above read: "Taste of Yorkshire – Sample Before You Buy."

The vendor, a cheerful woman in an apron dusted with flour, greeted them. "Go on, love, have a try! Wensleydale with cranberries, farmhouse cheddar, a bit of blue if you're brave."

Andrew gave Melanie a sidelong glance. "Are you brave enough for the blue?"

Melanie raised an eyebrow. "I survived a transatlantic flight. I think I can survive cheese."

The woman chuckled and cut a wedge, placing it on a small wooden skewer. Melanie popped it into her mouth and immediately made a face, somewhere between surprise and delight.

"Well?" Andrew prompted, grinning.

She swallowed, eyes wide. "It's... strong. Like it has an opinion about me personally."

Andrew barked a laugh that startled even him. "An opinion! That's one way of putting it." He picked up his own piece, chewed thoughtfully, then nodded. "Yes. Mine thinks I'm hopeless but forgivable."

The vendor laughed. "Best review I've heard all day."

They moved along the counter, sampling slivers of creamy Wensleydale studded with cranberries. Melanie sighed happily. "Oh, now this is more my speed. Sweet and gentle, just the right balance."

"Unlike blue cheese, which clearly needs anger management," Andrew teased.

She nudged him lightly with her shoulder. "Don't be cruel. Maybe blue cheese just had a rough childhood."

The banter rolled easily now, the earlier stillness at the fountain pen and ink stall settling into something lighter. They lingered over a tangy cheddar, debated the merits of smoked cheeses, and finally left the stall carrying a small, wrapped wedge of Wensleydale between them, "for later," the vendor had insisted.

As they stepped back into the market's paths, Melanie looked at Andrew, her eyes bright. "You know, if you'd told me a week ago that I'd be standing in the middle of England, laughing about cheese, I wouldn't have believed you."

Andrew's gaze softened, warmth spreading across his face. "And yet... here you are."

They had only just stepped away from the cheese stall

when the faint rise of a violin drifted across the square. At first, it was almost swallowed by the chatter of the market, but as they neared the corner, the sound lifted, clear, soulful notes dancing above the noise of the crowds.

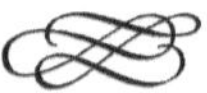

CHAPTER 17

A young man stood with his case open before him, bow sweeping gracefully across the strings. The tune was an old folk melody, threaded through with something wistful.

Melanie slowed to a stop, and lightly touched Andrew's arm. "Oh... listen."

The crowd around them blurred for a moment, just the music and the two of them in its center. Andrew glanced at her profile, the way she tilted her head slightly, as though catching every nuance.

"I used to play the piano," Melanie murmured, almost to herself. "Not well. But I loved the feeling of being lost in the sound."

Andrew smiled, quietly. "Then you and the violinist here have something in common."

They stood together until the tune ended, clapping softly as coins clinked into the case. Melanie fished in her bag, dropping in a few pounds with a shy smile. When the violinist bowed in thanks, Andrew leaned closer and teased, "Careful. He might serenade you next."

"And you'd be jealous," she shot back with mock prim-ness, though the pink in her cheeks gave her away.

They wandered on, their steps easy now, until a little doorway caught Melanie's eye. A wooden sign above proclaimed: "Curiosities & Charms."

"Oh, Andrew, look at that! It's practically calling us in."

Inside, the air smelled faintly of old paper and lavender. Shelves were crowded with mismatched treasures: old pocket watches, glass bottles, carved wooden animals, odd brass instruments whose purpose neither of them could guess.

Melanie picked up a small enamel brooch shaped like a teacup. "Well, that's darling."

Andrew turned over a tiny globe that fit in the palm of his hand. "If only international travel were as easy as spin-ning this."

She grinned. "Would've saved me jet lag."

At the back of the shop, Melanie found a tray of antique keys, each one unique. She held one up, its bow shaped like a heart, the metal worn smooth. "Oh, Andrew. Imagine the doors this might have opened."

He studied it, then her, before saying softly, "Maybe it's still waiting to unlock the right door."

The moment lingered, gentle and unhurried, before Melanie set the key carefully back. "Or at least the right journal," she said lightly, though her eyes held his for a beat longer than usual.

They left the shop with nothing purchased, yet both carried the weight of something found, something not for sale.

As they stepped back into the fading light of afternoon, the market winding toward evening, Andrew cleared his throat. "Shall we head toward supper? Or... dessert first again?"

Melanie laughed, linking her arm through his for just a second before letting go. "I think we've earned both."

The restaurant Andrew chose was tucked into a narrow lane just off the square. Inside, the air was warm with the scent of roasted herbs and baking bread. A hostess led them to a small corner table where a single candle flickered light between them, bringing to light Andrew's lined but kind features and catching the glimmer of silver threads in Melanie's hair.

She slipped off her coat, smoothing it over the back of her chair. "This feels... a little magical," she admitted, lowering her voice as though reluctant to disturb the hush.

"I thought you might like it," Andrew said, his voice modest but tinged with a secret pleasure. He unfolded his napkin across his lap, then met her gaze. "Some places seem meant for conversation."

The waiter brought menus, but for a moment neither of them opened theirs. The candle flame reflected in Melanie's eyes, and Andrew found himself almost forgetting what he'd meant to say. He cleared his throat, breaking the spell. "So... shall we try the specials? Or are you tempted by something else?"

Melanie laughed softly, leaning forward. "If I have learned anything today, it's that England has a way of surprising me with food. I'll trust your judgment."

When the plates arrived: a tender lamb stew for him, a delicately spiced fish dish for her, they both sighed at the first bite. Melanie dabbed at her lips with her napkin. "I think I could grow very fond of this country."

Andrew's eyes warmed. "And this country," he said gently, "could grow very fond of you."

The words hung between them, too heavy to be entirely casual, yet softened by the murmur of voices around them, the clink of cutlery, and the candle's small flame.

When at last they stepped back outside, the night air was cool with a slight breeze. Melanie drew her scarf closer, and Andrew instinctively offered his arm. She accepted, and together they strolled slowly along a cobbled street that led them toward the river.

Somewhere in the distance, a church bell chimed the hour. Melanie tilted her head back, catching the faint glimmer of stars above the rooftops.

"I don't think I'll forget this evening," she murmured.

Andrew glanced at her, his expression unreadable in the shadow, then said softly, "Nor will I."

They walked on, unhurried, letting the night enfold them. The street opened out to the riverside, where the water moved slow and dark beneath the lamps strung along the embankment. Across the river, the silhouette of the Minster loomed faintly, its towers softened by nightfall.

Andrew spotted an empty bench tucked a little apart from the others under a willow tree. "Shall we?" he asked, gesturing toward it.

Melanie nodded, and they sat side by side, the bench creaking lightly beneath them. For a while neither spoke, the only sound the lap of water against stone and the occasional splash of a duck settling in for the night.

Melanie folded her hands in her lap, then glanced at him. "It feels... rare, doesn't it? To just sit. To not rush anywhere."

Andrew smiled, looking out at the river. "I can't

remember the last time I stopped long enough to notice how the air smells after dark." He turned his head, studying her in faint light from the nearby streetlamps. "I suppose I have you to thank for that."

She ducked her head, warmth rising in her cheeks. "All I did was fly across the Atlantic."

"That," he said softly, "is no small thing."

They lapsed into quiet again, but this time it was full, not empty. Melanie found herself aware of the closeness of his arm, the way their shoulders nearly touched. She wondered if he felt it too, that small ache of wanting more and not daring to overstep.

After a long while, Andrew leaned back, exhaling. "It's strange," he murmured. "You sit here beside me, and I feel as though we've known each other for years. And yet... tonight feels like the beginning of something."

Her heart gave a sudden thump. She turned, met his eyes, and saw her own hesitance mirrored there, softened by something deeper.

"Yes," she whispered, her voice barely carrying over the river's hush. "I feel that too."

The moment stretched, sweet and trembling, before Andrew looked away with a small, rueful smile. "We should head back. Tomorrow will come quickly."

They rose together, neither in a hurry. As they walked back toward her hotel, Melanie thought she could still feel the river's quiet inside her, the echo of what had almost been spoken, and perhaps would be, in time.

At last, they reached the hotel's front steps; neither seemed eager to break the spell of the evening.

Andrew cleared his throat gently. "I was thinking... tomorrow morning, if you'd like, we could visit the museum gardens. They're quiet and lovely at this time of year."

Melanie's face brightened. "That sounds perfect. I'd love that."

They lingered there, words seeming reluctant to form. Melanie fiddled with the strap of her bag, her mind still on the conversation by the river.

"Well then," Andrew said, his voice soft, "until morning." He hesitated, long enough that Melanie wondered if he might step closer. But instead, he opened the hotel door for her, the old-fashioned courtesy bringing a smile to her lips.

"Until morning," she echoed, stepping inside.

For a brief moment, their eyes met, the air between them full of the weight of all that had gone unsaid. Then the door closed gently, and she was gone.

Reflections—Melanie

Melanie sat on the edge of her hotel bed, untying her scarf slowly, as though pulling herself out of the day thread by thread. She pressed a hand to her chest, where her heart still felt restless from their riverside talk.

It feels like the beginning of something, he had said. And she had felt it too. But would beginnings like this last?

Reflections—Andrew

Andrew, at home, set his keys on the hall table and leaned against the doorframe. He could still smell the faint trace of her perfume when she'd stood beside him, still hear her laugh echoing in his ears. For years his life had been tidy, predictable, empty in ways he didn't want to admit. Tonight, sitting by the river with her, he'd felt... alive. Younger, somehow.

He rubbed the back of his neck. *Careful,* he warned himself. *Don't go tumbling in too fast.* Yet even as he said it, he knew he was already tumbling.

CHAPTER 18

*M*elanie, the next morning before breakfast, tapped out a message to her friend Ruth back in Boston: *He's kind. He makes me laugh. I feel comfortable with him, though I'm nervous too. We walked by the river last night. It was beautiful. I can't explain it, Ruth. It feels like more than friendship. Am I being silly?*

The reply came minutes later: *Be careful, Melanie. Don't let your heart get carried away. I don't want you to get hurt.*

Melanie sighed, her fingers hovering over the phone. She typed, *I'll be careful,* though part of her wished for encouragement instead of caution.

Andrew, that same morning, had tea with his sister Margaret, who had been curious about Melanie from the start. Over toast and jam, she leaned forward. "So? What's she like?"

Andrew hesitated, then gave a small smile. "She's... genuine. Thoughtful. I find myself wanting to linger in every moment."

Margaret arched a brow. "You've known her a matter of

days in person, Andrew. Don't let your imagination do all the work."

"I know," he said quietly, stirring his tea. "But it doesn't feel imagined."

Margaret softened a little, reaching across to pat his hand. "Then enjoy it. Just don't lose your footing, dear brother."

The morning air was warm when Melanie stepped outside her hotel. Andrew was waiting, hands tucked in his coat pockets, the familiar tilt of his cap already making her smile.

"Ready for a bit of greenery?" he asked.

"More than ready," she said, falling into step beside him.

The Museum Gardens unfolded like a secret kept in the heart of the city, the wide lawns scattered with daffodils, ancient stone ruins draped in ivy, paths winding beneath budding trees. A few early walkers strolled by, but for the most part it felt like the gardens belonged to them alone.

They found themselves drawn to the ruins of the medieval abbey, its arches still rising gracefully despite centuries of weather. Melanie paused, resting her hand lightly on a cool stone pillar.

"It feels... timeless here," she murmured. "Like people have been standing in this same spot for hundreds of years, trying to make sense of their lives."

Andrew glanced at her, his voice low. "I like how you worded that; it's a reminder that our own small worries aren't so heavy in comparison."

But as the words left his mouth, another thought

tugged at him—except some worries aren't small at all. Like how many mornings like this I'll have before she goes home. He pushed it down quickly, offering her a smile when she turned toward him.

They wandered further, finding a bench beneath a budding cherry tree. Melanie settled with a sigh, lifting her face to the branches. A pair of squirrels darted nearby, chasing each other in spirals up the trunk.

She laughed softly. "They remind me of my grandchildren. Always chasing each other, never still."

Andrew tilted his head, watching her more than the squirrels. She spoke with such warmth, such affection, it made him ache a little. She has a whole life waiting back home, he thought. A daughter and grandchildren. How could I ever fit into that?

"Do you miss them?" he asked gently.

She nodded. "Of course. But... I think sometimes it's good to step away from what you know. To see the world from another angle." She hesitated, her smile faltering just slightly. "I'll have to take so many pictures before I go back. Otherwise, I'll wonder if I dreamed it all."

Andrew's heart gave a small, painful twist at the thought of her going back home. He tried to answer lightly: "If it's a dream, then I suppose I'd better stay in it as long as possible."

She turned her gaze to him, and for a heartbeat the unspoken hung between them. Then she smiled again, easing the moment. "Wise advice, Mr. Collins."

They sat quietly for a while, letting the garden's calm settle around them. Children's laughter rang from somewhere across the lawn, and a breeze carried the scent of damp earth and new blossoms. To any passerby, they looked like two old friends enjoying a pleasant morning.

But beneath their stillness ran an unspoken awareness, that time was not infinite, that endings were already approaching, though neither dared give voice to them yet.

After a time, Melanie gave a little stretch and stood. "If I sit here much longer, I might take root."

Andrew chuckled, rising beside her. "Nothing wrong with roots."

"Yes, but I'd prefer to keep moving, thank you. Besides..." She pointed toward the river path where a cluster of ducks had gathered, waddling hopefully near a couple tossing crumbs. "That looks like trouble waiting for us."

Sure enough, the ducks spotted them and began waddling closer.

"Oh no," Andrew muttered. "We've been marked."

Melanie laughed. "They're adorable."

"They're ruthless," he corrected, fishing in his pocket. He pulled out a small paper packet he'd bought earlier at a bakery stall. "Good thing I came prepared."

"You bought food for the ducks?" she asked, eyebrows lifting.

"Well," he said solemnly, although his lips were twitching, "I told myself it was for later. But really, it was for them. Never trust a duck, they'll guilt you into feeding them."

Melanie burst out laughing as he tore the packet open and scattered crumbs. The ducks surged forward, squabbling noisily.

"That one is glaring at you," she teased. "I think you're being judged for uneven distribution."

Andrew raised a brow at the stoutest duck in the group. "That one looks like he'd be happier at the cheese stall."

Melanie giggled, nearly doubling over. "Stop, I'll choke!"

As the ducks squabbled over the last crumbs, they strolled further down the path. Melanie tucked her arm through his for just a moment before letting go. "You make me laugh, Andrew. Even when you don't mean to."

"That's because life's ridiculous," he replied, though his smile betrayed how pleased he was. "Best to laugh at it before it laughs at you."

She tilted her head, studying him. "Were you like this when you taught? Making cheeky jokes at history's expense?"

Andrew chuckled. "Guilty. I once told a class that the Vikings invented fish and chips. Half of them believed me but the headmaster wasn't amused."

"Oh, I would've loved to be in that class," she said warmly. Then, after a pause, "I think your students were lucky. To have someone who saw the humor in things."

Her words settled into him, quiet and sure. He looked at her sidelong. "And I think your grandchildren are lucky to have someone who sees wonder in pressed flowers and duck squabbles."

Melanie smiled, and for a moment they walked in companionable silence, their footsteps in rhythm.

The tea shop Andrew led her to was tucked just off Stonegate, its sign painted with a teapot spilling golden swirls. Inside, the air smelled of warm sugar and butter, and the tables were small, each with a vase of fresh daffodils. They found a quiet corner near the window, where Melanie could watch the street while still feeling wrapped in the shop's cozy hush.

A waitress set down a tiered tray of little cakes and scones, their tops glistening. Melanie's eyes widened. "Andrew Collins, I think you're trying to send me home with an extra ten pounds."

He gave her his familiar smile. "Just making sure Massachusetts remembers Yorkshire properly."

She picked up a tiny sponge cake and held it aloft. "I don't think I've seen anything so perfect. Mine at home always slump in the middle."

Andrew spread clotted cream on a scone with deliberate care. "That's because you're too honest. Cakes, pies—any honest thing should slump a little. Means it's real."

Melanie laughed, shaking her head. "You always have a way of making flaws sound like virtues."

"Because they are," he said simply, before biting into his scone.

They sampled cakes and traded commentary like critics at a fine tasting. Melanie declared the Battenberg "a triumph in geometry," while Andrew insisted the Victoria sponge was "a national treasure." They ended up splitting a slice of lemon drizzle cake, forks clashing playfully in the middle of the plate.

At one point, Melanie leaned back, watching him with a soft smile. "Do you know what strikes me, Andrew? We've done nothing extraordinary these past few days. Just... walking, eating, talking, and a lot of sitting. And yet, it feels remarkable."

Andrew set his fork down, his expression thoughtful. "Perhaps that's what makes it remarkable. Ordinary things, shared. That's what I've been missing all these years, I think."

Her heart gave a little ache at that. She reached across the table, her hand lightly squeezing his before she pulled back. "Then I suppose we'd better keep at it, hadn't we?"

His smile was quiet but full. "I should like that very much."

———

When they'd finished their tea and gathered themselves to leave, Melanie asked lightly, "So, what will we do this evening? Another music night? More pudding?"

Andrew looked at her with a secretive grin, adjusting his cap. "That," he said, "is classified information."

She blinked, then laughed. "Classified? What on earth are you planning?"

"You'll find out in due course," he replied, eyes twinkling. "Let's just say it involves... York after dark. And perhaps a touch of suspense."

Her brows arched, amusement sparking. "You're enjoying this far too much. I'll have you know I don't like surprises."

"Then you're going to love this one," he said, grinning.

Melanie shook her head, half exasperated and half delighted. "Andrew Collins, you are impossible."

"And yet," he said as they stepped out into the sunlight, "you keep showing up anyway."

She laughed, but inside, anticipation fluttered in her chest. Whatever he had planned, she trusted it would be something she'd remember.

They lingered outside the tea shop for a moment, the sun sliding lower.

Andrew cleared his throat. "It'll be a later evening tonight. Perhaps we should each have a little rest first?"

Melanie smiled, secretly relieved. "That might be wise. I'd hate to yawn through your mystery surprise."

"Seven-thirty, then?" he suggested. "I'll meet you here."

"It's a date," she said lightly, then flushed at her own words.

He tipped his cap, the smile playing at his mouth. "Until then."

Melanie

Alone in her room, Melanie kicked off her shoes and lay back on the bed. The quietness of the room wrapped around her, and suddenly she felt the strangeness of it all, this city not her own, the days spilling one into the next like something dreamed.

She thought of Andrew's hand in hers across the tea table. How natural it had felt, touching him, and how dangerous too. What would happen when her return ticket called her back? Would this become only a sweet memory she carried alone?

Still, she smiled, remembering his mysterious tone. York after dark. A touch of suspense. Whatever the evening held, she trusted him. And that trust, she realized, was no small thing.

Andrew

Andrew sat in his armchair, the flat quiet except for the ticking of the mantel clock. He should have dozed, but his thoughts were restless.

He thought of Melanie's laughter spilling out in the tea shop, her eyes shining when she teased him. He thought of the ache in his chest when she'd touched his hand. At his age, he'd accepted that certain things were behind him. Yet here he was, waiting for evening with the anticipation of a young man.

Then came the shadow: She'll have to go home. The thought settled heavily. He stared into the quiet and admitted he was already afraid of losing what had only just begun.

Still, he smiled. Tonight, at least, was his.

<h1 style="text-align:center">CHAPTER 19</h1>

At seven-thirty sharp, Melanie found Andrew waiting outside the tea shop, cap pulled low against the chill. She had wrapped her scarf snug, her cheeks pink in the cool night air.

"So," she said, smiling. "Are you going to end the suspense?"

Andrew's eyes twinkled. "Follow me."

They joined a small crowd gathering near the Minster, where a man in a long cloak and wide-brimmed hat stood holding a lantern. His voice carried easily over the murmur of the group:

"York is the most haunted city in England. Tonight, I'll show you its shadows and the stories that never rest."

Melanie's eyes widened in delight. She turned to Andrew, whispering, "A ghost walk! You scoundrel. And you made me wait all day to find out?"

His grin was unrepentant. "Some suspense is good for the soul."

They wound through narrow cobbled lanes, the light from the lantern bobbing ahead. The guide spun tales of monks who still walked the abbey ruins, of headless Romans glimpsed by the river, of a grey lady said to appear at a shuttered inn.

Melanie clutched Andrew's sleeve more than once, laughing at herself each time. "I don't believe in ghosts," she whispered as they passed a darkened alley.

"Of course not," Andrew replied gravely. "But if one appears, you may stand behind me."

"Behind you?" she whispered, eyes dancing. "Shouldn't you be protecting me?"

He smiled. "At my age, self-preservation comes first."

She swatted his arm, stifling a laugh.

At one point, when the guide lowered his voice to a chilling whisper outside a shuttered inn, Melanie leaned close and murmured, "If I wake screaming tonight, it will be entirely your fault."

Andrew's heart leapt at her nearness. He whispered back, "Then I'll have to live with that guilt."

Melanie

The guide lowered his voice, and the group instinctively pressed closer together.

Andrew's hand found Melanie's, fingers warm and steady, and she felt that a rush of comfort followed by something else she didn't quite know what to do with.

She wanted him closer. Not urgently or desperately but just... closer.

She was suddenly acutely aware of the narrowness of the street, of the way his shoulder moved near hers but never quite touched, of how easily he *could* have drawn her in if he wanted to.

The thought surprised her with its intensity.

His thumb moved once against the back of her hand, a small, absentminded stroke, and her breath caught before she could stop it.

Does he feel this too? she wondered.

She told herself not to read into it. They were standing in public. It was dark. He was being respectful. Andrew was always careful.

And yet the wanting was there now — quiet, persistent and unanswered.

She tightened her grip on his hand, just slightly, as if testing whether he might respond.

He didn't pull away; but he didn't move closer either.

Melanie swallowed, smiling politely at the guide's next story while something tender and unsettled settled into her chest.

When the guide finally dismissed the group near Clifford's Tower, Andrew and Melanie lingered a moment apart from the others. The tower loomed dark above them, the night air cool on their faces.

Melanie shivered slightly. Andrew noticed at once, slipping off his scarf and draping it gently over her shoulders.

"You'll catch cold," he said softly.

She looked up at him, her eyes bright in the lamplight. "Thank you, Andrew."

For a heartbeat, neither moved. The city seemed to hold its breath around them.

Then Melanie smiled, stepping back just enough to ease the moment. "Well. I can't say I expected a ghost walk, but it was perfect."

Andrew returned her smile, though his chest ached with the unsaid. "I'm glad."

They began walking slowly back through the quiet streets, their footsteps in rhythm, their conversation hushed but warm, carrying with them not just the echoes of ghost stories, but the weight of something very much alive.

The streets were nearly empty by the time Andrew and Melanie reached her hotel. They stopped at the steps, the silence between them charged.

Melanie pulled Andrew's scarf a little tighter around her shoulders. "Thank you," she said softly. "For today, for the gardens, for the tea and cakes, for... this evening. It was wonderful."

Andrew's smile was gentle, his eyes lingering on her. "I'm glad you enjoyed it. I wasn't sure if ghost stories were your taste."

"They were perfect," she whispered. "Not because of the ghosts, though."

For a heartbeat, they stood in that quiet, the city hushed around them. Then Melanie reached out, her hand touching his arm lightly. "So... tomorrow morning. The museum gardens set a high bar. You'll have to outdo yourself."

"I'll do my best," he said, his voice low. "Sleep well, Melanie."

She gave a small smile, warm and lingering. "Good-night, Andrew."

He held her gaze for one last moment, then tipped his cap and stepped back as she slipped inside.

Reflections—Melanie

Alone in her room, Melanie stood by the window, looking out over the quiet street. The scarf still carried his warmth, and she pressed her cheek against it for a moment before folding it carefully over the chair and getting ready for bed.

She thought of the way he'd watched her during the ghost walk, the way he'd draped the scarf around her shoulders without hesitation. How natural it felt to be beside him, even in the shadowed streets.

Melanie lay on her back in bed, hands folded over her stomach, staring at the faint outline of the ceiling.

She could still feel the warmth of Andrew's hand in hers. She turned slightly onto her side, drawing the covers closer.

I wanted him closer, she admitted to herself, the thought arriving without shame, only honesty.

It wasn't about urgency or even need, but about connection. About the way something between them had begun to hum softly, insistently, beneath every shared glance.

She wondered if he felt it too—or if wanting had sharpened her imagination. Either way, the absence of something she couldn't quite name left a hollow place behind her ribs.

She reminded herself that wanting more didn't mean she was owed it. Still... wanting didn't simply disappear because it was inconvenient.

Melanie closed her eyes. *I will not rush this,* she told herself.

But I won't pretend I don't feel it or want him either. That, at least, felt honest.

But the thought she'd been avoiding crept in: I'll have to leave soon. This can't last forever.

Her heart twisted with both joy and fear. She whispered aloud into the quiet, "What will happen when I go home?"

Reflections—Andrew

Back in his flat, Andrew sat at the small desk, the journal open but untouched for several minutes.

Tonight frightened me, he finally wrote. He paused, then continued. *Not because of her, but because of what I felt standing beside her.*

He could still picture the way Melanie's fingers curled around his, the way her thumb pressed faintly against his skin as if asking a question he wasn't brave enough to answer. *I wanted to pull her closer,* he wrote. *And I didn't.* The admission sat heavily on the page.

I tell myself that this is respect. That I'm taking things slowly. But the truth is, I'm afraid of how deeply I already care. He exhaled.

If I let myself reach for her, I'm not sure I'd be able to retreat again.

Andrew closed the journal. And then the fear settled in again: *She'll be gone soon. Back across the sea. Back to her life where I'm only words on a screen again.*

The thought hollowed him, but then another followed, steadier. *At least I have these days. At least I've had her laughter here, not just in letters.*

He rose and crossed to his desk, opening the leather journal she had given him again. He dipped his pen, hesitated, then wrote:

Day Four. Ghosts may haunt this city, but none of them haunt me as much as the thought of her leaving.

CHAPTER 20

The National Railway Museum was alive with sound the moment they stepped inside: the low hum of visitors, the faint clatter of footsteps on polished floors, and the distant hiss of a steam engine demonstration. Vast halls stretched ahead, filled with gleaming carriages and iron locomotives that looked too grand, too improbable, to have ever moved across countryside tracks.

Melanie's eyes widened as she took it all in. "Goodness. I feel like a child walking into a toy box."

Andrew chuckled, adjusting his cap. "Except these toys weigh a hundred tons."

They wandered toward the Royal Carriages exhibit, where velvet-lined compartments and polished wood gleamed under the lights. Melanie pressed her hand to the glass, peering at a regal sitting room on wheels. "Imagine traveling like this! I'd feel I ought to be wearing pearls just to sit down."

"You'd be waving regally at every sheep in the field," Andrew teased. He tilted his hand in a royal wave, his face solemn.

Melanie laughed so suddenly she startled a child standing nearby. She shook her head, wiping at her eyes. "Stop it! You'll have me curtseying before the teapot."

"Well," he said with gravity, "if you insist on tea on board, I may oblige."

They moved on to one of the older locomotives, black and powerful, the steel shining as though new. Melanie ran her fingers along the barrier rope. "It's strange, isn't it? These once carried people to beginnings and endings, meetings and goodbyes. How many stories passed through one carriage, unseen?"

Andrew's eyes softened. "You always see the people first. I always see the history."

She turned to him, smiling. "That's why we make a good pair."

Andrew

They paused beside an old display case filled with letters showing thin, careful handwriting pressed beneath glass.

Andrew barely registered the words.

Melanie stood close beside him, her arm touching his arm when she shifted her weight, and the awareness of her was suddenly overwhelming.

He could feel the warmth of her and smell her faint, familiar scent. He thought how easily his hand could have slid to the small of her back. The stirring inside him, unfamiliar, startled him with how intense and real it felt.

Andrew folded his hands together in front of him, grounding himself. *If I start,* he thought, *I don't know if I'll know how to stop.* And that frightened him more than he wanted to admit.

Love, he was discovering, did not arrive gently. It arrived with weight and consequence.

He glanced at Melanie, watching her study the letters, her expression thoughtful, open.

She deserves certainty, he thought. *Not hesitation disguised as affection.*

So he stayed where he was. Careful and close, but not too close.

Melanie turned toward him then, smiling softly, and Andrew returned it, warm and sincere, even as something inside him ached with the effort of holding back.

They discovered a carriage open for visitors to step inside. Andrew held the door for her, and Melanie ducked into the narrow space, settling onto the upholstered bench. Andrew slid in beside her, and for a moment it was easy to imagine the train rocking, countryside flying past the window.

Melanie smoothed her skirt, glancing sideways at him. "If you could take a train anywhere, Andrew, where would you go?"

He tilted his head, considering. "Anywhere? Perhaps the coast. I used to love taking students to Whitby for the sea air and the abbey ruins." His lips quirked. "I could see us there, you know. Fish and chips on the pier, gulls circling like thieves."

She laughed, picturing it. "That sounds perfect."

Then she leaned back, her voice softening. "If I could take a train anywhere, I think... I'd want it to go between here and home. Back and forth, as many times as I liked. No airports, no leaving. Just one more stop after another."

Her words hung in the still air of the carriage, heavier

than she meant them. She glanced away quickly, smoothing her skirt again. "Silly thought."

"Not silly," he said quietly. "Not at all."

They sat a moment longer in the quiet carriage, lost in thoughts they didn't dare yet speak aloud. Then Andrew cleared his throat and rose, offering his hand.

"Come on," he said lightly, his smile returning. "There's a steam engine that needs inspecting. You can tell me if it passes your royal standards."

Melanie laughed. "Very well. But I'll expect velvet cushions."

———

Back in his car again, Andrew drove away from the city, hedgerows flashing past, fields opening wide beneath a pale spring sky. Melanie sat comfortably in the passenger seat, hands folded in her lap, sneaking the occasional glance at Andrew as he drove. He seemed at ease behind the wheel, humming faintly along with the radio, one hand steady on the gearshift.

"This is lovely," she said softly, more to herself than to him.

He glanced over. "Not too bumpy for you?"

"Not at all. I meant... being here. Out in the country. With you."

His lips quirked, and he returned his attention to the road. "Then I've done my job."

CHAPTER 21

They stopped in a village where stone cottages leaned close together, their roofs softened with moss. The pub stood square on the corner, its sign swinging faintly in the breeze: The Fox & Hound. A low doorway led them into a space that smelled of woodsmoke and roasted meat, a hum of voices rising and falling around the worn wooden tables. Andrew guided Melanie toward a small table near the window, the beams above low and dark with age.

Before they could sit, a familiar voice called out: "Andrew Collins, as I live and breathe. Sneaking into my local without so much as a hello?"

Andrew turned, already groaning under his breath.

A tall man with silver hair was striding over, two pints in hand. He grinned broadly. "Knew it had to be you. Haven't seen that cap in years."

Andrew shook his head, half-smiling. "Melanie, this is Nigel. Nigel, Melanie."

Nigel set his pints down and took Melanie's hand warmly. "So, you're the American pen pal. We were beginning to think Andrew had invented you. Too good to be true, and all that."

Melanie laughed, cheeks warming. "I assure you, I'm real."

"Good," Nigel said cheerfully, plopping himself into the chair across from them as though invited. "Because this man hasn't stopped talking about you for months. Letters this, emails that. Nearly drove me mad with it."

Andrew groaned, sinking into his seat. "Do you mind?"

Nigel ignored him, leaning conspiratorially toward Melanie. "I tell you, I've known him thirty years, and I've never seen him so careful about ironing his shirts as he has been this past week."

Melanie's eyes sparkled as she glanced at Andrew, who muttered, "Traitor," into his pint.

As their food arrived, plates of roast beef, Yorkshire pudding, and golden potatoes, the teasing softened. Nigel told a few stories from their school days, painting Andrew as both an earnest teacher and a surprisingly mischievous youth.

"And here I thought he was always so serious," Melanie said, smiling.

"Oh, he's serious, all right," Nigel chuckled. "Serious about his crossword puzzles and keeping the cricket scores straight. But he's also the man who once convinced half a class that Shakespeare invented the sandwich."

Andrew gave Melanie a long-suffering look. "This is what happens when you let him drink at midday."

Melanie laughed until her eyes watered, the warmth of it loosening something in her chest. Watching Andrew with Nigel, the fond teasing, the camaraderie, made him seem even more real, more rooted. He wasn't just the man of her letters, her trip, her private moments. He was part of a community, with a history and people who cared about him.

When Nigel finally rose to return to his mates at the bar, he clapped Andrew on the shoulder and spoke in low voice only he could hear, "She's good for you, old man. Don't muck it up."

After he left, Melanie turned her attention back to her meal. "This is one of those meals you can't rush. Everything about it says, slow down, take your time."

Andrew nodded, taking a sip of his ale. "That's what I like about village pubs. They've no interest in you hurrying out the door."

She studied him over the rim of her glass. "Do you ever think you've hurried through too much of life? Teaching, routines, everything expected of you... and maybe forgetting to notice what you wanted?"

He was quiet for a moment, turning her words over. "A fair question." His eyes lifted to hers. "I suppose I thought duty was enough. That if I did what was expected, the rest would follow. But the truth is, when the duty ended, so did the noise. And I was left with the quiet."

Melanie's heart ached at that. She reached across the table, her fingers brushing the back of his. "I understand. I lived in that quiet too, after my marriage ended. It can be heavy. But it doesn't feel so heavy now."

He turned his hand, letting his fingers curl around hers just briefly, before pulling back with a small smile. "Nor for me."

They ate in companionable silence for a while, the fire warming their shoulders, the pub's hum cocooning them. Outside, the village street was still, only the occasional passerby with a dog breaking the calm.

When the plates were cleared, Andrew leaned back,

studying her. "Would you like a walk before we head back? There's a footpath just beyond the village. Not far, but the view's worth it."

Melanie smiled. "I'd like that very much."

———

They left the warmth of the pub behind and followed a narrow path that wound past the last stone cottages and out into the fields. The air was cool and clean, carrying the scent of damp earth and budding hedgerows. Birds trilled from the branches above, and a brook gurgled softly somewhere out of sight.

Melanie pulled her scarf a little closer. "It's so peaceful here. Almost makes me forget the rest of the world exists."

Andrew smiled, hands in his coat pockets. "That's the trick of the countryside. It doesn't shout. It just waits for you to notice."

They walked in comfortable silence for a while, shoes crunching over the gravel. Then Melanie spoke, her voice softer. "When I was married, we never walked like this. My husband always thought it was a waste of time to just wander. I think... that's why I love it so much now. Walking feels like claiming time back, step by step."

Andrew glanced at her, his brow furrowing slightly. "I'm sorry, Melanie."

She gave him a small smile. "Don't be. It's past. But it makes me grateful for this time right now. For walking with someone who doesn't mind the slow pace."

"I more than don't mind," he said quietly. "I rather treasure it."

They came to a rise where the path opened out, giving them a view of the fields rolling away in shades of green and gold, the horizon touched with distant hills. They stood side by side, taking it in.

"It's beautiful," Melanie murmured.

Andrew nodded. "It is. But..." He hesitated, then went on, "It's more so with someone to share it."

The words hung between them. Melanie turned her head, and for a long moment their eyes met. No jokes, no teasing, just the simple, steady truth of two people seeing each other.

Later, as Andrew steered the car back toward the city, Melanie sat quietly, gazing at the fields slipping by. She thought of the walk, the stillness, the weight of his words. It's more so with someone to share it.

Her chest ached with both joy and the faint, unwelcome tug of worry: *What happens when I go home?* She pressed the thought aside, letting the hum of the car and the nearness of Andrew soothe her for now.

Andrew drove with his usual care, but his mind replayed the sight of her against the countryside sky, the softness in her eyes when she looked at him. He tightened his grip on the wheel. *She'll be gone too soon. And I don't know what I'll do with the quiet when she is.*

Still, when he glanced at her and saw her smiling faintly to herself, he couldn't help smiling too. For the moment, the road stretched ahead, and she was beside him.

CHAPTER 22

By the time they returned to York, the market stalls were still busy, lanterns strung overhead giving the square a festive glow.

Andrew took a few shopping baskets from his car. Melanie paused at the sight of the market square, her eyes bright. "Oh, this is perfect. You do realize, Andrew, that I'm going to insist on carrying half these baskets?"

He laughed. "We'll see. You may have to fight me for the bread."

They wandered among the stalls, choosing a crusty loaf, a wedge of cheese, some potatoes and carrots, a bundle of herbs tied with twine. Melanie picked up a small container of berries, holding them up to her nose. "They smell like summer. Let's get these too."

Andrew only nodded, secretly delighted by her enthusiasm. He bought a bottle of cider from a local vendor, tucking it carefully into the bag.

As they left the square, Melanie murmured, "It's funny. Shopping at a market in a foreign country should feel strange. But with you... it feels ordinary. Comfortable."

He glanced at her sidelong, warmth rising in his chest. "Ordinary's not a bad thing, Melanie. Sometimes it's the very best thing."

Andrew's flat welcomed them with the faint scent of books and the quiet tick of the mantel clock. Melanie slipped off her coat and looked around with interest at the cozy sitting room with its mismatched chairs, the stacks of books on the side table, the tidy but lived-in kitchen.

"It suits you," she said warmly. "Simple. Solid. Just enough."

He set the bags down and grunted softly. "That's one way of putting it."

They began cooking together, the kitchen filling with clatter and laughter. Melanie insisted on chopping vegetables, though Andrew teased that she was far too cautious with the knife.

"At this rate, dinner will be ready tomorrow," he quipped.

She swatted his arm with the wooden spoon. "Patience, Mr. Collins. Good things take time."

He pretended to sigh. "I'll keep that in mind."

When he over-salted the potatoes, she wrinkled her nose dramatically and declared, "Clearly you're trying to shorten my life."

"Or lengthen it by preserving you," he retorted, and her laughter spilled bright into the small kitchen.

They carried the simple supper: roasted chicken, potatoes, vegetables, bread and cheese, to the table, lit only by the soft lamp in the corner. Melanie poured cider into mismatched glasses, raising hers in a toast.

"To markets, and over-salted potatoes, and unexpected joy."

Andrew lifted his glass, his eyes steady on hers. "To company that makes the ordinary extraordinary."

They ate slowly, savoring both the food and the quiet intimacy. Conversation drifted easily, and at one point Melanie leaned back, her gaze soft. "You know, I think this is my favorite part of the trip so far. Not the grand sights or the tours. Just this...cooking and eating together."

Andrew set down his fork, his voice gentle. "So do I."

When the plates were cleared and the kitchen tidied, they sat in the sitting room with cups of tea, the radio playing softly. Melanie curled into the armchair, her hands wrapped around the cup, watching Andrew as he leaned back, looking oddly at peace.

"This feels like home," she said quietly, almost to herself.

Andrew's heart gave a painful, joyous thump. He met her eyes, and for a long moment, neither looked away.

The clock ticked steadily in the silence, wrapping them in a sense of belonging neither had expected to find.

It was late when Andrew pulled his car into the quiet street by Melanie's hotel. Neither of them moved at first, the soft hum of the engine filling the silence.

Melanie broke it with a sigh. "Thank you. For today. The museum, the countryside, the cooking... I don't think I've laughed and felt so at ease in years."

Andrew turned toward her, his expression gentle. "Then it was worth every salted potato."

She chuckled, then fell quiet, her smile lingering.

At the hotel steps, he walked her to the door, as he always did. The scarf he'd loaned her before was still looped around her neck. For a moment they stood together, unwilling to let the day end.

Melanie shifted her bag on her shoulder. "I should let you go. You've indulged me enough for one day."

His voice softened. "Melanie... you've given me more than you know."

Something unspoken pulsed in the quiet between them. She almost reached for his hand, almost leaned closer, but the weight of the moment held them still, balanced on the edge.

At last, Andrew tipped his cap, his smile a little wistful. "Goodnight, Melanie."

Her eyes shone as she answered. "Goodnight, Andrew. Until tomorrow."

Reflections—Melanie

She set her bag down and leaned against the door, her heart full and aching all at once. The time with him tonight had felt so natural. Chopping vegetables, laughing in his kitchen, sipping tea in mismatched cups. Ordinary things. The kind of things that made up a life together with someone.

She pressed a hand to her chest. This feels like home. And that scares me. Because home is supposed to be across an ocean. How can both be true?

His friend Nigel was a character, warm, blunt, full of stories. She had liked him almost immediately. But it wasn't Nigel she was thinking of now. It was Andrew, sitting across from her, pink at the ears, trying to look exasperated while his friend cheerfully exposed thirty years of history.

I've only ever known him through his words to me, she thought. Emails, always his words speaking directly to me. Today I saw him through someone else's eyes. Through the teasing of a friend who's seen him grumble over cricket and iron his shirts too carefully. And what I saw only made me love him more.

Love? Was that what this was? Her throat tightened, and she pressed a hand to her chest.

Nigel had said, "She's good for you, mate. Don't muck it up." She heard it again now, only this time as if it were spoken to her as well: *He's good for you, Melanie. Don't let this slip away.*

It frightened her, that thought. To feel so much, so quickly, after so many years of making herself small. But there it was. In the way Andrew's eyes softened across the table, in how his hand had found hers under the wood, steady and sure.

She closed her eyes, whispering into the stillness: "He is good for me. I have to believe that I am good enough for him, that I am enough."

Melanie stood by the window, watching the lights along the street blur softly in the glass. She replayed more of the day: the museum, and the quiet moments where Andrew had been close enough that she could feel his presence without touching him and she ached for the feel of him.

She let herself admit what she had been carefully skirting all day.

She wanted Andrew—not just his companionship, not just his voice and steady presence, but the warmth of him, the closeness she had felt standing beside him. The wanting didn't frighten her. What startled her was how natural it felt, how quietly it had arrived, without urgency or apology. She wasn't ashamed of it. She was simply aware, for the first time in a long while, that her heart—and her body—were awake again.

She pressed her palm lightly against the glass. *He wants me,* she thought, not with certainty, but with instinct, and that knowledge complicated everything. Because wanting someone who didn't quite reach back hurt in a very particular way.

She wondered whether he held himself back because she was older, because she was divorced, or because she wasn't quite what he'd imagined. The thought stung more than she expected.

Melanie straightened, drawing a slow breath.

No, she told herself firmly. *I will not disappear again.* She would not shrink her own feelings to make someone else comfortable. She would not pretend she wanted less than she did.

If Andrew was holding something back, she would let him, but she would not punish herself for wanting him.

Reflections—Andrew

Back in his flat, Andrew hung his coat and set the market basket aside. The kitchen smelled faintly of roasted herbs, the counters still a little damp from their washing up. For the first time in years, the room felt lived in.

He lowered himself into his chair, letting the quiet settle. But it wasn't the heavy quiet he'd known before. Tonight it felt full, echoing with her laughter, her voice, the soft scrape of her knife on the cutting board.

He closed his eyes. This is what I've missed. Not grand

events. Not noise. Just someone beside me in the ordinary hours.

The ache came then, sharp and sudden, at the thought of her leaving. But he didn't push it away this time. Instead, he whispered into the stillness: "Please... let there be more than this week."

He sat a while longer, the warmth of her presence still lingering, before rising to sit at his desk to write his thoughts.

Day Five. *Today Melanie met Nigel. God help me.*

He smiled faintly at the ink as it curved across the page.

Nigel has known me thirty years. Which is to say, he knows far too much. He teased, of course, about shirts ironed, letters written, and my apparently endless talk of Melanie. I wanted the floor to open and swallow me whole. And yet...

He paused, his pen tapping against the margin.

She laughed. She laughed with him, at me, and in that laughter, I saw her relax further into my world. She saw me not only as a correspondent or a man in her company for these days, but as Andrew-with-his-friends. Andrew, who has lived a life here, and is somehow still worth teasing over a pint.

The ink thickened where he pressed the nib harder.

It frightened me, how exposed I felt. To let her see me through Nigel's eyes, not as I hope to be, but as I am. And yet, I think she liked what she saw. God knows why, but she did.

He set the pen down, rubbing the bridge of his nose.

Perhaps that is the truest measure of this thing between us. Not just how she looks at me when it is only us, but how she looks when others hold the mirror. And tonight, when Nigel called her 'good for me,' she didn't flinch. She smiled. And I... believed him.

Andrew's pen hovered before he wrote. *Today nearly undid me. At the museum, standing beside Melanie, I felt the wanting sharpen— not fade. I felt how easy it would have been to touch her. And how impossible it felt to risk what that touch might awaken.*

He paused. *I am afraid of being the one who wants more.* The words surprised him. *I have lived too long telling myself I am content with what I have. That wanting deeply is foolish at my age.*

He had told himself many careful things about patience and respect, but alone with his thoughts, Andrew allowed the truth its proper name.

He wanted her. Not recklessly or urgently, but deeply, in a way that made restraint an act of will rather than indifference. The awareness settled into him with surprising calm. *Desire, I realize, is not what frightens me. It is how much I hope that she wants me the same way.*

He closed the journal gently, slipping it onto the bedside table.

And as he slid beneath the covers, he thought: *She is good for me, more than Nigel knows and more than even I yet understand. If I don't find the courage to step forward, I may lose her without ever knowing what we could have been.*

The thought stayed with him long after the light went out.

CHAPTER 23

The call came on the morning of her sixth day in York.

Melanie had just finished preparing for her morning outing with Andrew when her phone buzzed with Emily's name. She smiled, expecting a cheerful check-in.

"Hi, sweetheart!"

"Mom, oh, thank goodness you answered." Emily's voice was tight, hurried. "Jack has come down with some awful stomach bug, and Sophie's just started coughing. Daniel's away on business, and I...well, it's a bit of a madhouse here."

"Oh, Emily," Melanie said softly. "I'm so sorry. Have you called the doctor?"

"Yes, the office said there was a nasty virus going around. But honestly, I wish you were here. You always know what to do."

The words landed heavier than they should have. *I wish you were here.*

"I could...well, I could try to come home sooner," Melanie heard herself say. "Change my flight, perhaps."

"Would you?" Emily exhaled audibly. "That would be wonderful. I hate to ask. I just didn't get much sleep last night and I feel exhausted."

"You didn't have to ask," Melanie said, though her heart sank as she spoke.

When the call ended, she sat still, phone in hand, the room suddenly too quiet.

Andrew met her in the hotel lobby. "There you are. I thought we might...Melanie? What's wrong?"

She turned, her smile too quick, too bright. "I think I'll have to go home early. Emily needs me. The children are sick, and she's...well, she's alone with them."

"Oh," he said softly. "I see."

Something flickered in his eyes, disappointment, yes, but also that quiet resignation she'd once seen in herself.

"Of course," he said after a beat. "Family first. Always."

His politeness was unbearable.

"I'll see about changing my ticket," she murmured.

He nodded, trying to smile. "If you need a lift to the station..."

But she couldn't bear the look on his face and interrupted gently, "I'll manage."

After he left, she sat back down and pressed her fingers to her temples. What had she done? Why did doing what she thought was the right thing feel like betrayal?

The train station was crowded when she arrived to ask about changing her ticket. She queued quietly, rehearsing her practical tone. Just a family emergency. Nothing serious.

Ahead of her in line, an older woman and her grown daughter were speaking in low, affectionate voices.

"You didn't have to come, Mum," the younger woman said, shifting a heavy tote. "I'd have managed the move fine."

"Nonsense," the older woman replied. "I like feeling useful."

The daughter smiled wryly. "You're more than useful. You're everything. But it's your turn to have a life, remember? I'm a grown adult, you shouldn't have to rescue me from any little thing that, quite honestly, I am fully capable of dealing with myself. Go have your adventures."

The older woman chuckled. "At my age?"

"At any age."

Something inside Melanie loosened. It was such a simple exchange, but it struck straight through her confusion.

All her life, she'd equated love with sacrifice, and here just now, two strangers were showing her another kind of love: one that gave permission instead of guilt. And when she really thought about it, she had a habit of rescuing her daughter and always being there for her. In doing so, her daughter just expected it.

I think I've enabled her and that needs to stop. Going all the way home early from England because Emily was tired and her grandchildren had a virus? What am I thinking?

Her throat tightened, tears pricking. She stepped out of the queue and sank onto a bench. For once, she wanted to choose herself.

She rose, pulled out her phone, and dialed Emily again.

"Emily," she said gently when her daughter answered,

"I've been thinking. You'll be all right, won't you? You've got the doctor, and Daniel will be home on the weekend."

A long pause. Then a softer voice. "Yes, Mum. We'll manage. Are you sure?"

"I'm sure," Melanie said. "You need to know you can do this without me always rushing in. And I need to...well...no, I want to stay a little longer."

Emily hesitated, then sighed. "Okay. You deserve it. It really was selfish of me to even think you should come home. I'm sorry, Mum."

When the call ended, Melanie laughed through her tears, quiet, astonished laughter. She gathered her bag, left the station, and walked into the rain.

When she reached Andrew's door, she hesitated, not from uncertainty, but to steady the warmth rising in her chest. She knocked once.

He opened it almost immediately. Relief flashed across his face before he masked it with careful politeness.

"Melanie."

Andrew."

He stood aside. "Come in, please." He huffed a small laugh, tension easing. "You didn't go?"

"I did. For a while. I thought I had to."

He gestured for her to sit. She took a spot across the table from him and he set a cup of tea in front of her.

"I've spent my whole life being needed," she said quietly. "And it's wonderful, mostly. But it's also... a kind of cage, isn't it? You start to believe the only way to love is to give yourself away."

Andrew nodded slowly, his throat tight. "Yes. I know that one. Different shape, same feeling."

She looked at him, searching. "You do?"

He smiled ruefully. "After my father died, my mother leaned on me in ways she didn't mean to. I learned to stay small. Reliable. The kind of man people count on, but don't quite see."

The words fell softly between them, heavy with understanding.

Melanie's eyes softened. "It's strange. You and I, both learning how to be seen."

"Seems we're good at practicing it on each other," he said.

She laughed quietly, and the sound shimmered through the room like candlelight. "Emily will be fine. I realized she doesn't need me to fix things anymore. And maybe... maybe I need to learn that, too."

He reached across the table, hesitated, then laid his hand gently over hers. "You've earned your own joy, Melanie. The world will survive if you stop rescuing it for a week."

CHAPTER 24

The spring air carried a faint chill as Melanie and Andrew walked up the slope toward Clifford's Tower. The mound was steep, the stone keep rising solidly at the top, its walls weathered by centuries of sun and rain. Melanie paused halfway, catching her breath, though she smiled at Andrew's mock-offended glance.

"Don't look at me like that," she said, adjusting her scarf. "I told you I wasn't built for English hills."

Andrew laughed. "You've conquered transatlantic flights, ghost walks, and Yorkshire cheese. I think you can manage this."

"Just barely," she said, though her laugh made the climb easier.

At the top, the city spread out below them: rooftops clustered close, church spires punctuating the skyline, the Minster rising tall and solemn in the distance. The morning light gilded the stones, softening their age.

Melanie leaned against the wall, gazing out. "It's beautiful. All those lives down there, layered one over the other. How many people have stood here and looked out like this?

Hundreds of years of them. Each with their own worries, their own loves."

Andrew joined her, resting his hands on the cool stone. "That's history, really. Not the dates and kings. Just... people. Trying, failing, hoping. Leaving echoes behind."

She glanced at him, a smile tugging at her lips. "And you thought you only saw the history while I saw the people."

The corners of his eyes crinkled. "Perhaps I've been influenced by certain company."

They fell into a thoughtful silence, looking out over the city together. For Melanie, the rooftops and lanes shimmered with both strangeness and familiarity, as though she had already lived here in some forgotten chapter. For Andrew, the familiar streets looked new, colored by her presence beside him.

After a while, Melanie spoke softly. "Do you ever wonder how much of your life will be remembered? Not by history books, but... by people."

Andrew tilted his head. "Sometimes. When I was teaching, I thought about it more. If a student remembered one lesson, one story, then perhaps that was enough." He looked at her steadily. "And you? What will your grandchildren remember?"

Her throat tightened unexpectedly. "I hope they'll remember my stories. My pies that never quite came out even. Maybe... that I laughed easily, even when life didn't make it easy." She gave a self-conscious smile. "Not much, really."

Andrew's voice was low. "It's everything."

The words settled between them, heavier than the stone beneath their hands. Melanie felt a tremor of warmth and fear both, and she looked away, blinking at the rooftops as though memorizing them.

After a pause, she said briskly, "Well. If nothing else, they'll remember I climbed this hill without keeling over."

Andrew chuckled. "With some theatrical sighs for effect."

"True," she admitted with a grin. "But I'll take my victories where I can find them."

As they descended the hill together, Andrew thought of the weight of her words, the way she had looked with the city stretching out behind her. She thinks she's leaving only small echoes. She doesn't see how deeply she's already shaping mine.

And Melanie, walking beside him, thought of his quiet "It's everything" and felt her heart stumble in its step. Why does it scare me more to leave him than it did to fly across an ocean to meet him?

By early afternoon, the sun had broken through the clouds, turning the River Ouse into a sheet of rippling silver. Melanie stood at the dock, eyeing the boat that bobbed gently against the moorings. "Well," she said, tilting her head, "it looks sturdier than the one I imagined. I was half expecting a rowboat with peeling paint."

Andrew smiled. "That comes later, once you've passed the intermediate course. Today, you're on the beginner's cruise."

"Oh good," Melanie replied dryly. "I'd hate to capsize on my holiday."

They boarded with the small crowd, finding seats near the railing. The boat eased away from the dock with a soft shudder, and soon they were gliding past green banks and stone bridges.

Melanie leaned over the rail, watching ducks paddle in lazy arcs. "Do you think they recognize every boat that goes by?"

Andrew followed her gaze. "I imagine they just hope each one carries someone daft enough to toss bread."

She laughed. "You would know, you're practically on a first-name basis with the ducks at the Museum Gardens."

"Ruthless creatures," he said solemnly, and she nearly spilled her tea laughing.

As the guide droned amiably over the loudspeaker about the history of the river, Melanie leaned close. "I wonder if he makes up half of this. He could tell us the Romans built this bridge with toothpicks, and I'd believe him."

Andrew chuckled. "Want me to test it? I could raise my hand and ask how many toothpicks exactly."

"Don't you dare," she said, though her eyes sparkled.

He sipped his tea and gave her a sidelong look. "I must say, you're braver than I expected."

"Braver?"

"Coming all this way. Trusting me enough to get on a boat I didn't personally inspect."

Melanie smiled, her voice softening. "Well, you've proven yourself so far. No ghosts have gotten me. No ducks have devoured me. If this boat sinks, I'll blame the river, not you."

"High praise indeed," Andrew murmured, though the warmth in his chest was far more than her teasing tone suggested.

As they passed under a low stone bridge, Melanie ducked her head dramatically. "Oh my! I nearly lost my hat."

Andrew gave her a skeptical glance. "You're not wearing one."

"Details," she said loftily.

He shook his head, chuckling. "You'd make a dreadful sailor."

"And you'd make a dreadful pirate," she shot back. "Too polite. You'd open the treasure chest and apologize to it."

Andrew's laugh rumbled low and genuine, the kind that startled even him. "Then it's fortunate we're neither."

Melanie smiled, watching him laugh, her heart catching at the sight.

The boat looped back toward the dock, sunlight reflecting off the water and Melanie thought to herself how amazing sharing a simple boat ride with him was.

And Andrew, glancing at her out of the corner of his eye, thought: If this were the whole of life, boats, laughter, and her beside me, it would be enough.

They chose to eat their evening meal at a small bistro tucked into one of York's winding lanes, its windows glowing warmly against the dusk. Inside, the tables were close together but not crowded, the air carrying the scent of roasted vegetables and fresh bread.

Andrew pulled out Melanie's chair before sitting across from her. "No ghostly candles tonight," he teased.

Melanie smiled as she set her bag down. "Good. I'd like to see what I'm eating for once."

The waitress brought them menus written on chalkboard paper. Melanie studied hers with a little frown.

"Explain to me again what a ploughman's is? Every time I hear it, I imagine a man with a pitchfork serving bread."

Andrew chuckled. "Not far off. Cheese, bread, pickles, sometimes ham. The pitchfork is optional."

"Hmm," she said, still studying the board. "And if I order that, will you promise not to steal my cheese?"

"No promises," he replied, eyes twinkling.

In the end, Melanie ordered a ploughman's board "for the cultural British experience," and Andrew chose a simple shepherd's pie.

As they waited, Melanie leaned her elbows lightly on the table. "Do you often come here?"

"From time to time," Andrew said. "Mostly when I need a meal that feels like comfort. The shepherd's pie never judges me."

Melanie laughed softly. "We could all use less judgment in our lives." Then her smile faded just slightly. "Do you ever think about how fast this week is going? Tomorrow's Day Seven already."

Andrew swallowed hard. "I do. It feels both short and long, doesn't it? Like we've only just begun and also like... we've known each other a while."

Her eyes softened. "That's exactly it." She paused, as though considering, then said quietly, "I think that's rare. And I don't want to take it for granted."

The waitress arrived with their plates, breaking the moment. Melanie laughed again when she saw the generous spread of bread, cheese, and pickles. "Well, if nothing else, I'll be remembered for conquering a ploughman's."

"And for fending off my attempts to steal from it," Andrew added.

They ate slowly, their conversation meandering, books,

travel dreams, family stories. At one point Melanie described how her grandson once tried to teach her video games, and Andrew nearly choked laughing at her impression of the boy's exasperated sighs.

By the time two servings of sticky toffee pudding arrived, the mood had lightened again. Melanie scooped up the last bite and said firmly, "No regrets. Worth every calorie. I could eat this every night and never tire of it."

Andrew smiled, leaning back with quiet contentment. "A sentiment I can agree with wholeheartedly."

They walked together back through the lamplit streets toward her hotel, the cobblestones slick from an earlier drizzle. The city was quieter now, the day fading into evening calm.

Outside the hotel, they paused as they always did. Melanie smiled up at him, her cheeks flushed from the walk. "Thank you for today, Andrew. For everything. I think this has been another one of my favorite days."

He tipped his cap, his voice low. "Mine too."

For a moment they stood in silence, the air thick with all that remained unsaid. Then Melanie touched his arm gently, her smile lingering. "Goodnight."

"Goodnight," he echoed, his eyes holding hers before she slipped inside.

CHAPTER 25

Melanie was waiting outside her hotel when Andrew arrived, his hands tucked in his coat pockets, a trace of amusement on his face.

"You're early," he said.

She smiled. "I was restless. Besides, you promised to show me your everyday York today. No more castles or ghost stories. I want to see the real Andrew Collins."

His mouth curved into his familiar smile. "Dangerous request. The real Andrew is far less glamorous than you might think."

"I'll take my chances," she said, looping her arm lightly through his as they set off down the street.

Their first stop was the bakery. The air inside was warm and fragrant; the shelves stacked with crusty loaves and sugared pastries. Melanie inhaled deeply. "Oh, I could live here."

Andrew nodded to the woman behind the counter, who greeted him by name. "You'd be broke within a week," he murmured to Melanie.

She chose a small currant bun, and he bought his usual loaf, teasing her as they left. "You've officially crossed into local territory now. You'll be speaking in Yorkshire vowels next."

From there they wandered into a little bookshop, the kind where narrow aisles smelled of paper and dust. Melanie ran her hand along the spines reverently. "Now this," she whispered, "feels like home."

Andrew watched her, the corners of his mouth softening. "I suppose if one had to be haunted, this wouldn't be the worst place."

"You're thinking of ghosts again."

"Occupational hazard," he replied with a grin.

They had just left an antique shop when a familiar voice rang out from across the cobbled street.

"Andrew?"

He turned, blinking in surprise. A woman in her early sixties with a brisk stride and a tartan scarf was waving, a shopping bag swinging from her arm.

"Margaret," Andrew said, his voice warm though touched with a hint of nervousness. "Well, this is unexpected."

Melanie felt a sudden flutter in her chest. His sister. His family.

Margaret reached them, her eyes sharp but kind as they flicked from Andrew to Melanie. "So this is the American visitor you've been keeping such a secret."

"Not a secret," Andrew corrected, faintly pink. "Simply... private."

Margaret arched a brow, then turned to Melanie,

extending her hand. "I'm Margaret. I've heard quite a bit about you."

Melanie felt a flush rise to her cheeks, but she extended her hand warmly. "Yes, I'm Melanie. It's lovely to meet you."

Margaret's lips twitched. "He didn't mention you were this lovely, though. Typical Andrew, downplays everything important."

Andrew sighed, muttering something about exaggerations, but Melanie caught the faint smile tugging at his mouth.

Rather than stand in the street, Margaret insisted they step into a nearby café. The three of them settled at a small round table, cups of tea arriving shortly after.

"So," Margaret said, folding her hands. "You've crossed the Atlantic to see my brother. That takes courage, or foolishness." Her eyes twinkled. "Which was it?"

Melanie laughed softly. "Maybe a bit of both. But mostly hope."

Margaret studied her, then nodded as though satisfied. "Fair enough. I'll tell you something about Andrew: he can be dreadfully stubborn and far too cautious. He'd have happily kept writing emails forever, if you hadn't pushed him."

Andrew groaned. "Margaret..."

But Melanie only smiled. "I might have nudged a little. But he came through."

Margaret's expression softened as she glanced at her brother. "I'm glad he did. It's good to see him smiling again. It's been... a long time."

The care in her voice was unmistakable, and Andrew reached to squeeze her hand briefly. "I'm doing all right,

Margaret. Better than all right." His eyes slid to Melanie, the words carrying more than he spoke aloud.

When they rose to leave, Margaret kissed Andrew's cheek and then Melanie's. "Take care of him," she said warmly.

As they stepped back into the street, Andrew exhaled slowly. "Well. That could have gone worse."

"She loves you," Melanie said gently, slipping her arm through his. "And I like her. She sees you very clearly."

Andrew smiled. "Yes. That's the problem. I'm glad you like her though. Some people think she is too serious and distant."

"It's funny," she said quietly. "Running errands and chatting with your sister, it feels so... normal. Like this could be an ordinary Saturday."

Andrew met her gaze, his voice steady. "Would you like it to be?"

Her heart gave a sudden thump. She looked away from him then, not sure if he meant what she wanted him to mean.

Andrew leaned back and said lightly, "Well. Next stop, the greengrocer. Nothing more glamorous than carrots."

Melanie laughed, though her chest ached with what she hadn't said.

The greengrocer's stall was bright with color: carrots bundled with leafy tops, deep purple beets, glossy apples stacked in pyramids. Melanie picked up a tomato, turning it in her hand.

"They smell richer here," she said. "As though they remember the soil."

Andrew gave her a sidelong smile. "You're romanticizing vegetables."

She wrinkled her nose. "Guilty. But don't tell me you don't hear stories when you look at them."

"Only tragic ones," he said gravely, holding up a knobby potato. "This fellow led a rough life."

Melanie laughed so hard she startled the vendor, who chuckled and slipped an extra apple into her bag "for the joy," he said.

With bags in hand, they strolled back toward Andrew's flat. The streets were lively but not crowded, the air mild for March.

Melanie tilted her head thoughtfully. "Do you ever miss teaching?"

Andrew slowed, considering. "Parts of it. Not the meetings or the bureaucracy. But the students... yes. There's something about sparking curiosity in someone else and watching them light up."

She smiled. "You still do that, you know...spark curiosity. You've been teaching me all week."

He gave a small laugh. "I hardly think cheese tastings and ghost stories count."

"They count," she said firmly, meeting his eyes. "More than you realize."

Her words lingered in the air between them, quiet but certain.

Back at Andrew's flat, they unpacked their bags in easy rhythm. Melanie sliced the bread while Andrew warmed soup on the stove. The simple meal of crusty bread, cheese, apple slices, and steaming bowls of vegetable soup felt richer for being shared.

They sat at his kitchen table, the soft tick of the clock keeping them company.

Melanie stirred her soup idly. "Do you know, I think this

is my favorite kind of meal. Nothing fancy, nothing fussy. Just... nourishing."

Andrew nodded. "There's a kind of honesty in it. Food that doesn't pretend to be more than it is."

She glanced up at him, her smile tinged with something deeper. "A little like you, perhaps."

He ducked his head, embarrassed but warmed. "I'll take that as a compliment."

"It was meant as one," she said softly.

After a while, Melanie leaned back in her chair. "You know, when I told my daughter I was coming here, she worried. Said I was being reckless, flying across the ocean to meet a man I only knew on paper."

Andrew looked at her sharply. "And what do you think? Was she right to worry?"

Melanie shook her head, her expression steady. "No. I knew I was not being reckless. I trusted you. And the moment I met you at the station, I was positive."

The silence stretched, full of all the things they weren't quite ready to name. Then Melanie cleared her throat, lightening her tone. "Besides, you're far too proper to be dangerous. Except to potatoes."

Andrew laughed, tension breaking, though the truth of her words settled deeply in him.

CHAPTER 26

The air outside was cool, the afternoon stretching before them as Andrew guided Melanie toward Coppergate.

"Where are we going?" she asked, her hand tucked in his arm.

"You'll see," he said, his tone sly. "It's something every schoolchild in York is dragged to at least once. Thought you should have the honor."

When they reached the entrance, Melanie read the sign aloud. "Jorvik Viking Centre. Ohhh... Vikings!" Her eyes widened with delight. "Andrew, this is wonderful!"

He chuckled. "Just wait. You've never smelled a Viking street until you've smelled one recreated."

Inside, they climbed into the slow-moving carriage that carried visitors through a reconstruction of Viking-age York. The lights dimmed, and the sounds of traders and animals filled the air. A woman's voice chanted in Old Norse as the car glided forward.

Melanie gasped softly. "Andrew, it's like stepping back in time!"

He watched her more than the animatronic figures. Her wide-eyed wonder, the way she leaned forward as if afraid to miss a detail, made his heart swell. "It's quite something," he agreed. "Though I must admit, the smells are… rather authentic."

As if on cue, the scent of smoke and tar drifted through the air, mingling with less pleasant odors. Melanie wrinkled her nose, laughing. "Goodness! That's… vivid. Did people really live like this?"

"Oh yes," Andrew said, pleased to play the historian. "York was Jorvik, a major Viking city. Traders, craftsmen, warriors… all crowded together. And I daresay the perfume of the place would have been even stronger in reality."

She nudged his arm playfully. "You sound like their tour guide. Should I be imagining you in a helmet, swinging a sword?"

He gave her a sideways look, dry but amused. "If you must."

"I think you'd make quite a good Viking," she teased, eyes dancing. "Strong, stoic, slightly terrifying, but only on the outside."

The carriage jolted past a smithy, sparks flashing, and Melanie gripped his hand instinctively. Andrew turned his palm over, holding hers securely.

"You're safe," he said quietly, and realized in that moment it wasn't just a jest. With her hand in his, he wanted to promise safety always. He didn't let go of her hand.

When the ride ended, they stepped into the gallery with glass cases for artifacts of jewelry, tools and fragments of bone. Melanie lingered over a delicate silver brooch.

"It amazes me," she murmured, "how something can

last a thousand years. And here we are, looking at it like it's new."

Andrew studied her profile in the soft light, her expression full of reverence. "Some things do last," he said softly.

They left Jorvik with the early dusk settling over York, the air cool and tinged with woodsmoke. Melanie looped her arm through Andrew's as they walked, her eyes still bright from the afternoon.

"I have to say," she began, trying to keep a straight face, "I'll never forget it. The sights, the sounds, the... smells."

Andrew gave her a sidelong look. "Authenticity, Melanie. History is never tidy."

She laughed, then leaned closer, lowering her voice as if confiding a secret. "You know, I think I rather like the idea of you as a Viking. Tall, brooding, a little fierce. I can picture you standing on the prow of a longship, staring down the horizon."

His ears reddened. "Don't be ridiculous."

"I'm not," she insisted, her grin mischievous. "You'd make a very fine Viking. The sort people would follow."

He shook his head, though his mouth twitched as if fighting a smile. "If I were a Viking, I'd have been the one cataloguing the spoils, not swinging the sword."

"Oh, the scholarly Viking," Melanie teased. "With a horned helmet tilted sideways on his head while he's writing in his journal."

He groaned, but her laughter made his heart feel dangerously light.

Back at Andrew's flat, he set out a simple supper: bread, cheese, and fruit. Melanie helped slice the apples, brushing her hand against his more than once, each time sending a quiet spark through them both.

They ate at the table, but lingered long after the food was gone, their conversation meandering, from the artifacts at Jorvik to what York might have looked like centuries ago.

"You know," she said, stifling a yawn, "I think the Viking ride might be one of my favorite parts of this trip."

"Really? I thought yesterday and the day before and the day before were your favorites." he asked, surprised.

"Mmm." She smiled. "Because I got to see you as a Viking. And trust me, Andrew, you'd have been formidable."

He chuckled low in his chest, "You're impossible."

By the time the dishes were cleared and the last crumbs of bread tucked away, twilight had settled across the city. Andrew switched on a lamp in the sitting room, the light softening the edges of the room.

"Tea?" he asked, already filling the kettle.

Melanie smiled. "I wouldn't say no. You make a very proper cup."

He chuckled. "Years of practice. Survival skill, really."

While he busied himself in the kitchen, Melanie wandered to his bookcase. She trailed her fingers along the spines, pausing now and then to read a title. "You've read all these?"

"Most of them," he called back. "Some I keep just to look intelligent."

She laughed, pulling one slim volume from the shelf. It was well-worn, its pages softened with use. She opened it carefully, then looked over her shoulder as he entered with the tea tray. "This one's loved."

Andrew glanced at it and gave a small smile. "Poetry. I used to read a piece or two before lessons. The students groaned, of course, but I like to think it stuck."

Melanie returned the book to its place, touched by the thought. "Do you ever read them aloud now?"

He set the tray down and shrugged. "Not often. The walls don't applaud."

"Then maybe you'll read one to me some time," she said lightly, though her eyes held his.

His throat tightened at the simple request, and he only nodded, pouring the tea carefully to hide it.

They settled into their chairs, cups warming their hands, the radio humming softly in the background. For a while they spoke of little things: the weather forecast, tomorrow's plans, the stubbornness of his old radio that always drifted off station.

Then Melanie's voice grew quieter. "You know, when I first thought about this trip, I was terrified. Not of flying, or of being in a new place. But of being disappointed. Or worse... disappointing you."

Andrew looked at her, startled. "Disappointing me? Melanie..."

She waved a hand gently, as if to soften the moment. "I know it's silly. But when you spend so long in letters, you build an image. I thought, what if I didn't fit the picture in your head?"

He set his cup down firmly. "You have never fit into a picture, Melanie. You've been more than I imagined. More than I dared hope for."

The words slipped out before he could temper them, and silence followed, heavy but not uncomfortable. Melanie's eyes softened, glimmering in the lamplight.

"Thank you," she said, her voice barely above a whisper.

When at last it grew late, Andrew walked her back to her hotel. The air was cool, the streets quieter than usual, their footsteps echoing softly.

At the hotel steps, they paused as always. This time, Melanie didn't look hurried to go inside. She lingered, turning slightly toward him.

"I don't want to sound like a broken record," she said, "but... thank you. Today felt like... life. Not a holiday, not an escape. Just... life. And I needed that."

Andrew's throat tightened. He tipped his cap, his voice low. "So did I."

They stood in the quiet a moment longer, the distance between them charged. Melanie smiled gently, touched his arm with her fingertips, then whispered, "Goodnight."

"Goodnight," he echoed, watching as she slipped inside.

CHAPTER 27

Reflections—Melanie

Melanie lay back against her pillows, replaying the café scene over and over. Margaret's sharp wit, the way Andrew shifted uncomfortably in his chair, the tenderness between them when his hand squeezed hers.

She smiled into the dark. I liked her. She was honest, quick, unafraid to say what she saw. And what she saw was him, the real Andrew, not just the one he shows me when it's only us. She loves him fiercely, that much is clear. And she wants him happy.

She remembered Margaret's words: "It's good to see him smiling again."

Smiling again. Which means he has smiled like this before, and then... stopped. But now? Now it's back. And I'm part of why. The thought humbled her.

A lump rose in her throat. "Oh, Andrew," she whispered

softly into the quiet. "You don't even know what you've given me."

Sleep came slowly, but when it did, it carried with it the image of Andrew smiling, not for Nigel, not for Margaret, but for her.

Reflection—Andrew

Day Seven. Today we ran into Margaret. Chance, but perhaps the right kind of chance. I worried, of course, because she's my sister, and sisters see more than you want them to.

She wasted no time, naturally. Teasing me in front of Melanie, pointing out my stubbornness, reminding us both of my tendency to overthink. I ought to be irritated, but the truth is... I was grateful. Grateful that Melanie could see me through family eyes, not polished, not arranged, but simply as I am.

And Melanie laughed. She wasn't put off by Margaret's sharpness. She held her own, answered with warmth, even teased me back. Watching the two of them together, for just a moment, I glimpsed what it might be like, a future where my sister and the woman I love sit at the same table as though it were always meant to be.

He paused, his hand tightening around the pen.

Margaret said it's been a long time since she's seen me smile like this. She's right. Too long. And tonight, as I write this, I can't help but think perhaps she saw the truth I haven't dared say aloud. That I am in love, and it shows on my face whether I speak it or not.

I have not written this before, not even here, and perhaps tonight is the right night to set it down. Margaret's words have been echoing in my mind since the café: "It's good to see you smiling again." Why did I stop? Why did I let myself go so long without joy?

There was a woman, years ago. A colleague, Veronica. She laughed at my dry remarks, sought me out in the staff room, even walked home with me when her car was in for service. I thought...well, I don't know what I thought. That perhaps she saw me. The me I never trusted anyone to want. I cared for her more than I admitted, even to myself.

But I hesitated...always I hesitated. She wanted boldness, certainty, declarations. I offered caution, pauses, the kind of love that builds quietly. And before I could find the courage to speak, she was gone. Married another man. Settled elsewhere. She deserved happiness, of course she did. But in her leaving I heard only this: that no one would ever wait for me. That I was too slow, too unsure, too little.

That was the day I stopped smiling, I think. Not all at once, not dramatically. But a slow dimming. Smiles became polite, then rare, then almost foreign. Margaret saw it. Everyone must have, though no one said it aloud. I told myself I was content with books, with letters, with my students. But the truth was, I had folded myself into smallness, convinced I was better unseen than unwanted.

And then Melanie replied to my letter. Just a letter, at first. Then another. And another. And somehow, through words on a screen, she coaxed a smile out of me. Not polite, not forced, but real. The kind I thought I'd lost. She doesn't demand I be more than I am. She simply... sees me. And God help me, I think she always has.

CHAPTER 28

The road wound through rolling moors, wide skies stretching pale blue above them. Heather was only just beginning to tint the hills with purple, and sheep dotted the fields like stray clouds. Melanie sat gazing out the window, her hands folded in her lap, a small smile on her lips.

"It's wild," she murmured. "So open. Almost too big for my eyes."

Andrew glanced at her, warmed by her wonder. I've driven this road countless times, and yet with her it feels like the first time again.

The sea air greeted them before they reached the town, sharp, salty, and alive. Whitby spread out below, its red-roofed houses climbing the hillside, the harbor dotted with fishing boats. Above it all, the ruins of Whitby Abbey stood stark against the sky, their gothic arches jagged like teeth, beautiful and haunting both.

Melanie stepped out of the car and inhaled deeply. "Oh... Andrew. I can smell the salt. It's wonderful."

He smiled, his heart tugging at the joy in her face. "Best air in England, if you ask me."

And one day soon she'll breathe Massachusetts air again, he thought, a pang tightening his chest. He pushed it away, offering her his arm. "Come along, then. We've a hundred and ninety-nine steps to climb before you earn your fish and chips."

Her eyes widened. "Steps?"

He grinned. "Yes. Steep ones. But worth it."

The climb to the abbey ruins left Melanie breathless but laughing, and when they reached the top, the view swept the effort away. The North Sea stretched endless and silver, the wind tugging at their coats. The abbey ruins rose around them, arches and pillars silhouetted against the restless sky.

Melanie stood still, hair blown loose from her scarf, eyes wide. "It feels... otherworldly. As if the past is still alive here."

Andrew nodded, his gaze not on the ruins but on her. *She looks as though she belongs here. And yet she doesn't. She belongs across the ocean. What am I doing, letting myself hope?*

She turned to him suddenly, catching his expression. "You've gone quiet."

He cleared his throat. "Just thinking how many storms these stones have seen. And still they stand."

Her smile softened. "That's reassuring."

More than you know, he thought.

Later, they descended into the town, their legs grateful for the downhill stretch. The harbor was lively with gulls wheeling overhead, their cries sharp. They found a bench overlooking the boats and shared a paper parcel of fish and chips, the steam rising in the cool air.

Melanie bit into hers and laughed. "It's scandalous, Andrew. I've never tasted anything this good. I'll be ruined for American fish forever."

He chuckled, watching the grease glisten on her fingers as she dabbed them with the flimsy napkin. *How can something so simple, sitting on a bench with fish and chips, feel like everything I've wanted?*

Melanie glanced at him, catching the softness in his eyes, and her chest gave a small ache. *How will I leave this? Him?*

They strolled the stone pier after lunch, the sea wind bracing, gulls darting close. Melanie held her scarf tight, laughing when the wind nearly pulled it free. Andrew steadied her with a hand at her elbow, the warmth of his touch steadying her more than the pier beneath her feet.

"This place is alive," she said, her cheeks pink with cold. "The air, the water, everything. It feels like it doesn't need people, but it lets us borrow it for a while."

Andrew looked out to the restless horizon. *Borrow. That's the word. Borrowed time. Borrowed days. And what happens when she gives them back?*

He said only, "A fair observation," though his voice carried more weight than he meant.

She glanced at him, hearing it, and tucked her hand briefly through his arm. Neither spoke of the ache rising in them both.

When they reached the sea, the tide was low and glittering. Gulls wheeled above the promenade, and a cool breeze carried the scent of salt and lavender.

"Still glad you stayed?" he asked.

"More than I can say."

They walked along the shore, their footsteps parallel, the waves lapping softly beside them.

"I think the sea approves of your decision."

She smiled, the wind teasing her hair. "Then it's settled. I'll listen to the sea from now on."

The sun was low as they wound back through the moors. Melanie rested her head lightly against the seat, drowsy but content. She thought of the abbey's arches against the sky, of Andrew's hand steady at her elbow. *This week is slipping like sand through my fingers. What will I do when it's gone?*

Andrew kept his eyes on the road, but his thoughts churned. *I can't ask her to stay. She has her family, her roots. But if she goes...will I ever feel this alive again?*

CHAPTER 29

By the time they returned to York, dusk had folded itself over the city, a few shop windows were still lit, but the noise of the day had fallen into quiet.

Andrew parked near Melanie's hotel, then hesitated. "Are you tired? I could walk you in, let you rest after the day."

Melanie shook her head quickly. "No, not yet. I'd like a little more time." She glanced at the small café across the street and pointed towards it. "Maybe a cup of tea? It would be nice to sit and relax for a little while. Somewhere quiet... maybe that little café?"

Andrew followed her gaze and smiled. "That sounds about right."

They found a corner table in the nearly empty café, the windows fogged faintly from the steam of kettles. The waitress brought them a pot of Earl Grey and two small cups. The scent rose warm and familiar, wrapping around them.

Melanie curled her hands around her cup. "I feel like the sea is still in me," she said softly. "Like it's rocking in my chest."

Andrew stirred his tea, his spoon clinking lightly. "It does that. Leaves you feeling both alive and small."

Her gaze lifted to him. "Do you ever feel small, Andrew?"

He gave a short laugh. "All the time. Though today, standing by those ruins... it wasn't the abbey that made me feel small. It was realizing how quickly time runs out, how fast days slip by." He hesitated, then looked down into his cup. "Like this week."

Melanie wanted to answer, to tell him she felt the same ache, but the words tangled in her throat. "Then we'll just have to hold onto each moment while we have it."

Andrew

It had been happening all day. He noticed the way she laughed without checking herself, the way she had reached for his arm earlier without thinking, and the way her presence felt... woven into him now.

I love her. The thought didn't arrive with fireworks. It arrived with gravity.

Andrew's hands stopped stirring his tea. Love meant risk; love meant being seen and believing someone might actually stay. And that was the part of him that had learned not to hope.

He stirred his tea again, giving himself a moment to breathe, to steady the sudden tremor beneath his ribs.

Melanie turned. "Are you all right?"

"Yes," he said quickly. "Of course." But he didn't smile the way he usually did and didn't meet her eyes for quite as long. Something, just a fraction pulled back.

He told himself it was nothing…just tiredness and the day catching up with him.

But he knew better. It was fear.

And it had just quietly taken a seat between them.

When the café closed, they stepped back into the cool evening, the air carrying the faint scent of rain. Their footsteps echoed on the cobblestones as they strolled toward the hotel, their hands brushing now and then.

Melanie broke the silence with a small laugh. "You know, back at the pier I thought I might lose my scarf entirely. If it had gone, you'd have seen me chase it straight into the sea."

Andrew smiled. "I wouldn't have let you. I'd have gone in after it myself."

She looked up at him, eyes bright. "Not for the scarf, surely."

"No," he said softly. "Not for the scarf."

Outside the hotel, Melanie hesitated, reluctant to end the night. She turned to him, her voice low. "Thank you. For today. For the sea, the abbey, the fish and chips. I'll never forget it."

Andrew looked down at her. "Nor I. We made memories."

For a long moment, they simply stood there. Then Melanie touched his sleeve, lingering just a second longer than usual. "Goodnight, Andrew."

"Goodnight, Melanie," he whispered, his voice thick.

As she disappeared inside, he remained on the pavement, staring after her until the door closed. His chest ached but mingled with it was something fierce and unde-niable: *I don't want to lose this. I can't.*

Reflections—Melanie

The room was still, the hum of the city muffled by heavy curtains. Melanie sat on the edge of the bed, still wrapped in her scarf, as though reluctant to shed the day. She could taste the salt air lingering on her lips, hear the crash of waves in her memory.

She closed her eyes, remembering his words, "Not for the scarf."

Her heart ached with the truth she hadn't spoken aloud: she didn't want to leave. Not yet. Not when she had only just begun to see what a life with him might feel like.

But her grandchildren's faces rose in her mind: waiting, expecting her return. Two worlds tugging, neither one easy to release.

Melanie lay back against the pillows. *I don't want to leave this yet.*

Reflections—Andrew

Andrew sat in his armchair, a cup of tea cooling on the table beside him. But he wasn't looking at the tea. He was staring at the scarf draped neatly over the back of the chair where Melanie had laid it nights before.

He thought of her laughter on the pier, her eyes shining against the backdrop of the abbey, the quiet courage in her voice when she said they'd have to hold onto each moment. And then her words at the hotel: "I'll never forget it."

He rubbed a hand over his face, his chest heavy with a

longing he hadn't felt in years. *I don't want her to leave. Not yet...not at all.*

But he could see no way forward. Her family was an ocean away. His life was here, stitched into York's cobbles and quiet routines. And yet the thought of returning to those routines without her was unbearable.

He leaned back, closing his eyes, and whispered into the still room: "Please let there be more."

The clock ticked on, steady and indifferent, but Andrew held onto the hope as though it were the only anchor left to him.

CHAPTER 30

The morning broke pale and cool, the sky a soft wash of grey. Melanie met Andrew outside her hotel, a little paper list folded in her pocket.

"I need to find something for my grandchildren," she confessed, smiling a little sheepishly. "They've been very patient with Grandma going on an adventure without them."

Andrew nodded, his smile warm. "Then we'd better do it properly. York has no shortage of trinkets to delight small hands."

They wandered into the Shambles Market, where stalls spilled over with knitted scarves, painted cups, jars of honey, and tiny carved animals. The cobbled lane buzzed with chatter and the scent of roasting nuts.

Melanie stopped at a table of hand-painted wooden toys, picking up a little train with careful fingers. "Jack will love this. He's crazy for anything with wheels."

Andrew picked up a small carved cat from the same stall, its back arched playfully. "And this one? Perhaps for Sophie?"

Melanie smiled, touched. "She would adore it." She hesitated, then added softly, "You're good at this."

Andrew shrugged, but his throat tightened. Because it feels like choosing for my own.

The café was small, tucked into one of the quieter lanes, with lace curtains in the windows and mismatched china cups. They chose a corner table; their shopping bags piled at their feet.

Melanie wrapped her hands around the warm cup, inhaling the faint citrus of Earl Grey. "I think I'm done," she said, smiling faintly. "If I buy anything else, I'll need another suitcase."

Andrew arched a brow. "And that would be such a terrible tragedy?"

She laughed, shaking her head. "I'd never get it through customs." She fell quiet for a moment, gazing out the window at a boy tugging his mother's hand along the cobblestones. "It's strange, though. I came thinking I'd want to bring back as many things as I could... to remind me. But it turns out the things I want to remember most won't fit in a suitcase."

Andrew stirred his tea slowly, his spoon clinking against the cup. I know what you mean, he thought, but what came out was, "You'll have your photographs. And your journal."

"Yes," Melanie agreed softly. "But they won't capture everything." She looked at him then, as if to add something more, but the words tangled. *Say it, Melanie. Tell him you'll miss him, not just the sights.*

Instead, she smiled lightly. "You'll just have to come to Massachusetts one day. Then I can return the favor."

Andrew's heart leapt, but he covered it with a smile. "And risk your grandchildren teaching me video games? I'm not sure I'd survive it."

They left the café and wandered the cobbled streets, the market slowly winding down. The air smelled faintly of roasted nuts and damp stone. Melanie stopped at a stall of hand-knit scarves, running the soft wool through her fingers.

"You'd look well in blue," Andrew said, surprising himself.

She glanced at him, amused. "Are you suddenly my stylist?"

"Purely observational," he said, the corners of his eyes crinkling as he smiled. "Besides, you're safer with scarves than hats. Less risk of it blowing off your head."

She laughed, tucking the scarf back on the pile. "True." But as they walked on, she thought, *He notices me. Even in such small ways. When was the last time someone really noticed me?*

Later they paused at a shop window filled with fountain pens, bottles of ink in jewel tones arranged like treasures. Melanie lingered, her face softening. "They're beautiful," she whispered. "I used to think pens had personalities. That the right one could change how you write."

Andrew studied her quietly. *That's why she brought me the journal. She's given me her heart in small, thoughtful ways. And what have I given her in return? Only my silence when it matters most.*

He wanted to say something, but the words caught in

his throat. Instead, he said lightly, "Then perhaps one will find its way into your suitcase yet."

She smiled, though inside the ache grew sharper. *I don't need a pen. I need you. But how can I ask for that, when an ocean waits between us?*

They chose to have supper at a small inn with low beams and a fire burning in the hearth. The dining room was nearly empty, just a few couples scattered at other tables. A vase of daffodils sat between them, their yellow heads nodding gently in the lamplight.

The food was simple, Andrew with a lamb stew, Melanie with a savory pie. They ate slowly, the conversation meandering at first, about how lamb-based meals were not as common in restaurants in the United States, the peculiar accents they'd overheard, how English pickles seemed to appear on every plate, and then, gradually, the talk grew softer.

Melanie set down her fork and leaned back. "It's odd. The more ordinary the setting, the more I find myself wanting to freeze it. Just this, this table, this fire, your ridiculous commentary on pickles." She laughed quietly. "It's the everyday things I'll miss most."

Andrew swallowed. He wanted to reach across the table, to take her hand, but he settled for his words. "That's because the everyday things matter most." He hesitated, then added, "And they're the hardest to leave behind."

She looked at him steadily, her eyes glimmering in the firelight. For a moment, the room seemed to narrow to just the two of them.

Tell him, she thought. *Tell him you don't want to go.*

But instead, she said softly, "Then let's not talk about leaving tonight. Let's just... let it be."

Andrew nodded, though his heart ached. *If I agree, does it mean I'm accepting the end?*

They finished their meal quietly, then lingered by the fire with cups of tea, speaking little. The silence between them was not uncomfortable but weighted with all that neither dared voice.

He walked her back to her hotel, but instead of parting at the hotel door, Andrew paused, his hand lingering at his side. "Would you... walk a little?" His voice was quiet, almost tentative.

Melanie hesitated only a heartbeat before nodding. "Yes. I'd like that."

They turned together, their footsteps soft on the cobbles as they made their way toward the Ouse. The river lay dark, rippling with the reflection of bridges and the occasional passing boat.

Melanie broke the silence first, her voice low. "When I go home, I think I'll dream about this city. Not the big things, though the Minster, the abbey, the sea... they'll stay with me. But it's the sound of the cobbles underfoot. The way the air smells near the river. Even the ducks." She laughed softly. "I'll miss the ducks."

Andrew smiled faintly. "And I'll miss seeing it all through your eyes."

She turned her head, catching the weight in his gaze, and her breath caught.

For a moment she wanted to tell him, everything, but the words hovered unspoken.

Instead, she slipped her arm lightly through his. They walked in silence for a while, the water whispering beside them.

At a bench overlooking the river, they stopped. Melanie sat, Andrew beside her, silent. Melanie had been talking, something about her grandchildren, about how Jack was obsessed with anything that had buttons, when she realized Andrew hadn't said anything for a while. She glanced at him.

He was listening. She could see that. His gaze was on her, his expression gentle and attentive. But something was different. Not colder or distant, just... slightly farther away.

"You're very quiet tonight," she said softly.

"Am I?" he asked, and smiled, the same warm smile she loved. But it didn't quite reach his eyes the way it had earlier.

Melanie felt a small, unwelcome ache stir in her chest. She told herself not to read too much into it. People had moods. People got tired. It was foolish to assume anything meant something.

And yet...

When they started walking back and paused by the railing, the place where they had lingered together so many times before, she waited, half unconsciously, for him to stand a little closer.

He didn't. It wasn't obvious and it was only a few inches...but it felt like miles.

Her heart tightened. *Did I imagine everything? Did I lean too far, too fast?*

Andrew still smiled, spoke kindly and still walked beside her.

But Melanie suddenly felt as if she were standing on the edge of something uncertain, unsure whether to step forward or pull back.

She folded her hands together, hiding their faint tremble.

Finally, she spoke, her voice barely more than a whisper. "I don't want this to end."

Andrew's hand tightened on the railing. His heart hammered, but he forced himself to answer carefully. "Nor do I."

She turned her face toward him, her eyes glimmering in the soft light. For a long moment they simply looked at each other, the world narrowing to the quiet rush of the river and the space between them.

Tell her how you feel, you coward. Andrew lifted a hand slightly, then let it rest back on his knee. *But what if she doesn't want me that way?*

Melanie's fingers twitched, aching to close the gap. *Say it, Melanie. Tell him. But if you do, how can you bear to leave?*

When they finally rose and walked back, the silence between them was tender, not empty. Outside her hotel, Melanie turned to him. "Thank you," she said softly. "For not letting the night end too soon."

Andrew tipped his head, his throat tight. "It was my pleasure."

She touched his sleeve briefly, lingering. "Goodnight, Andrew."

"Goodnight, Melanie."

And when she slipped inside, the absence of her arm in his was sharper than he had expected, leaving him standing alone under the lamplight with only the echo of her words: *I don't want this to end.*

Reflections—Andrew

Andrew sat in his armchair long after returning, the fire in the grate burned down to embers. His hands rested loosely on his knees, but his mind replayed the night in merciless detail.

He closed his eyes, jaw tightening. *Why didn't I kiss her? Why didn't I tell her I'm falling in love with her?*

He had wanted to. God, he had wanted to. The moment had been there, hanging in the air like a ripe fruit waiting to be picked. But he had hesitated, as he always did, afraid of frightening her and discovering that the tenderness in her eyes was not what he hoped it was.

A hollow laugh escaped him. "Coward," he muttered into the empty room.

The truth gnawed at him: he was afraid. Afraid that if he kissed her, he would never want to let her go. And she had a family, a life an ocean away. *What right do I have to want more?*

Still, when he finally dragged himself to bed, it was her face he saw as his eyes closed, her voice whispering, *I don't want this to end.* And the ache in his chest told him what he already knew: neither did he. But fear held him hostage.

Reflections—Melanie

Melanie lay in bed staring at the ceiling, the room quiet except for the faint hum of traffic beyond the curtains. Her scarf still carried the scent of salt and woodsmoke from their walk, and she pressed it to her cheek as though it could anchor her.

Her mind replayed the bench by the river, the way his hand had hovered, the way his eyes had searched hers. She had been certain he would lean closer, that the moment was building toward a kiss. But then... nothing.

Her heart twisted. *Why didn't he? Didn't he want to?*

She closed her eyes, remembering the warmth of his arm beneath her hand, the weight of his gaze. *But maybe... maybe he doesn't see me that way. Maybe I'm just something temporary for him, a pleasant interlude. Maybe I'm not enough.*

The thought hollowed her. She rolled onto her side, blinking back tears.

Yet even as doubt pricked, another truth pressed close, stubborn and undeniable: she had felt something in him. Something steady and yearning, held back only by fear.

"Why didn't you kiss me, Andrew?" she whispered into the dark.

The silence gave no answer, but her heart knew the question mattered less than what it revealed: she wanted him to.

CHAPTER 31

The morning broke grey and cool, a mist hanging low over York. Melanie stood in the hotel lobby, her suitcase at her side, the paper bag of souvenirs tucked carefully on top. The hum of voices around her felt distant and muffled.

Andrew arrived right on time, his cap in his hand, his smile faint but steady. "Ready?"

"As I'll ever be," Melanie whispered.

They walked together to the train station, her suitcase wheels rattling over the cobblestones. Neither spoke much. The city seemed quieter than usual, as if it too knew this was the end.

The train sat waiting, its engine idling with a low growl, the smell of diesel sharp in the cool air. Passengers milled about, checking tickets, loading luggage.

Melanie's throat felt tight. She turned to Andrew, managing a wobbly smile. "Well. This is it."

He nodded, but his hands clenched around the brim of his cap. "I wish it weren't."

Her chest ached at the raw honesty in his voice. She

reached out, brushing his sleeve with trembling fingers. "These days... they've meant more than I can say. You've meant more."

Andrew swallowed hard. His mind screamed with everything he wanted to say: *Stay. Don't go. I can't bear the quiet without you.* But the words lodged in his throat. He had never been good at grand declarations.

Instead, he said softly, "You've changed my days, Melanie. Changed me."

She blinked rapidly, willing back tears. "And you've changed me."

The boarding call echoed over the loudspeaker. Melanie's stomach dropped. She turned to her suitcase, fumbling with the handle.

Andrew's heart pounded. He watched her preparing to walk away, and a sharp panic gripped him. *This is it. If I let her go without telling her, without showing her, I'll regret it every day that follows. Don't be a coward, Collins. Be brave. For her.*

Before he could second-guess, he reached out, his hand closing gently over hers where it gripped the suitcase handle. She looked up, startled, her eyes wide and shimmering.

"Melanie," he said, his voice rough. "Before you go..." He let the fear fall away, leaned in, and kissed her.

It wasn't rushed. It wasn't dramatic. It was steady and tender, the kind of kiss that carried the feelings of days unsaid, the promise of all that had been growing between them. Melanie's breath caught, then she melted into it, her free hand lifting to his shoulder.

For Andrew, the world fell away: the hiss of the train, the murmur of passengers, the chill of the morning. There was only her. The softness of her lips, the warmth of her presence, the certainty that he had done the one thing he couldn't leave undone.

When they finally broke apart, Melanie's cheeks were wet with tears, but her smile was radiant, trembling with both sorrow and joy.

"I'll never forget this," she whispered.

"Nor I," Andrew said, his voice unsteady, but sure. "Not for all my days."

The driver called again, sharper this time. Melanie took a shaky breath, then squeezed Andrew's hand tightly. "I'll write as soon as I'm home."

"I'll be waiting," he said, his fingers gripping hers as though they might anchor her in place.

She pulled her hand free at last, lifted her suitcase, and stepped onto the train. Andrew stood rooted as she found a seat by the window. Their eyes met through the glass, her hand lifting in a final wave.

He raised his in return, his chest aching as the train pulled away, carrying her out of sight.

Andrew remained on the pavement long after the train had gone, the mist curling around him. His lips still tingled with the memory of her kiss. For the first time in years, the ache in his chest was sharp and alive, not dull and resigned.

"She'll come back," he whispered into the morning air. "She has to."

And though the street was empty, the hope in his words made him believe it might be true.

Melanie

The train pulled steadily from York station, the whistle sharp, the station sliding slowly out of sight. Melanie pressed her forehead to the cool glass, her eyes straining for one last glimpse. But Andrew's figure was already swallowed by distance.

Her chest ached. The kiss still lingered, soft, steady, unforgettable. She touched her fingers lightly to her lips, her heart tumbling with every mile. *Why now, when I'm leaving? Why not sooner?*

She blinked rapidly, fighting the sting in her eyes. Around her, passengers murmured, pages turned in newspapers, luggage thumped into racks. Ordinary life going on. Yet for her, everything had shifted.

He kissed me. He wanted me. But what happens now? Letters, yes. Calls, perhaps. But will it be enough? Will he be enough, half a world away? Or worse, will I? I don't want this to end.

Hours later, buckled into her seat on the plane, the cabin hum surrounding her, Melanie stared at the scatter of clouds beyond the window. The Atlantic stretched unseen below, the same ocean that would soon separate her from him again.

She closed her eyes. The scent of salt air at Whitby, the warmth of his hand at the café table, the quiet weight of his gaze by the river, each memory folded close inside her like treasures. But it was the kiss she clung to most fiercely.

He was brave, finally. Brave enough to show me what I longed to know. And now I have to be brave too. Brave enough to believe this isn't goodbye.

Tears pricked her eyes, but a small, steady smile curved her lips. She whispered under her breath, unheard by anyone but herself: "I'll come back to you, Andrew. Somehow."

Andrew

Andrew let himself into the flat, the silence closing around him with cruel familiarity. The scarf she had worn was still draped neatly over the chair. Her laughter seemed to linger faintly in the air, ghostly but sweet.

He moved mechanically, coat hung, kettle boiled, cup set down untouched. At last, he crossed to the desk and opened the leather journal Melanie had given him, the one she had chosen with such care.

He dipped his pen, hesitated, then began to write:

Day Ten. She has gone. I brought her to the train and watched as it carried her away, and though I knew it would, I wasn't ready. I will never be ready. The flat is too quiet. The city too large. I feel as though I've lost something I only just discovered. And yet, I kissed her and she kissed me back. Brave, beautiful Melanie. For that moment, I felt alive again. I don't know what will happen, but I know this: she has changed everything. And I cannot, I will not, go back to the silence I knew before.

He set the pen down, pressing the page flat with his hand. The ache in his chest was sharp, but it carried something new as well—hope.

Leaning back, he whispered into the empty room, "Write to me soon, Melanie. Please."

And though the silence answered only with the faint tick of the clock, Andrew felt that somewhere across the ocean, she was holding onto the same hope too.

CHAPTER 32

Melanie

In Massachusetts, Melanie's life resumed with her book club, her grandchildren's visits, her quiet evenings and her volunteer times at the library. But every time she checked her email, her heart leapt at the sight of Andrew's name. Their letters, once steady, became daily again. When they managed a video call, seeing his face and hearing his voice along with the sound of his laugh filled her house like sunlight.

With each day apart, she realized the truth: she didn't just enjoy his company. She yearned for it. She missed the streets of York, the taste of scones and the sound of his voice beside her instead of in her ear; those things had become part of her in a way she hadn't expected.

Andrew

The days after Melanie's departure passed in slow, echoing stretches. Andrew wrote daily in the journal she had given him, his words spilling out with more honesty than he could ever manage aloud. Emails crossed the ocean through the internet, his words answered by hers, each new email notification carrying comfort and ache in equal measure.

Andrew walked the city with her ghost beside him, every café where she had laughed, every bench where they had sat shoulder to shoulder. He wrote pages in the journal she had given him, but the ink never seemed enough. At night, he found himself whispering her name into the quiet flat.

CHAPTER 33

Andrew—Four weeks later

The flat was too quiet without her.

Andrew sat at the small table looking out the window, journal open, pen resting against the page as rain traced thin, uneven lines down the glass. York looked the same, but something in it had shifted. Or perhaps something in him had.

He wrote her name without thinking. *Melanie.* He'd done that more than once since she left.

I hope she comes back, he wrote, then paused, the words suddenly feeling incomplete. Hope alone felt... passive. As though love were something that simply happened to you, rather than something you stepped toward.

He leaned back, rubbing his hand over his face, the memory of her laughter still warm in his chest. Her careful way of noticing things. The way she'd stood beside him on the river walk, shoulder just close enough to feel without touching.

Why was he waiting?

The thought arrived quietly, but once there, it refused to leave.

Why shouldn't I go to her?

Andrew stared at the sentence as if it might argue back.

He was almost sixty. He had routines. A life that fit him well enough.

And yet...

He picked up the pen again, his heart thudding a little harder now.

If she crossed an ocean for me, he wrote slowly, *why am I sitting here pretending patience is the same thing as courage?*

The answer settled into him with a surprising calm.

He didn't want to wait and wonder. He wanted to see her world, and he wanted to walk beside her life the way she had walked beside his.

Andrew closed the journal, his decision suddenly solid and unmistakable.

Tomorrow, he would tell her.

Melanie

She answered on the second ring. "Andrew?"

"I was hoping you'd be awake," he said, smiling despite himself.

"I always am when it's you," she replied, warmth threading through her voice. "What's wrong?"

"Nothing's wrong," he said quickly. Then, more carefully, "At least, I don't think it is. I've been thinking."

She laughed softly. "That sounds dangerous."

"Quite," he agreed. "Melanie... I don't want to wait for you to come back again."

There was a pause on the line. Not tense, just attentive.

"I think," he continued, heart in his throat now, "that I should come to Boston. See you. See where you live. Where your life is."

The silence that followed stretched just long enough for doubt to flicker.

Then Melanie inhaled sharply. "Andrew."

"Yes?"

"I was hoping you'd say that."

He closed his eyes, relief washing through him.

"I don't want you staying in a hotel," she added quickly, excitement bubbling now. "That would feel... distant. I have the little apartment over the garage, you remember I mentioned it? You could stay there."

"I remember," he said, smiling.

"The kitchen is shared," she went on, already planning. "Which really just means we'll end up making tea at the same time and talking far too much."

"That sounds perfect," Andrew said softly.

She laughed then, full and unguarded. "I can't believe you're coming."

"Neither can I," he admitted. "But I want to. Very much."

When they said goodnight later, Andrew sat for a moment longer with the phone in his hand, heart light and steady.

For the first time in a long while, he wasn't waiting for life to come to him.

He was going to meet it halfway.

Melanie

The little apartment over the garage had always been tidy, but that morning Melanie found herself moving through it with a different kind of care.

She opened the windows first, letting in the fresh air. The curtains stirred, pale and familiar, and for a moment she simply stood there, hands resting on the sill, smiling at nothing in particular.

He's coming, she thought, the words still bright and unbelievable.

She smoothed the quilt on the bed; the blue one she'd chosen years ago because it reminded her of sky just after rain. She straightened the small table near the window, set a lamp where the light would be kind in the evenings. Nothing extravagant. Just... welcoming.

This wasn't about impressing him. It was about making space.

She paused in the doorway, suddenly aware of her own heart beating a little faster. There was excitement, yes, but also something steadier beneath it. A sense of rightness she hadn't felt in a long time.

Back downstairs in the kitchen, she heard the familiar sound of the back door opening.

"Mom?"

"In the kitchen," Melanie called.

Emily came in with a bag of groceries, eyeing her mother curiously. "You're in an unusually good mood. Should I be suspicious?"

Melanie laughed. "Probably."

She poured tea while Emily unpacked groceries, then said, almost casually, "Andrew's coming to visit."

Emily froze mid-motion. "Wait...Andrew Andrew?"

"Yes. Andrew Andrew. The very one."

Emily's face lit up. "Mom, that's wonderful!"

"He'll stay up here," Melanie said, gesturing toward the stairs. "In the apartment. The kitchen's shared, of course."

Emily grinned. "Of course it is. I know that, Mom."

Melanie smiled too, but her voice softened. "It feels... brave. And a little terrifying."

Emily leaned against the counter. "Good terrifying or bad terrifying?"

"The kind that reminds you you're alive," Melanie said after a moment.

Emily nodded thoughtfully. "You know, you've spent so much of your life taking care of everyone else. It's nice to see someone coming to you for a change."

Melanie felt something warm and almost tearful rise in her chest. "I didn't realize how much I needed that until now."

Emily reached over and squeezed her hand. "I think he's good for you."

"I think so too," Melanie said quietly.

Later, back upstairs, Melanie placed a small vase on the table and added a single sprig of lilac from the yard. She stood back, surveying the room one last time. She turned off the light, already imagining the sound of footsteps on the stairs, the way his voice would fill the small space.

CHAPTER 34

Andrew

The flight had seemed endless. Hours of stiff joints, restless dozing, and the odd clatter of meal trays. Andrew had spent most of it staring out at the expanse of cloud, thinking of Melanie. Each hour closer filled him with a mixture of anticipation and doubt. *What if I don't fit here? What if I'm only ever a guest in her life, never more?*

When the plane finally touched down in Boston, he felt both relief and a surge of nerves. The terminal was crowded, loudspeaker announcements blending with the rumble of rolling suitcases. He followed the stream of passengers through customs, clutching his passport a little too tightly.

And then he was through the sliding doors, standing in the arrivals hall with his cap in hand, scanning the crowd.

He saw her before she saw him. Melanie, standing on tiptoe, her scarf bright against the sea of strangers, eyes searching. She looked just as she had in York, alive, vibrant, warm, only here, in her own world, she seemed to shine even more.

"Melanie," he whispered to himself, and then she spotted him.

Her face lit up, a smile breaking like sunlight. She hurried forward, weaving past people until she was in front of him.

"Andrew!"

He dropped his bag without thinking and opened his arms. When she reached him, she rose onto her toes and kissed him. He made a soft sound of surprise before kissing her back, hands settling at her waist as if that was where they had always belonged.

When they finally pulled apart, Andrew rested his forehead briefly against hers.

"Hello," he said, voice unsteady.

Melanie smoothed her hair, suddenly aware of the people all around them. "Welcome to Massachusetts," she said lightly, though her voice shook with happiness. "You survived the flight?"

"Barely," Andrew admitted with a grin. "Your American version of tea will need to revive me."

She laughed, slipping her arm through his. "We'll see to it."

They retrieved his bag, Melanie fussing with the handle when he tried to take it. "Nonsense, I'll manage," he protested, though his heart warmed at her stubbornness.

As they walked out into the cool evening air toward the car park, Andrew felt a strange sensation, the disorientation of being both completely out of place and completely at home, simply because she was beside him.

Melanie stopped at her car and Andrew reached for the

left front side door, then froze. "Wrong side again," he muttered under his breath.

Melanie laughed, delighted. "See? Now you know how I felt in York. Don't worry, you'll get the hang of it by the time you leave."

He settled into the seat, shaking his head, but her laughter eased his nerves. As they drove out of the airport and onto the highway, the city lights of Boston spread before them.

"Everything feels... larger," he said quietly, peering at the wide lanes, the expanse of sky.

Melanie smiled. "That's America for you. Big roads, big portions, big everything. But I live on the outskirts of Boston, it's nothing like this."

Andrew glanced at her with affection. *It doesn't matter where we are. If she's here, it's enough.*

The roads around Logan were a tangled knot of ramps and lanes, signs sprouting overhead in every direction. Andrew gripped the armrest as Melanie navigated with practiced ease, darting into a lane that seemed to appear from nowhere.

"Good lord," he muttered. "It's like a racetrack designed by a madman."

Melanie laughed, checking her mirrors. "Welcome to Boston traffic. Consider it your initiation."

He shook his head, eyes wide as a vehicle thundered past on the left. "You do realize half of these cars could swallow mine whole? That one looked like it was hauling an entire house."

"That was just a pickup truck," she teased.

"Pickup?" he echoed faintly. "What do they pick up… elephants?"

Melanie's laughter bubbled over, and the sound eased some of his tension. He allowed himself a small smile. If she can laugh at it, perhaps I'll survive.

As the skyline receded behind them, the lanes widened into long stretches of highway. The neon signs gave way to clusters of trees, their leaves just tipping into summer green. Andrew relaxed as the ride went on, still wide-eyed.

"It does feel different," he admitted softly. "The scale of it. Even the sky feels larger somehow."

Melanie glanced at him, warmth in her eyes. "It's strange, isn't it? I felt the same in York, only in reverse. Everything closer, more intimate. Here, you get space whether you want it or not."

He nodded, his gaze drifting to the open horizon. Space I wouldn't mind, so long as she's in it.

By the time they turned off the highway into Melanie's town, the light was fading, the streets lined with clapboard houses and neat lawns. American flags fluttered here and there. Children rode bicycles down quiet lanes. It was smaller, calmer than the roar of Boston, and Andrew felt some of the tightness in his chest ease.

"This is home," Melanie said simply, slowing the car. Her voice carried pride but also a trace of nerves, as though she were seeing it through his eyes.

Andrew took in the main street, the diner with its neon sign, the brick library with its white steps, the little café with chairs stacked for the night. "It's… charming," he said honestly. "Quieter than I expected."

Melanie smiled, relieved. "Just wait. My house is even quieter. Unless the grandchildren are over."

Her home sat on a tree-lined street, pale blue siding

with a tidy porch and flowerbeds just beginning to bloom. Andrew carried his suitcase up the steps, pausing to take in the small wind chime tinkling gently in the breeze.

"It suits you," he said softly. "Warm and welcoming."

Inside, the house smelled faintly of cinnamon and books. Photos of her daughter, her grandchildren and Melanie herself in younger days lined the hallway walls. Andrew lingered on them a moment, struck by how full her life here was. And yet she made space for me.

"Come in, come in," Melanie urged, taking his coat. "You must be exhausted."

Before he could answer, footsteps sounded on the steps, and then two children came rushing in, a boy of about eight and a younger girl.

"Grandma!" the girl squealed, flinging herself at Melanie's waist. Then she peered up at Andrew with wide eyes. "Is this him?"

Andrew blinked, startled, then chuckled. "I suppose it must be. Unless you were expecting another Englishman to wander in."

The boy grinned. "Say something! Say something in your accent!"

Andrew raised a brow, his lips twitching. "Something."

The children collapsed into giggles, and Melanie swatted them gently. "Manners, you two. This is Andrew. Andrew, this is Sophie and Jack."

Andrew crouched a little, smiling. "A pleasure. I'm very glad to meet you."

Jack tilted his head. "Do you like baseball?"

Andrew hesitated. "I... admire it. From a safe distance."

More giggles. Melanie rolled her eyes fondly. "You'll have to excuse them. They've been far too excited for this day."

Andrew straightened, his chest warm. "As have I," he said softly, his gaze resting on her.

After the children were coaxed home with promises of another visit, Melanie settled Andrew in her living room with a cup of tea. He felt something rub against his ankles and reached down to pet Haiku, who was making herself known.

Andrew sipped and glanced around, taking in the bookshelves, the quilt draped on the sofa, the framed picture of Melanie with her daughter. "It feels... lived in, but in the best way."

Melanie smiled faintly. "I was nervous, you know. Letting you see this part of my life. It's one thing for me to walk York's streets with you. But this, this is who I am every day."

He set the cup down, leaning forward slightly. "And I'm glad. I wanted to see it...to see you here."

Her heart swelled at his words, the sincerity in his voice. She reached across, her fingers touching his hand. "Then welcome to my home, Andrew."

He covered her hand with his, his throat tight. *I can't believe I'm with her again.*

Melanie lit a single lamp in the sitting room and brought in a plate with a few slices of apple pie.

"You shouldn't fuss over me," Andrew protested, though his eyes twinkled at the sight.

"Nonsense," Melanie replied, setting it down. "Pie fixes everything, even jet lag."

He chuckled, taking a fork. "Then here's to American pie medicine."

They ate slowly, the warmth of the room cocooning them. Outside, the occasional car passed, but otherwise the town had grown hushed for the night. Andrew leaned back in his chair, letting out a soft sigh.

"You were right," he said. "It is quieter here. Different from York. But not empty."

Melanie tilted her head, curious. "What do you mean?"

He gestured slightly with his fork. "There's a... fullness. A sense of life woven into the walls. Your family, your years here. It doesn't feel lonely the way my flat does when I walk in."

Her throat tightened at the honesty in his words. She reached over, laying her hand on his. "You're not alone anymore, Andrew. Not really."

He turned his palm to clasp hers, the warmth steadying him. If only I could believe this might last, he thought.

They sat like that for a moment, the silence gentle. Then Melanie smiled softly. "You should rest. You've crossed an ocean today, after all."

"True," he admitted, though his eyes lingered on her face. "But if every evening ends like this, I'll find crossing oceans rather worth it."

Her cheeks flushed, and she squeezed his hand before rising. "Come on then. I'll show you the apartment."

The stairway off the kitchen led up to the apartment over the garage. It was simple but inviting: a desk and chair, a recliner, a bathroom with a shower, and a quilted bedspread on the bed and a vase of fresh flowers on the nightstand in the small bedroom. Andrew set his suitcase down and turned to Melanie in the doorway.

"It's more than I deserve," he said softly.

Melanie shook her head. "It's exactly what you deserve."

They lingered at the doorway longer than necessary, neither quite ready to end the day.

Andrew reached for her this time, slowly, giving her every chance to step away.

She didn't. Instead, she stepped in to meet him.

The kiss was soft, unhurried, and deep, a promise rather than a question.

"Goodnight, Melanie," he said, resting his thumb briefly against her hand.

"Goodnight, Andrew, sleep well," she replied, warmth blooming in her chest as she turned and went down the stairs.

Reflections—Melanie

The house was quiet in a way it rarely was.

Melanie moved slowly through the kitchen, turning off a light that was already dim on the way to her bedroom. Upstairs, Andrew's footsteps had faded, the guest room door closing softly, not with distance, but with care.

The kiss at the airport replayed in her mind. It was as if they had picked up exactly where they'd left off at York station, without apology.

And the goodnight kiss had felt like something settling into place.

This is real, she thought.

Not a holiday version of love or a pause from life. But

something that would exist alongside laundry, schedules, grandchildren, and mornings that began too early.

Melanie pressed her palm briefly to her chest.

She wasn't nervous.

She wasn't wondering if she should be here.

For the first time in a long while, she felt chosen, and that she was choosing in return.

Reflections—Andrew

Andrew sat on the edge of the bed, the quilt soft under his palms, and exhaled slowly. The strangeness of America, the noise of Boston, the laughter of the children, all of it swirled in his mind. But stronger than all of it was the certainty that he was where he needed to be.

Boston feels... lived in, he wrote.

Not temporary.

He thought of Melanie's kiss at the airport, how natural it had felt, how easily his hands had gone to her waist, as if his body had known what his mind was still catching up to.

I didn't hesitate, he wrote.

And that may be the most telling thing of all.

The goodnight kiss lingered with him, the softness of it, and the unspoken understanding that neither of them needed to rush.

I am not afraid tonight, he continued. *That surprises me.*

He closed the journal slowly.

This was not the careful distance of emails or the tentative longing of York.

This is not a visit. This is a beginning.

CHAPTER 35

*A*ndrew woke to the smell of coffee and something warm baking. For a moment, he didn't know where he was. He heard the faint chime of a clock in the hall and the hum of traffic outside. Then memory caught up, and his heart filled with quiet joy. *Her house. I'm here.*

He dressed quickly and followed the scent to the kitchen. Melanie was at the stove, her hair pinned up loosely, wearing an apron dotted with flour. Sunlight spread across the counters, catching on the glass canisters lined neatly on the shelf.

Andrew leaned against the doorway, watching her with a small smile. "If I'd known there'd be pie and fresh coffee every morning, I'd have crossed the ocean sooner."

She turned, laughing, a spatula in hand. "You're not getting pie for breakfast. Blueberry muffins. And scrambled eggs, if you behave."

"Then I'll do my best," he said gravely, moving to the table.

Melanie poured him a cup of coffee and set a plate

before him. "So, your first American breakfast in a real American kitchen. Thoughts?"

Andrew studied the spread as though it were a museum exhibit. "Portions generous. Coffee strong enough to strip paint. And I note the muffins are, how do you say, not stingy with the blueberries."

Melanie laughed, settling opposite him. "We don't do stingy when it comes to blueberries. Or much of anything, really. You'll notice."

He took a sip of coffee and raised a brow. "Indeed. I suspect by the end of this trip, I'll have to roll myself back onto the plane."

She swatted at his arm lightly across the table. "Nonsense. You'll walk just fine."

They ate with companionable ease, Andrew savoring each bite, Melanie enjoying the way he observed even the simplest details of her world as though they were worth noting.

Halfway through their second cup of coffee, a knock sounded at the front door. Melanie glanced at the clock and set her cup down. "That'll be Emily," she said, her tone tightening just slightly.

Andrew straightened in his chair, nerves prickling. The daughter. The one who worried about her mother crossing the ocean. *What will she think of me?*

Melanie opened the door, and a woman in her mid-thirties stepped inside, her hair pulled back neatly, her expression alert but cautious.

"Mom," Emily said, hugging Melanie quickly before her gaze flicked toward Andrew. "So, this is Andrew."

Andrew rose at once, smoothing his shirt. "Miss Emily, a pleasure to meet you. I've heard much about you."

Her brows lifted slightly at his formal tone. "Likewise. Though I'm not sure what my mother's told you."

"That you are wise, efficient, and occasionally exasperated by her," Andrew said with a small smile.

Emily blinked, then laughed despite herself. "That sounds about right."

They moved into the sitting room, Emily perching on the sofa while Andrew sat carefully in a chair, feeling every inch the foreign guest.

"So," Emily began, her gaze steady, "you've come all the way from England. That's quite a trip for... a friend."

Andrew inclined his head. "It is. But then, your mother has a way of making oceans feel rather small."

Melanie shot him a look, and Emily tilted her head, studying him. "That's... very poetic."

Andrew shrugged, a faint smile tugging at his mouth. "Old teachers don't shed their habits easily."

There was a small silence, not unfriendly, before Emily said more softly, "You have a new fan club. Jack couldn't stop imitating your accent. Sophie told me you have kind eyes."

Andrew's throat tightened. He glanced at Melanie, who smiled gently, then back at Emily. "Then I am honored. Children often see what adults overlook."

Emily held his gaze another moment, then nodded slowly. "Well. I suppose we'll just have to see what you make of Boston."

Andrew exhaled quietly, tension loosening. Not approval, not yet. But perhaps permission to try.

When Emily finally rose to go, Melanie walked her to the door, murmuring something Andrew couldn't catch. Emily gave him a final look before leaving, not unfriendly, but measured.

Andrew sank back into his chair, letting out a slow breath. "Well," he said dryly, "*that* wasn't an examination at all."

Melanie laughed, coming back to him. "You did fine. She'll come around." She reached for his hand briefly, squeezing. "Thank you for being yourself."

He smiled faintly, his heart still pounding. "I'm not sure I know how to be anything else."

CHAPTER 36

After Emily left, Melanie insisted they walk into town. "It's small," she said as they set out along the shaded sidewalk, "but everything important is here."

Andrew carried himself a little stiffly at first, conscious of being out of place. Every step feels like I'm in her story, not mine. But as they passed tidy clapboard houses with porches and rocking chairs, the warmth of the neighborhood seeped in.

The main street stretched just a few blocks, a mix of brick and wood-front shops, American flags fluttering and hanging baskets spilling with flowers. A bell over the door jingled as they stepped into a café, the smell of coffee and cinnamon thick in the air.

"Melanie!" the barista called cheerfully from behind the counter. "Your usual?"

Melanie smiled, waving. "Maybe later, Sarah. This is my friend Andrew, visiting all the way from England."

Sarah's eyes widened. "Oh! Welcome! You've come a long way."

Andrew inclined his head politely, lips twitching.

"Indeed. And so far, the muffins and traffic have both left an impression."

Sarah laughed, and Melanie slid her arm through his as they left.

Outside, Andrew murmured, "So you're well known here. You walk into a shop, and they know your order before you sit down."

Melanie shrugged, a little self-conscious. "That's small towns for you. Everyone knows everyone. Sometimes it's comforting, sometimes it's suffocating." She glanced at him. "York isn't like this?"

He shook his head. "Not quite. People nod at you, yes. But not everyone knows the way you take your coffee."

And yet, he thought, there's something enviable about it. She belongs here in a way I never quite have anywhere.

They stopped at the library, a modest brick building with white columns. Inside, it smelled of polished wood and well-loved books. The librarian greeted Melanie by name, asking after her daughter and grandchildren.

Andrew trailed beside her as she walked through the aisles, her fingers brushing spines as though greeting old friends.

"You belong here," he said softly.

Melanie turned, surprised. "What do you mean?"

He shrugged. "You move among the shelves as though they know you. As though you've left a piece of yourself in every aisle."

Her heart caught at his words. He sees me. Not just the surface, but the marrow of me.

"Perhaps I have," she admitted. "Books have been constant when people haven't."

Andrew nodded, thinking of his own flat, of shelves filled but always silent. "Then I'm glad they kept you company."

She smiled faintly, touched by the gentleness in his voice.

Later, they crossed the town green, where children played tag around the bandstand. An elderly man tipped his cap to Melanie, and she waved in return. Andrew walked slowly, taking it all in: the rustle of leaves overhead, the clatter of a bicycle on the path, the chatter of neighbors calling across the street.

"It feels... open," he said quietly. "As though you could walk the same square a hundred times and still be greeted as though you'd been missed."

Melanie glanced at him, her voice soft. "And in York, it felt close, as though every step carried history with it. Both ways of belonging, I suppose."

He looked at her then, smiling, as he thought. *And where do I belong now? With her, yes. But which of these worlds could hold us both?*

On their way back, Melanie guided him into the café again, insisting on coffee and a slice of her favorite lemon cake. They sat by the window, watching traffic slide past.

Andrew forked a bite of cake, brow lifting. "Sweet mercy. You didn't tell me it was dangerous."

Melanie laughed. "Dangerous?"

He nodded solemnly. "Yes. If I lived here, I'd eat this daily and perish within the month."

She laughed, shaking her head. "You're impossible."

But as she watched him savor another bite, her heart swelled. *He fits here more easily than he realizes. And how quickly I want him woven into these small rhythms, these ordinary hours.*

They walked back to the house slowly, hand in hand, Melanie pointing out familiar spots, the church, the bookshop, the ice cream stand that would open come summer.

Andrew listened quietly, committing each detail to memory. *This is her world. Her air. Her belonging. And I've been allowed into it. How can I ever go back without it?*

Melanie glanced at him, noting the thoughtful set of his brow. "You're quiet."

He looked at her, the weight of his thoughts softened by his smile. "Just listening to the story of your town and the story of you in it."

Her cheeks warmed, and she reached for his arm, her voice tender. "Then I'll keep telling it."

CHAPTER 37

The sun was sinking low, covering the clapboard houses with amber light as Melanie unlocked her front door. Andrew followed, carrying a small paper bag of vegetables from the grocery store they'd stopped at on the way home.

"Nothing fancy," Melanie warned as she set her keys on the counter. "Just a roast chicken with some potatoes and carrots."

Andrew placed the bag down with exaggerated solemnity. "After last night's pie and this morning's muffins, you could serve me boiled shoe leather, and I'd still sing your praises."

Melanie laughed, giving him a playful nudge with her shoulder. "Good. Because I'm saving the boiled shoe leather for tomorrow."

She tied an apron around her waist and handed him a second one, faded blue with a frayed hem. "Here. If you're helping, you'll need this."

Andrew slipped it over his head, eyeing the floral pattern skeptically. "I assume the flowers are compulsory."

"Absolutely," she said firmly, hiding her smile as she handed him a knife. "Carrots first. Think you can manage?"

"Madam, I was raised on Sunday roasts," he replied. "Carrots are in my blood."

He set to work at the counter, carefully slicing, while Melanie busied herself with the chicken. Every so often she glanced sideways at him, warmed by the sight of his tall frame bent seriously over the chopping board, the ridiculous apron knotted around his waist.

Andrew caught her look once and arched a brow. "What?"

"Nothing," she said innocently. "Just... you look comfortable in my kitchen."

His knife paused. Something tightened in his chest at her words, and he forced a smile. "Well, I'll try not to disgrace myself with uneven carrots then."

When the chicken went into the oven and the vegetables were simmering, Melanie leaned back against the counter, arms folded, watching him rinse the knife.

"You're a good helper," she said.

He glanced over his shoulder, smiling. "Don't spread that around. You'll ruin my reputation."

Her laughter softened into a smile as she moved closer, taking the dish towel from him to dry the knife.

Melanie's heart gave a little leap. *This feels so ordinary. And yet at the same time, so much more.*

They set the small table in her dining nook, nothing elaborate, just plates, silverware, and a vase of tulips her grandchildren had brought over last week. The smell of roasted chicken filled the house.

Andrew carved while Melanie poured the wine. He tasted a bite and closed his eyes with exaggerated bliss.

"Perfect. You could give the Yorkshire kitchens a run for their money."

Melanie rolled her eyes, though her cheeks warmed at the praise. "Stop flattering me and eat before it gets cold."

They ate slowly, conversation flowing easily. They talked about her volunteer work at the library, about his favorite walking paths in York, about the strange differences between American and British sayings.

"So, what do you call it?" Melanie asked at one point, pointing at the breadbasket.

"A bap."

She laughed. "That sounds made up."

"It does not," he protested. "You Americans are the ones calling them 'rolls,' as though they're meant to roll away down the table."

Melanie chuckled, her eyes bright. This is what I wanted him to see, my home, my rhythms and how easily he fits in them.

After the dishes were washed, Andrew insisting on doing the drying while Melanie teased him about streaks on the glasses. They carried their tea into the sitting room, Melanie curled into one end of the sofa, with Andrew settling down next to her. For a while they sipped in silence, the quiet hum of the house wrapping around them.

At last Melanie said softly, "It feels strange. Having you here, in this room. I used to imagine it sometimes, when we were writing. But imagining isn't the same."

Andrew set down his cup, his gaze steady on her. "No. It isn't. And I think I prefer the real thing."

Her smile wavered into something tender. "So do I."

When the evening grew late, they took their cups out to the kitchen. Andrew paused at the doorway leading up the apartment, his hand lightly on the frame.

For a heartbeat, both of them waited, but then she smiled up at him as he tipped his head down, their lips meeting and her hands slid around his shoulders.

"Goodnight, Andrew," she said softly.

He looked at her a long moment before answering. "Goodnight, Melanie."

CHAPTER 38

The next morning after breakfast, they walked one street over to Emily's house, a neat two-story with bikes strewn in the yard and chalk drawings bright on the driveway. Andrew stepped out cautiously, adjusting his jacket as though he were walking into an inspection.

"Relax," Melanie murmured, touching his arm. "They've been waiting for this."

Emily opened the door, wiping her hands on a dish towel. "Come in, come in," she said warmly, though her eyes flicked toward Andrew with that same assessing look as the day before.

Not long after, the children had pulled him into the living room and laughter had filled the house.

"Andrew!" Jack shouted. "Come on, you have to play with me!"

Andrew blinked. "Play what exactly?"

Jack grinned, tugging at his sleeve. "Video games! You'll be terrible at it, but that's okay."

Behind him, Sophie appeared, quieter but grinning,

holding a stuffed rabbit. She looked up at Andrew with wide eyes. "You came to visit us."

Andrew crouched slightly, smiling. "Of course I did. Wouldn't miss the chance to be humiliated by your brother."

Jack whooped in triumph, dragging him toward the living room. Melanie followed, laughing under her breath.

The living room was cozy, the television already displaying bright colors and animated characters. Jack thrust a controller into Andrew's hands.

"Okay," Jack explained rapidly, "this button jumps, this one punches, and this one does special moves. Don't worry if you lose, Grandma always does."

Melanie, settling onto the sofa, raised her brows. "Thank you, Jack. I feel so appreciated."

Andrew studied the controller as though it were a bomb. "Jump, punch, special moves. How hard can it be?"

The screen exploded into action. Andrew's character stumbled forward while Jack's darted nimbly, leaping and spinning.

Andrew pressed a button at random. His character promptly fell into a hole.

Jack collapsed in laughter. "You didn't even move! You just fell!"

Andrew shook his head, grinning despite himself. "Clearly I was testing gravity."

Melanie chuckled, leaning forward. "Careful, Jack. Don't underestimate him. He's a quick learner."

Sophie, perched beside her, hugged her rabbit. "I think he's funny."

Andrew glanced at her with mock seriousness. "Thank you, Sophie. Finally, someone on my side."

She giggled, hiding her face in the rabbit's ears.

By the second round, Andrew had figured out the jump button. He managed to hop over Jack's character once, which he celebrated far too enthusiastically.

"Did you see that?" he exclaimed, looking at Melanie. "I leapt!"

Melanie laughed so hard she nearly spilled her tea. "You leapt right into a trap, Andrew."

Jack howled with laughter. "Grandma's right! You're the worst!"

Andrew clutched his chest dramatically. "The worst? And here I thought we were friends."

Jack grinned wickedly. "We are friends. That's why I have to beat you."

By some miracle, and perhaps Jack's mercy, Andrew managed to land a single hit in the third round. He froze, staring at the screen.

"Did I just...?"

"Yes!" Sophie cried, bouncing. "You hit him!"

Andrew pointed triumphantly at the screen. "Mark the day. History has been made."

Jack groaned. "Beginner's luck!"

Andrew leaned back, scup. "I'll take it."

Melanie shook her head fondly, watching the way he laughed with them, how naturally he slipped into their chatter. *He belongs here more easily than he believes. And oh, how quickly they've claimed him.*

When Jack finally relinquished the controller, Sophie climbed into Andrew's lap without hesitation, rabbit in tow.

"Do you like it here?" she asked earnestly.

Andrew blinked, touched. "Very much. Especially when I get to meet clever young ladies like you."

She smiled shyly, burrowing into his shoulder.

Melanie's heart swelled at the sight. This is what I wanted, for them to see him, and for him to see them. For our worlds to touch and hold together, even just for a little while.

Emily appeared in the doorway then, arching a brow at the scene, Andrew with Sophie curled on his lap, Jack proudly explaining his latest high score, Melanie laughing quietly on the sofa.

"Well," Emily said, her voice tinged with surprise but softened by amusement. "It looks like you've survived initiation."

Andrew met her eyes over Sophie's head and gave her a small smile. "Barely. But I wouldn't trade it."

By midday, Emily suggested they all get some fresh air. "Let's go to the park," she said, glancing at her mother. "The kids can run, and there's that hot dog cart Jack loves."

Melanie agreed, and soon they were walking the short distance to the town green, the children skipping ahead, Andrew and Melanie trailing with Emily beside them.

The park was alive with weekend families: children racing up slides, parents chatting on benches, people walking dogs, and a group tossing a frisbee near the trees. The smell of sizzling hot dogs drifted on the breeze from the vendor's cart.

"Ah," Andrew murmured, sniffing the air. "So, this is the famed American cuisine. Hot dogs."

Melanie smirked. "Don't act so superior. You loved my lemon cake yesterday."

"Cake is art. This, I suspect, is alchemy of questionable nature."

Jack overheard and whirled around. "Hot dogs are the best! You'll see."

Emily rolled her eyes but smiled. "One with mustard for Jack, ketchup for Sophie...and Mom?"

"Mustard and relish," Melanie supplied.

Andrew hesitated when asked his order, then said dryly, "I'll take one of these hot dogs with everything. For science."

The vendor handed him a condiment covered hot dog cocooned inside of a bun on a napkin, steam rising. Andrew studied it solemnly. "It seems harmless enough." He took a cautious bite and then blinked. "Well. That's... oddly delightful."

Jack laughed. "I told you!"

Melanie laughed, nudging Andrew's arm. "Welcome to America."

They sat on a bench while the children raced to the playground. Andrew finished his hot dog, brushing crumbs from his lap. "I retract my earlier suspicion. This may be the crown of civilization."

Melanie chuckled. "Careful, or you'll have to smuggle some back to York."

Emily sipped from her soda, watching him. "You're good with them," she said quietly.

Andrew turned, surprised. "With Jack and Sophie?"

She nodded. "Not everyone knows how to listen to children. You do. That matters."

Andrew felt a flush creep up his neck. "They're good children. Curious, full of energy. It's not so different from teaching, really. Only with fewer exams and more... video game defeats."

Emily smiled faintly, the reserve in her gaze softening a little more.

Melanie watched the exchange with a warm ache in her chest. *He's winning them over. Piece by piece, without even trying.*

Jack ran up breathless. "Andrew! Watch me!" He scrambled up the climbing frame and leapt dramatically onto the slide, landing in a heap at the bottom.

Andrew applauded gravely. "Remarkable form. You could win an Olympic gold medal."

Jack grinned, puffing out his chest.

Sophie padded up with her stuffed rabbit, holding it out to Andrew. "Mr. Whiskers wants to sit with you."

Andrew accepted the rabbit solemnly, placing it on his knee. "Mr. Whiskers, you have excellent taste in company."

Sophie giggled and nestled beside him.

As the afternoon waned, they gathered the children and walked back toward Emily's house. Andrew walked beside Melanie, lowering his voice. "I'd forgotten what it feels like. The noise of children and the way they tumble over words in their excitement. It makes the world... brighter somehow."

Melanie looked at him, her heart tightening. "I'm glad you feel that. They like you, Andrew. More quickly than I even expected."

He smiled faintly, though inside he thought, *And I like them. Which makes the thought of leaving all the harder.*

CHAPTER 39

$\mathcal{E}$mily's dining room was cozy, with a wooden table worn smooth by years of meals and homework sessions. The smell of roast pork and herbs filled the air, and Andrew found himself easing into a chair with Sophie at his side and Jack already chattering away about school.

Emily's husband, Daniel, entered just as Melanie was setting down a bowl of green beans. He was broad-shouldered, with kind eyes and the same cautious curiosity his wife carried. He extended a hand across the table.

"So, you're Andrew," Daniel said warmly. "We've heard quite a bit about you."

Andrew rose slightly to shake his hand. "I can only hope it wasn't all dreadful."

Daniel chuckled, settling into his seat. "Depends on who you ask."

Emily shot him a look, though her lips twitched with amusement.

As they began to eat, Jack peppered Andrew with questions about England.

"Do you drink tea all the time? Like, every day?"

Andrew, spearing a potato, nodded solemnly. "Without fail. It's the law. If you miss a day, they send you to Scotland as punishment."

Jack's eyes widened before Melanie stifled a laugh. "Don't listen to him," she said. "He's full of tall tales."

Sophie leaned over her plate, curious. "Do you have ducks in England?"

Andrew smiled. "Plenty. And they are likely just as bossy there as they are here."

Daniel grinned, listening. "You've got their attention, that's for sure. Jack doesn't usually sit still this long at dinner."

Andrew inclined his head. "I'm honored." He paused, then added more softly, "I was a teacher, once. Perhaps it never quite leaves you."

Melanie glanced at him with quiet pride. *He slips into this family space as though it's always been his.*

Halfway through the meal, Emily leaned her chin on her hand, watching him. "So, Andrew... England to Massachusetts. That's not a small leap. What made you decide to come?"

Everyone grew quiet. Andrew's eyes flicked to Melanie, then back to Emily.

"Your mother," he said simply. "Letters and calls are one thing. But sometimes you need to cross an ocean to prove to yourself what matters."

Emily studied him for a moment, then nodded slowly. "Fair enough."

Daniel reached across to refill Andrew's glass. "Well, we're glad you did. Even if the Sox are still better than whatever you've got back home."

Andrew arched a brow. "Cricket, sir. A game of grace and strategy. Unlike your... baseball contraptions."

Jack groaned dramatically. "Baseball is way better! I'll prove it!"

Laughter rippled around the table, the tension broken.

When the plates were cleared and goodnights exchanged, Melanie and Andrew stepped back out into the night for the short walk back to her house.

Melanie smiled. "You did well tonight."

He chuckled. "Like an exam?"

"Maybe a little," she teased. "But you passed. Daniel likes you, and Emily's warming. That's no small thing."

Andrew's smile softened. "I liked them too. You've a strong family, Melanie. It's easy to see where your kindness comes from."

She smiled, touched. *How is it he always knows what to say?*

Back at her house, Melanie set down her keys and turned to him, her smile gentle but weary. "Thank you for today. For being patient with all of it."

Andrew shook his head. "There was nothing to endure. Your family... they welcomed me. That's more than I dared hope for."

They stood for a moment in the quiet hallway.

Andrew's heart thudded. *I should kiss her again. Here, in her world. Not leave it hanging like some unfinished sentence.* But his courage faltered, his hand tightening uselessly at his side.

Melanie's pulse quickened. *Doesn't he remember? I do. Every moment. Why doesn't he kiss me?*

But neither moved.

Instead, Melanie smiled softly, covering the ache with warmth. "Goodnight, Andrew."

His voice was low, rough with what he didn't say. "Goodnight, Melanie."

As she closed her bedroom door, her hand lingered on the knob, heart racing. In his guest room, Andrew sat heavily on the bed, cursing himself. *Next time, Collins. Be brave next time.*

CHAPTER 40

The drive to the Boston Science Museum was noisy with Jack's endless chatter and Sophie's giggles. Emily had to work for a few hours and was meeting them there.

"Grandma, wait until you see the lightning show! And the dinosaurs! Andrew, did you know they have a T-Rex?"

Andrew gave both Jack and Sophie, both in the back seat, a solemn nod. "A T-Rex? Remarkable. I suppose I'll have to keep my wits about me in case it gets loose."

Jack snorted. "It's not real! It's just bones!"

Andrew leaned forward conspiratorially. "Ah, but you see, in England we have a saying: 'Never trust a dinosaur exhibit. They bite when you least expect it.'"

Jack groaned, but Sophie giggled, clutching her rabbit tighter.

Melanie glanced at him in the mirror, smiling at the ease with which he slipped into their world.

The museum buzzed with families and school groups. As they walked in, Andrew looked up at the enormous globe suspended from the ceiling. "Well," he murmured, "I suppose I've traveled half of that already."

Melanie nudged him. "And you've still got the other half to go."

She shepherded the children toward the dinosaur exhibit first. Jack ran ahead, tugging Andrew by the hand. "Come on! You have to see this!"

Andrew stood before the towering T-Rex skeleton, eyes widening. "Good heavens. That's... rather more impressive than the textbooks let on."

Jack puffed up proudly. "I told you!"

Andrew studied the teeth closely, lowering his voice. "You know, I think he's looking at me."

Jack burst out laughing.

Later, they crowded into the theater for the famous lightning show. Sparks cracked, thunder rattled, and the children squealed with delight.

Andrew leaned toward Melanie, speaking over the noise. "I feel as though I should be taking notes. Very educational and extremely electrifying."

She rolled her eyes, stifling laughter. "Don't start with the puns."

"Too late," he said, his grin boyish.

When one bolt lit up the room in brilliant white, Melanie jumped slightly. Andrew reached over and took her hand, steadying her. For a moment, neither moved. Then Sophie climbed into her lap, and the spell was broken.

Still, Melanie felt the warmth of his touch long after.

* * *

Emily found them as they were deciding what to look at next and suggested the butterfly garden before lunch. Soon they were wandering through the warm, humid air filled with fluttering wings. Sophie gasped as a bright blue morpho landed on her shoulder.

"Look, Andrew!" she cried.

Andrew bent close, his voice hushed. "You must be very special indeed, Sophie. They don't land on just anyone."

Her face lit with pride.

A smaller brown butterfly brushed against Melanie's hand. She lifted her eyes to Andrew, and for a moment it was only the two of them, the hush of the garden, the fragility of wings.

"It suits you," he said softly.

Her breath caught, and she smiled faintly. "I'll take that as a compliment."

They sat with paper trays in the museum café with chicken fingers for the children and sandwiches for the adults.Andrew leaned back in his chair, looking around.

"Your museums," he said to Melanie, "are... exuberant. No half-measures. Dinosaurs, lightning, and all those butterflies.

Melanie laughed. "Well, we like to put on a show."

He smiled, watching her. "That much is clear."

After lunch, Emily thanked them for coming, and the children clung to Andrew with noisy goodbyes.

"That was wonderful," Melanie said as they walked back to her car. "Thank you for being so patient with them."

Andrew shook his head. "They were the delight. I learned more about dinosaurs in three hours than in three decades."

She chuckled. "And now you're an expert."

CHAPTER 41

By the time they crossed over toward the Prudential Center, Andrew had already noticed the peculiar-looking vehicle parked at the curb. It was painted bright yellow, with cartoon ducks splashed across the side and a driver in a plastic Viking helmet waving at passersby.

Andrew stopped in his tracks. "Melanie. That contraption is... alarming."

She grinned, tugging his hand. "It's the Boston Duck Tour. Trust me, you'll love it."

"It's part bus, part boat." He squinted. "Surely that violates some sort of engineering principle."

"Or makes it brilliant," she countered, eyes twinkling. "Come on. It's one of the best ways to see the city."

Inside, the seats were already filling with families, couples, and tourists with cameras slung around their necks. Their guide, a middle-aged man with boundless cheer, greeted them with a booming voice.

"Welcome aboard! By the end of this tour, you'll all be

certified Bostonians. And yes, that means you'll have to learn how to pahk the cah in Hahvahd Yahd."

The crowd laughed. Andrew muttered under his breath, "This is going to be excruciating."

Melanie stifled a giggle. "Oh, admit it. You'll secretly enjoy every minute."

As the Duck rumbled into traffic, the guide launched into a lively history of Boston. They passed Copley Square, with its mix of old stone churches and glass towers, then trundled past the State House with its gold dome gleaming in the sun.

"Look at that," Melanie whispered, pointing. "I always love how the dome catches the light. It feels like Boston's crown."

Andrew tilted his head, thoughtful. "It is rather splendid. I'll allow it."

Their guide peppered the commentary with jokes, pointing out Fenway Park, Boston Common, and the swan boats in the Public Garden. Every so often, he had the passengers quack at pedestrians.

Melanie quacked gamely, laughing until her sides hurt. Andrew, at first stoic, eventually gave in with the softest "quack" under his breath. She heard it, her grin triumphant.

"There it is," she teased. "Your inner Viking is quacking."

At last, the Duck lumbered down a ramp and splashed into the Charles River. A cheer went up from the passengers as the skyline spread wide across the water, glass skyscrapers reflecting the sun, sailboats dotting the rippling blue.

Andrew's hand tightened on Melanie's as the vehicle

bobbed. "Well," he admitted, "this is... unexpectedly marvelous."

She leaned against him, her eyes shining. "Isn't it? I love this part because the city looks completely different from here."

He studied the view in silence for a moment, the breeze tugging at his graying hair. "It's beautiful," he said at last. "Almost as beautiful as watching you enjoy it."

Melanie blushed. "You're learning flattery again."

"Observation," he corrected gently, echoing his own words from their ice cream in the park.

They sat together as the Duck glided along the Charles, the hum of the engine mingling with the laughter of children and the guide's playful banter. For Andrew, the city might still feel foreign, but with Melanie's hand warm in his, it already felt like home.

By the time they returned to Melanie's neighborhood, the sunlight had disappeared and evening had arrived. They decided against anything elaborate for supper, instead slipping into a small corner restaurant just a block from her house. The kind of place with wooden tables, low lamplight, and the smell of garlic and fresh bread hanging in the air.

Melanie ordered a simple pasta with marinara; Andrew chose baked haddock. When the breadbasket arrived, Melanie tore off a piece and held it out to him.

"Quack," she whispered, her eyes dancing.

Andrew groaned, but leaned forward to take it, biting gently from her fingers. "You will never let me live that down, will you?"

"Not a chance," she teased.

They lingered over the meal, conversation drifting from

the Duck Tour to the history they'd heard earlier in the day at the Science Museum.

They walked home slowly hand in hand. Once back at her house, Melanie smiled at him, "Thank you for today. It meant a lot, having you there."

Andrew looked at her. *Say it. Tell her you thought of the kiss. Tell her you want more.*

Instead, he only nodded, his voice rough. "It meant a great deal to me as well."

Their eyes lingered on each other, both remembering York, both feeling the weight of it.

"Goodnight, Andrew," she whispered.

"Goodnight, Melanie," he said softly, watching her step toward the hallway leading to the stairs to her bedroom, the unspoken ache pressing heavier with every passing day.

CHAPTER 42

The community center smelled faintly of coffee and paper, and there were folding chairs arranged in a circle. Melanie's book club had gathered, a half-dozen women of similar age, their voices lively with gossip before the official start.

"Ladies," Melanie said, guiding Andrew in, "this is Andrew. Visiting from England."

A hush fell, followed by eager smiles.

"Well, well," said one of the women, her sharp eyes twinkling. "So, this is the Andrew we've heard about."

Andrew straightened, lips twitching. "I can only hope the reports were favorable."

"Oh, very," another chimed in, grinning at Melanie. "She's been quoting you for months."

Melanie flushed lightly. "Not true."

Andrew glanced at her, warmth tugging at his chest. She talks about me here. Even in her world, I have a place.

The book of the month was a historical novel set in Italy, but the group kept veering off topic.

"So, Andrew," a woman asked, leaning forward. "Do you prefer Jane Austen or the Brontës?"

Andrew smiled. "Depends. Do I want to be amused or haunted?"

Laughter rippled through the room.

Another woman eyed him thoughtfully. "And how do you find our Melanie as a travel companion?"

Andrew hesitated, then met Melanie's gaze. "Unfailingly brave. And entirely too modest."

Melanie's heart gave a small leap.

The women exchanged knowing looks, and Melanie quickly steered the conversation back to the book, though her cheeks remained pink.

When book club finished and they stepped outside, the sky had turned heavy, clouds rolling low. A drop of rain splashed on Melanie's cheek.

"Looks like we're in for it," she said.

Andrew offered his arm. "Then we'd best make haste. I refuse to drown before lunch."

By the time they reached her house, the rain was falling in earnest, pattering against the windows, turning the world soft and grey.

After taking her jacket off, Melanie rummaged in her cupboard, pulling out a worn recipe card. "Well, if we're trapped inside, you might as well learn my mother's lasagna. It's a family classic."

Andrew slipped off his jacket, rolling up his sleeves.

"Lasagna. I accept the challenge. Though I warn you, garlic bread is my true calling."

She handed him a loaf and some butter. "Then you can prove it."

The kitchen soon filled with the scent of simmering sauce and garlic.

Andrew stirred carefully, tasting with a wooden spoon. "Mmm. Needs more..." He paused dramatically. "...wine."

Melanie laughed, swatting his shoulder. "You just want another glass for yourself."

"True," he admitted with a grin.

As they layered noodles and sauce, their conversation grew quieter, more thoughtful.

Melanie placed the final layer of pasta. "I didn't cook this for years after my marriage ended. Too many memories. It was his favorite."

Andrew looked at her, his expression gentle. "And now?"

"Now..." She exhaled slowly. "Now it feels like mine again. Ours, tonight."

He swallowed, moved. "I know something of that emptiness. I told myself I was content with solitude, but... it wasn't true. I was just afraid to admit the loneliness."

Melanie slid the dish into the oven, then turned, leaning against the counter. "And are you afraid now?"

Andrew met her gaze steadily. "Yes. But less so with you."

Her throat tightened, and for a moment they simply looked at each other, the rain tapping steady against the glass.

When the lasagna emerged golden and bubbling, they sat at the table with steaming plates and warm garlic bread.

Melanie lifted her fork, smiling faintly. "You've passed the garlic bread test."

Andrew smirked. "My proudest achievement yet."

But beneath the teasing, both felt the gravity of what they'd shared. The fears, the loneliness, the quiet hope, and the fragile beginnings of something deeper.

CHAPTER 43

The rain hadn't let up by nightfall, drumming softly on the roof and windows. Melanie set two cups of tea on the coffee table while Andrew fiddled with the remote.

"I'm told Americans take their movies very seriously," he said dryly. "I'm prepared to be educated."

Melanie laughed, curling onto the sofa with her quilt tucked around her legs. "Well, I'm not going to show you anything too serious. Tonight calls for comfort. Something familiar."

They settled on a classic romantic comedy, the kind both had likely seen years ago. The screen lit the room in flickers of light, and her living room felt warm and cozy.

Andrew sat next to Melanie on the sofa, their cups sending up little curls of steam.

Ten minutes in, Andrew tilted his head. "So, we're meant to believe they don't notice they're perfect for each other until the last five minutes?"

Melanie chuckled, sipping her tea. "That's the rule. Suspense."

He shook his head. "Utterly unrealistic."

She smiled at him over the rim of her cup. "Says the man who warned my grandson about man-eating dinosaurs."

Andrew's lips twitched. "Fair point."

Halfway through, a clap of thunder rolled outside, making the windows rattle. Melanie startled slightly. Andrew glanced at her, concern flickering in his eyes.

"All right?"

"Yes," she said quickly. "I just...well, storms make me jumpy."

He hesitated, then cleared his throat. "Would you... would you mind terribly if I sat nearer?"

Her heart skipped. "I think I'd like that."

Andrew moved closer, careful and deliberate, leaving just enough room to give her choice. She shifted the quilt so that it was over both their legs and leaned against him, his warmth settling her more than the tea in her hands.

A few minutes later, as the heroine on the screen fumbled awkwardly through a deJulietion of love, Andrew leaned closer, his voice pitched low, as if sharing a confidence meant only for her.

For the rest of the movie, their commentary grew softer, their laughter more hushed, each moment of shared humor drawing them closer. When the credits finally rolled, neither moved to rise.

Melanie's head rested against his shoulder, the steady rhythm of his breathing beneath her ear. Her eyes stung suddenly, not from sadness but from how right this felt.

Andrew looked down at her, his hand resting gently on her arm. *So simple, this closeness. And yet it felt like the bravest thing he had done in years.*

Reflections—Melanie

Melanie slipped into bed, the rain still pattering gently on the windows. She drew the quilt up to her chin and closed her eyes, but her body hummed with a nervous, joyful energy.

The warmth of Andrew's arm around her shoulders lingered like a physical echo, the steady comfort of his presence still pressed against her skin. For years, she had watched couples tucked together in cafés or parks, believing that kind of closeness had passed her by. But tonight, on her own sofa, she had felt it, the ease of leaning into someone, the joy of belonging.

She smiled into the dark. He asked permission. So careful, so respectful. *And when I said yes, he looked as though the whole world had lifted from his shoulders.*

Her chest tightened with something tender, almost fierce. *Oh, Andrew. You don't see it, do you? You don't see how much you mean.*

Sleep came slowly, carrying her into dreams with the warmth of his arm still wrapped around her.

Reflections—Andrew

Andrew sat on the edge of the bed, the small lamp casting a pool of light over the desk where Melanie had thoughtfully set his journal and pen. He opened to a fresh page, his hand lingering before the words began to flow.

Day Five. Tonight, I sat with her on the sofa, a film flickering before us, the rain loud outside. I asked her if I might sit closer. And she said yes. Not reluctantly, not politely, but with warmth.

She leaned into me, and I into her, and for the first time in years I felt steady and complete..

He paused, pressing the pen against the page, his throat tight.

I have spent so long believing myself too late for such things. That love, or even companionship, was for others, for younger men, for those less worn by life. But tonight proved me wrong. She made me brave enough to ask. And braver still, she welcomed me nearer.

He wrote slower now, the words weighted.

I fear the ocean that lies between us. I fear the days when I will return to silence. But for now, I will not let those fears eclipse the truth: I held her close, and she held me in return. That memory will carry me further than I thought possible.

Andrew set down the pen and closed the journal, his hand resting on its worn cover. The rain tapped steadily at the window, and for the first time in years, he went to sleep with hope alive in his chest.

CHAPTER 44

The ferry rocked gently as it pulled away from Hyannis, the salty wind tugging at Melanie's hair. She held onto the railing; her cheeks flushed with the sea air. Andrew stood beside her, one hand gripping his cap, the other braced against the rail.

"Remind me again why you insisted on this?" he said with mock severity as a spray of saltwater caught his sleeve.

"Because..." Melanie replied, smiling at him, "Nantucket is magic. And I wanted you to see it."

Andrew gave her a sidelong look. "Magic, hm? I'll hold you to that."

By midday, they were walking along cobblestoned streets lined with grey-shingled houses draped in roses. Shops overflowed with seaside trinkets, art prints, handwoven baskets, and Nantucket t-shirts.

Andrew slowed at one shop window displaying fountain pens crafted from driftwood. "Now that," he murmured, "is something special."

Melanie's lips curved into a smile. *He always notices the fountain pens.*

They stopped at a small café near the harbor, the breeze carrying the smell of salt and fried fish. Sitting outside with clam chowder and fresh bread, Andrew watched the sailboats drift in and out.

"It feels... timeless," he said softly. "As though the world beyond this island has stopped."

Melanie stirred her chowder, then looked at him. "Sometimes I think that's why people come here. To feel as though they can step out of time for a while."

He met her gaze steadily. "I think I'm beginning to understand."

They wandered the wharf, stopping to watch fishermen mend nets and children tossing breadcrumbs to gulls. Melanie led him toward Brant Point, where the lighthouse stood white against the blue sky.

She slipped her arm through his, her voice warm. "You're not tired, are you?"

"Not at all," he replied, though he leaned into her just slightly. "I've a suspicion you could walk me into the ground, but I'll endure."

She laughed softly. It feels so natural, his arm against mine. As though we've walked this way all our lives.

Near the dunes, they found a quiet stretch of beach. Melanie slipped off her shoes, letting the sand curl between her toes. Andrew hesitated, removed his own socks and shoes, then followed, grumbling good-naturedly.

"The things I endure for you," he muttered, wincing as the sand shifted under his feet.

Melanie laughed, the sound carried off by the wind. "Don't pretend you don't like it."

He smiled at her then, soft and unguarded. "With you, I like nearly everything."

Her breath caught, her heart tightening at the quiet truth in his voice.

Melanie leaned into his side, her head resting lightly on his shoulder. Andrew let out a long, slow breath, his arm wrapping around her as though it had always belonged there.

Andrew thought, *This is what I'll remember. Her warmth against me, the sea around us, and the impossible wish that time might hold still.*

They returned late, the ferry ride still clinging to them with its salt and sway. Melanie set a kettle on the stove while Andrew loosened his collar and took down the cups from the cupboard, both of them moving through the kitchen in an easy, unspoken rhythm that no longer felt new...just right.

As they carried their tea into the sitting room, Melanie flicked on the old radio perched on the shelf. A song drifted out, slow and tender, with a steady rhythm meant for holding someone close.

Andrew set his cup down, listening.

It's the perfect moment, he thought, not because it was uncertain, but because it wasn't.

Melanie stood near the window, humming softly, her head tilted as she recognized the tune. She turned when she felt his gaze, smiling with the quiet confidence that had grown between them over the last day.

"Melanie," he said gently.

"Yes?" she replied, already warm with expectation.

He stepped closer, offering his hand, not hesitant now, but deliberate. "Would you dance with me?"

Her smile bloomed, soft and luminous. "I'd love to."

He drew her into the center of the room, his hand settling at her waist with the same care he had shown her all evening, all week. Her other hand rested easily on his shoulder, familiar now. They swayed together, unhurried, the world narrowing to the music and the warmth they already knew.

Melanie leaned closer, her head resting against his chest, listening to the steady thump of his heart.

I could stay like this, she thought. *I could stay like this for a very long time.*

Andrew held her as though she were something precious, not fragile, but deeply valued. The ordinariness of it struck him then: the quiet room, the radio humming, and the ease of her body fitting against his.

So simple, he thought. *And yet this is everything.*

They spoke only a few quiet words.

"You're very graceful," Melanie murmured, smiling.

"That'll be the music," he replied softly. "Though I won't deny enjoying the company."

When the song slowed to its final notes, they didn't step apart. Andrew looked down at her, his expression open now and no longer guarded.

"I've been thinking about this," he said quietly. "About you, and about us."

Her eyes shimmered. "I know," she said. "So have I."

He bent then and kissed her, slow, certain, and lingering. Not the ache of reunion or the relief of finally daring, but something steadier.

Melanie kissed him back, her hands curling into his shirt, joy settling warm and sure in her chest.

When they finally drew apart, she laughed softly. "I like that you ask," she said. "Even when you don't have to."

Andrew smiled, his forehead resting against hers. "I never want to stop choosing you," he murmured.

They stood there a moment longer, still swaying to the fading hum of the radio, both knowing that whatever lines had once existed between them had already been crossed—gently, willingly, and together.

Reflections — Melanie

Melanie stood at the window for a long moment before turning out the light, the faint hum of the radio still echoing somewhere in the house below. Her body felt warm in that particular way that came not from heat, but from having been held.

The dance replayed itself in her mind, not the steps, but the feeling of his hand at her waist, the quiet certainty in the way he'd asked her, as though choosing her was something he meant to keep doing.

She smiled softly.

So much of her life had been spent bracing, for disappointment, for obligation, and for the next thing that would ask more of her than she had to give. Tonight had asked nothing. It had offered instead.

Melanie rested her hand against her chest, feeling her heart steady beneath her palm.

This wasn't urgency and it wasn't fantasy. It was something quieter and far more powerful: the sense of being met exactly where she was, without needing to explain or diminish herself.

When she finally lay down, sleep came easily.

And for once, she didn't wonder whether she was asking too much by wanting this. She simply let herself want him, and trust that wanting was allowed.

Reflections — Andrew

Day Six. Andrew wrote the date slowly, then paused.

Tonight we danced.

He almost smiled at how ordinary the words looked on the page, how little they revealed of what the moment had meant.

I asked her, he continued. *Not because I was unsure, but because I wanted to choose her, and have her choose me, even in something small.*

The memory settled warmly in him: Melanie's weight against his chest, the ease of her laughter, the quiet understanding in her eyes when he spoke of them—not someday and not hypothetically, but now.

I am not afraid tonight, he wrote, surprised again by the truth of it. *Not of wanting her and not of what this might become.*

There were still oceans, logistics, and still questions he didn't yet have answers for.

But tonight had taught him something important.

Love does not always arrive in a rush, he wrote. *Sometimes it comes as steadiness and choosing.*

Andrew closed the journal gently and for the first time in a long while, he felt no need to guard his heart from what lay ahead.

CHAPTER 45

The rain had cleared, leaving the air fresh and bright. Melanie stood at the stove, humming softly as she scrambled eggs, her cheeks still warm from the memory of last night's kiss. Every so often she found herself pausing, smiling into the pan like a schoolgirl.

Andrew wandered in, his hair still tousled from sleep. "Smells marvelous. And if I'm not mistaken, you're humming the tune from last night."

She laughed, flustered. "Am I? Well, it got stuck in my head."

"It's stuck in mine as well," he admitted, moving to pour himself coffee. He leaned against the counter, watching her with fondness. *She looks so at home here, and yet, she let me in. Into this kitchen, into her world, into her arms, and I don't want to leave it.*

They sat across from each other, eggs and toast between them. For a moment they ate quietly, but the silence wasn't awkward; it was warm, full of unspoken things.

Finally, Melanie said softly, "I didn't sleep much last night."

Andrew raised his brows. "Regrets already?" His tone was light, but he looked at her intently all the same.

She reached across, brushing his hand. "No regrets. Just... replaying everything." Her cheeks flushed. "Over and over."

His heart eased, his smile deepening. "Good. Because so was I."

"So," Melanie said, sipping her coffee. "What do you want to do today? No grandchildren, no book club, no obligations. Just us."

Andrew tilted his head, thoughtful. "I think I'd like to see more of your Massachusetts. Not just Boston and ferries and museums, but your everyday places. The ones that matter to you."

Melanie smiled. "Then I'll show you. There's a little antique shop in the next town you'd love. And afterward, maybe we can take a walk by the river trail. It's simple, but... it's where I go to think."

Andrew nodded, touched. "Then I'd be honored to walk where you think."

When the dishes were washed, Andrew reached to take the dishtowel from her hand. "May I?"

She arched a brow. "Drying dishes again? You're becoming alarmingly domestic."

He smirked. "And you mind?"

Melanie paused, looking up at him. "Not in the least."

Their eyes lingered, the memory of last night sparking again. For the first time in years, Melanie felt not just contentment, but possibility.

The little shop sat on a corner of the next town over, its windows cluttered with curiosities: brass candlesticks, old maps, stacks of yellowed books, and glass bottles catching the sunlight. A small bell chimed as Melanie pushed open the door, the air inside heavy with the mingled scents of old wood and lavender polish.

Andrew's eyes lit up. "Now this is dangerous. I may never leave."

Melanie laughed softly. "I thought you'd say that."

They wandered slowly through the narrow aisles. Andrew paused at a shelf of leather-bound books, running his fingers reverently along the cracked spines. "So many forgotten voices, sitting in silence. I always want to take them all home, but then I'd need a second house."

Melanie smiled, watching him. He looks alive here, like he's stepped back into his old life, but lighter somehow.

On a table near the back, Andrew spotted a fountain pen with a carved wooden body. He picked it up carefully. "Look at this. Made by hand, you can see the care in it. Imagine the letters it's written."

Melanie's heart warmed. "You and your pens."

"They're storytellers," he said simply, setting it down. "Like us."

She touched his sleeve, her eyes soft. "You're not done telling yours, Andrew."

His throat tightened, but he smiled. "Nor you, Melanie."

At another shelf, she lifted a small porcelain rabbit and held it out to him with a mischievous grin. "For Sophie's collection."

He chuckled, accepting it. "She'll insist Mr. Whiskers has a cousin now."

Afterward, they drove back toward her town and stopped at the river trail. The path wound beneath tall maples, their leaves dappling the afternoon sunlight across the water. The air smelled fresh, tinged with earth and moss.

They walked side by side, their hands brushing now and then until finally Andrew reached and laced his fingers through hers. She squeezed gently, smiling up at him.

"It's beautiful here," he murmured. "Peaceful. I can see why you come to think."

Melanie nodded. "It helps me breathe. Helps me remember what matters. I came here a lot after my marriage ended."

Andrew glanced at her, his voice low. "And what did you think about?"

She sighed. "About whether I'd ever be enough. For anyone. About how much of myself I'd given away, and if there'd be anything left to give again."

He stopped walking, turning to face her, his hands holding hers. "Melanie, you are more than enough. You've always been more than enough."

Her eyes shimmered, and her throat tightened. "And you, Andrew? What did you think about all those years alone?"

He hesitated, then spoke softly. "That maybe I'd missed my chance. That perhaps the world had decided I'd had enough of love. But then..." He squeezed her hands. "Then came you."

A silence stretched between them, filled only by the rush of the river. Melanie stepped closer, laying her hand against his chest. "I don't want to miss this chance, Andrew. Not with you."

He cupped her cheek, his thumb brushing lightly over her skin. "Nor I, love."

Their kiss was gentle, unhurried, the kind that grows out of a thousand small moments and slowly blooms. When they parted, Melanie rested her forehead against his.

"This feels new," she whispered. "And yet like I've known you forever."

Andrew's smile was tender. "Perhaps both can be true."

CHAPTER 46

The sun was sinking as they returned to her house, the time at the river still lingering in their minds. Melanie set her bag down on the counter and exhaled softly.

"Nothing fancy tonight," she said, slipping off her shoes. "How about omelets? Quick and easy."

Andrew rolled up his sleeves with a grin. "Point me to the eggs. After yesterday's lasagna triumph, I think we're ready for Act Two."

Melanie laughed, handing him a whisk. "We'll see if you pass this test."

The kitchen filled with the clatter of pans and the aroma of sautéing onions. Andrew cracked eggs with exaggerated care, earning Melanie's amused look.

"You know," he said as he stirred, "it occurs to me that cooking together may be the most dangerous thing we've done. One wrong move and we've got scrambled eggs on the ceiling."

Melanie shook her head, smiling. "You worry too much. Relax, you're doing fine."

He stole a piece of cheese from the cutting board, and she smacked his hand playfully. "Hey!"

Andrew grinned. "Chef's privilege."

She shook her head but couldn't stop her own laughter. *He makes the simplest things fun.*

They sat across from each other with plates of fluffy omelets, garlic bread leftover from the lasagna night, and glasses of wine. The room was warm, with the night air drifting softly through the open window.

Melanie lifted her fork. "I have to admit you've got a knack for omelets."

Andrew smirked. "Add it to my CV: teacher, reluctant traveler, competent egg cook."

Melanie looked confused. "CV? I don't think that's a term I'm familiar with."

"Job history, academic achievements, that sort of thing. I think it is the same as what Americans call a resume."

She laughed as she looked at him. "Then you can add good company to yours."

After the dishes were cleared, they carried their tea into the sitting room. Melanie tucked herself into her usual spot on the sofa, and Andrew sat next to her and slid his arm around her shoulders, pulling her to him.

She flipped through channels absently, landing on an old black-and-white movie. The screen flickered, soft music playing.

Andrew leaned back, studying her profile in the lamplight. "It's extraordinary, isn't it? That we sat across an ocean writing letters for months, and yet here I am, in your sitting room. As though it was always meant to be."

Melanie turned to him, her smile faint but full of feeling. "Sometimes I think it was."

The movie played on, but neither really watched it.

After a long silence, Andrew spoke softly. "I've thought of kissing you again all day."

Melanie's breath caught. "And what stopped you?"

His lips curved faintly. "Nothing now."

He leaned in, his lips finding hers, the kiss unhurried but lingering, deepening as her hand slid to the back of his neck. When they finally parted, Melanie whispered, "I could get used to this."

Andrew smiled, his voice low and steady. "Then let's make sure you can."

They sat like that for a while longer, the movie forgotten, the night soft around them, until they said goodnight with another long kiss in the kitchen.

Reflections—Melanie

Melanie sat at her vanity, brushing her hair slowly. The house was quiet except for the faint tick of the hallway clock.

She smiled to herself, remembering the way Andrew had kissed her on the sofa and how his arms had felt around her. She could still feel the warmth of his hands, and how her body seemed to awaken under his touch.

So many years I wondered if closeness like this was over for me. And yet here it is, not just tenderness, but safety. With him, I feel seen and wanted.

She set her brush aside and slipped into bed, her heart full. *How quickly the extraordinary has folded into the everyday. And how dearly I want to keep it.*

Reflections—Andrew

Andrew opened his journal again, the pen poised as he sat at the small desk. He wrote steadily, his words flowing more easily now than they had in years.

Day Seven. Tonight I kissed her again. Properly, with time enough to savor it, with the courage to linger. And she kissed me back, not out of politeness or curiosity, but because she wanted to and because she wanted me.

He paused, closing his eyes, the memory warming him all over again.

Her laughter fills the house like light. Her touch steadies me, soft yet certain. I have been afraid for so long, of being not enough, of being too late. But tonight, as we sat together, I began to believe that perhaps I am neither. Perhaps, for her, I am simply right.

CHAPTER 47

The next day dawned bright, the sky a flawless blue. By noon, the smell of charcoal drifted from Emily and Daniel's backyard, mingling with the laughter of children.

Melanie had just set down the platter of watermelon when the gate latch clicked.

"Oh good, Tom's here," Emily murmured under her breath. "Try not to provoke him, everyone."

Behind Tom, another voice called cheerfully, "You say that like it's hard, Em!" A second man stepped through the gate beside Tom, slightly shorter, with soft silver at his temples, crinkled eyes, and a grin that looked permanently ready for laughter.

"And Oliver's come too," Melanie said brightly, turning with delight. "Well, now the afternoon's properly balanced. What's a cookout without my favorite cousins."

Oliver swept forward and gave her a delighted hug. "How could I miss your famous overambitious cookouts?"

"They are perfectly ambitious," Melanie scolded, laughing. "And you always eat seconds."

"And thirds," he admitted proudly. "It's loyalty, Melanie."

Tom grunted. "It's gluttony."

Oliver clutched his chest. "You wound me, Thomas. I show up to support family and you insult my character before I've even smelled a burger."

Andrew watched the exchange with quiet amusement as Oliver turned toward him, eyes bright with interest.

"And you must be the Englishman," Oliver said warmly. "Andrew, is it? Lovely to finally meet the voice that's stolen our Melanie halfway across the Atlantic."

Andrew flushed. "I hope not stolen. Merely…borrowed but probably not giving her back!"

Oliver laughed, delighted. "Oh, I like him," he announced cheerfully.

Tom exhaled through his nose. "You like everyone. That's your second-greatest flaw."

"And your first is being allergic to joy," Oliver shot back. "It's terribly inconvenient at parties."

Emily groaned. "Here we go."

Oliver clapped Tom's shoulder. "Lighten up, brother. You've scared three mosquitoes and a very polite bird since you arrived."

Andrew chuckled before he could stop himself.

Tom eyed him, but something like approval flickered there too. "History man, eh?"

"Yes," Andrew replied. "It's a particular passion."

Tom nodded once. "Good. Means we won't have to discuss sports."

Oliver leaned closer to Andrew conspiratorially. "He pretends he's frightening. But once he starts talking about Roman aqueducts and things written in the margins, you won't shut him up for hours."

"That's slander," Tom muttered.

"It's biography."

Melanie watched them all with softened eyes. She adored this, the contrast, the affection, the rhythm between her cousins.

"You boys behave," she said fondly. "This isn't a wrestling match. It's a welcome."

Oliver beamed. "We're welcoming with spirit."

Tom glanced toward Andrew again, more thoughtfully now. "Kids like you," he said simply, nodding toward Sophie and Jack attempting English accents on the lawn.

"Do they?" Andrew asked.

"Means you're alright," Tom replied.

Oliver slung an arm around Tom's shoulders. "Hear that? He's welcoming you into the inner sanctum. Took me years to achieve that level of tolerance."

"You've still not achieved it," Tom said flatly.

Oliver grinned at Andrew. "He says that, but last Christmas he brought me an extra present. That was an emotional declaration."

Tom pushed his arm away. "Don't get sentimental."

Andrew found himself feeling unexpectedly grounded in the teasing warmth, as if he had gently stepped into the fabric of Melanie's life rather than hovering beside it.

Oliver lowered his voice slightly. "You make her happy," he said in a tone that still carried humor but held sincerity beneath it. "That matters more than you know."

Andrew inclined his head. "It matters to me too."

Tom nodded once, the same small gesture of acceptance as before.

"Just don't muck it up."

Oliver sighed theatrically. "Always the poet."

Tom turned to the grill again, muttering about hotdog buns, while Oliver stayed a moment longer beside Andrew.

"Welcome to the family," he murmured lightly. "We're a dramatic lot. But we mean well."

Andrew smiled. "I can see that."

From across the lawn, Melanie looked back at him, her face full of quiet ease, joy, and belonging.

And Andrew realized something gentle and profound:

He wasn't just visiting Melanie's world anymore; he was being woven into it.

"Andrew!" Jack called, darting across the lawn. "Say 'tomato!'"

Andrew blinked, amused. "Tomato."

Jack collapsed in laughter. "You said it funny! Say it again!"

Andrew obliged, exaggerating. "To-MAH-to."

Sophie, perched on the swing, chimed in with a giggle. "Say 'bottle of water'!"

Andrew arched a brow. "Bo-OH-o-wa'er."

She squealed with delight. "You sound so different! Like a movie!"

Melanie, setting down the potato salad, shook her head, laughing. "Don't torment the poor man."

Andrew laughed. "I've never had such an enthusiastic audience!"

They gathered at the table, paper plates piled with hamburgers, hot dogs, potato salad, and watermelon. The children chattered endlessly, trying to mimic Andrew's accent with comical results.

"Would you pass the 'po-tah-to' salad?" Jack asked in a dreadful imitation.

Andrew pretended to consider. "Well, since you asked

so politely..." He handed it over with mock formality, earning more giggles.

Emily, watching the exchange, leaned closer to Melanie. "They adore him."

Melanie's chest swelled, her smile soft. "I know."

Daniel lifted a beer toward Andrew. "You're one of us now. No going back."

Andrew raised his glass of lemonade with equal solemnity. "Then I shall endeavor to live up to the honor."

<hr>

Tom stood slightly apart from the main cluster of chairs; plate balanced carefully in one hand. He had positioned himself where he could see everyone without being directly in the flow of conversation.

Noise pressed in from multiple directions with overlapping voices and the children laughing. Tom focused on his food, grounding himself in the familiar order of it.

"Too loud?" Andrew asked quietly, stepping beside him.

Tom considered the question seriously. "Not intolerable," he said. "But noticeable."

Andrew smiled. "Fair enough."

They stood in companionable silence for a moment.

"I hear you're in research," Andrew said.

"Yes." Tom nodded. "Historical analysis. Patterns over time."

"That sounds... absorbing."

"It is," Tom said. Then, after a pause, added, "Predictable in a way people are not."

Andrew chuckled softly.

Tom glanced at him. "That wasn't meant humorously."

"I know," Andrew said. "That's why it was funny."

Tom accepted this, nodding once.

Across the yard, Oliver called out, "Tom! You're interrogating Melanie's man again!"

"I'm not," Tom replied calmly. "We're having a conversation."

Andrew laughed outright then, and Tom felt, faintly and unexpectedly, that he'd said the correct thing.

Melanie watched from a distance, a small smile tugging at her mouth. Tom caught her eye briefly and looked away, comforted by the fact that she never required him to perform.

As dusk settled, they gathered around a small fire pit. Jack carefully roasted a marshmallow until it only just caught fire, then blew it out, while Sophie carefully turned hers until it was golden.

Andrew attempted one himself, only to have it burn black, and slide off the stick into the flames.

Jack shouted. "You're terrible at this!"

Andrew threw up his hands. "Clearly I require remedial training."

Melanie leaned close, slipping another marshmallow onto his stick. "Here. Try again." She rested her hand lightly on his shoulder, the warmth of her touch sparking something deeper than the firelight.

When he managed a perfect golden brown, Sophie clapped. "See? You're not so bad!"

Andrew smiled. "High praise indeed, but it's all due to my trainer."

By the time they walked back to Melanie's house, the stars were bright above. She slipped her arm through his as they strolled. "You were wonderful today. They truly like you."

Andrew looked down at her, his smile tender. "I like them, Melanie. And I like what it means, that I'm... accepted, in your world."

Her hand squeezed his arm. "You are."

The smell of woodsmoke still clinging to their clothes as Melanie set a kettle of water to boil for tea and Andrew wandered into the sitting room, loosening his collar as though he were shedding the day.

She soon joined him, carrying their tea. They both sat close at the end of the sofa, their legs stretched out toward the coffee table.

"Today was... something," Andrew said, cradling his cup. "I haven't laughed like that in years." He stopped, swallowing.

Melanie turned to look at him. "And did it feel good?"

He met her gaze steadily. "It felt like coming back to life."

Melanie set her cup down, tucking her legs beneath her. "I was nervous about today, you know. Introducing you to more of my family, letting all of them see us together. I wondered if they'd judge me, or you."

Andrew tilted his head. "And now?"

She smiled faintly. "Now I see how wrong I was. They like you, Andrew. Truly. They see what I see."

"And what is it you see?"

Her cheeks warmed, but her voice was steady. "A man who is kind. Who listens. Who makes me laugh again. A man who fits in my world without even trying."

Andrew's chest ached with tenderness. He set his cup aside and shifted nearer, his hand brushing hers. "And you,

Melanie... you've given me more in these days than I thought I'd ever have again."

He leaned in slowly, and when their lips met, it was gentle at first, then deepened into something warmer, more certain. Melanie melted into him, her hands sliding around his shoulders.

They lingered like that, sharing quiet kisses and smiles, before finally parting for their rooms.

Reflections—Andrew

In his guest room, Andrew sat for a moment with his journal open, staring at the blank page. For once, the words came easily:

Tonight she kissed me back as though there was no doubt at all. No hesitation, no distance, just warmth. I feel like a man reborn. And if I had to leave tomorrow, this would be enough. But oh, how I hope there will be more.

CHAPTER 48

The drive down to the Cape was quiet in the best way, the kind of silence filled with comfortable glances and the hum of shared thought. When they reached the coast, the air carried that unmistakable tang of salt and seaweed. Gulls flew overhead, their cries sharp against the endless rush of surf.

Melanie breathed deeply, her scarf tugged by the breeze. "I always feel small here," she murmured. "But not in a bad way. More like... reminded that the world is bigger than my worries."

Andrew slipped his hands into his pockets, gazing out at the horizon where sky melted into sea. "I think I could stand here forever and still not take it all in."

They walked slowly along the strand, shoes in hand, wet sand cool beneath their feet. The tide whispered in and out, scattering shells and fragments of driftwood.

After a while, Andrew spoke, his voice quiet. "Melanie, do you ever wonder... if we've come too late to this? To... us."

She glanced at him, her heart catching. "All the time."

His jaw tightened. "I fear the ocean between us, the miles that will stretch when I'm back in York. And I fear…" He hesitated, then pushed on. "I fear I'm too old to begin again."

Melanie stopped walking. She touched his arm gently, making him meet her eyes. "Andrew. You're not too old. We're not too late. Maybe we're just… exactly on time."

He swallowed hard, her words sinking deep. On time… perhaps even now, life is still generous enough to give us this.

As they walked further, Melanie's gaze caught on a glint in the sand. She stooped, brushing away grit, and lifted a smooth bluish green fragment of sea glass, worn soft by the sea, shaped uncannily like a heart.

"Look," she said, holding it out to him, her smile tender. "It's almost perfect."

Andrew took it reverently, the cool weight in his palm oddly powerful. "A heart," he murmured. "The sea's way of giving us a sign."

She pressed it back into his hand, closing his fingers around it. "Keep it. In your pocket. And when you touch it, you'll know I'm thinking of you."

His chest ached, eyes stinging. "Melanie…"

But words failed him. Instead, he slipped the sea glass into his pocket, his hand lingering over it as though anchoring himself to her.

They walked on, and eventually Andrew stopped again, turning to face her fully, the wind tugging at his hair. "I can't pretend any longer. I love you, Melanie. Not in some fleeting, passing way, but with everything I have left."

Her breath hitched, tears glimmering as she reached for his face. "I love you too, Andrew. I didn't expect it, didn't dare hope for it. But I do. I love you."

The sea roared behind them as he kissed her, slow and certain, sealing the truth between them. When they drew back, both were smiling through tears.

Andrew held her close, his voice rough. "Then no ocean will be enough to undo it. We'll find a way."

Melanie rested her head against his chest, the sound of his heartbeat steady under her ear. "Yes," she whispered. "We will."

The drive home from the Cape was quieter than usual, but it wasn't silence of uncertainty, it was full, content, and brimming with the unspoken after their confessions by the sea. Melanie's hand rested lightly on Andrew's thigh as she drove, his fingers over hers now and then, each touch a reassurance: *We said it. It's real.*

When they returned, the house was dark and hushed. Melanie flicked on the kitchen light. "Hungry?" she asked with a smile.

Andrew chuckled. "When am I not?"

They settled on something simple: reheated lasagna and fresh salad. Nothing fancy, but it felt like a feast. Andrew insisted on setting the table while Melanie poured the wine.

As they ate, Melanie found herself laughing more easily than she had in years, at Andrew's dry wit, at his mock complaints about American bread, at his very British way of turning every ordinary thing into commentary.

At one point she set down her fork, smiling softly across the table. "I keep thinking this is all a dream. That I'll wake up, and you'll still be across the ocean, and none of this will have happened."

Andrew nodded and reached across, covering her hand with his. "It's no dream, Melanie. I love you." His voice wavered, but he pressed on. "Even if tomorrow carried me away forever, I'd still know it was true."

Her eyes stung with tears, but she squeezed his hand. "And so would I."

They carried their wine into the sitting room. Melanie lit a candle on the coffee table, its small flame lighting up the dark.

Andrew sat beside her on the sofa, not at the far end, not even with space between, but close enough that their shoulders touched. He slipped his arm around her, and she leaned into him, her head on his chest.

They didn't rush to talk. The candle flickered, the clock ticked softly, the house wrapped itself around them.

Finally, Melanie whispered, "Andrew?"

"Yes, love?"

"I don't want to waste another day. I've spent too many already."

He smiled and kissed her hair, his voice steady. "Neither do I."

They sat like that until the candle burned low, their kisses unhurried, threaded between murmured words and quiet laughter.

They parted for the night reluctantly, both knowing tomorrow would bring the ache of departure. But for tonight, at least, they rested in the certainty of love, fragile and fierce all at once.

CHAPTER 49

Sunlight was streaming through his bedroom window when Andrew woke. For a long moment he simply lay there, listening: the faint rattle of Melanie in the kitchen, the clink of china, the scent of coffee drifting down the hall. His chest ached already at the thought of leaving, but he forced himself up. *Don't mourn the hours yet. Live them.*

When he entered the kitchen, Melanie turned with a smile. She had made pancakes, stacked high on a platter, a bowl of strawberries and jug of real maple syrup beside them.

"Pancakes?" Andrew asked, eyes widening. "You're trying to ruin me for English breakfasts forever."

Melanie laughed softly. "It's your last morning here, I wanted it to be special."

He crossed to her, brushing a kiss across her cheek before she could hand him a plate. "Then it already is."

They ate slowly, stretching out the meal with sips of coffee and conversation. But under every word lay the same truth: this is the last morning.

They spent the late morning strolling through her garden, Melanie pointing out the peonies that would bloom in another week, the lilacs fading now at spring's end.

Later, they sat together on the porch swing, Melanie tucked under his arm. They rocked gently, not speaking much, only savoring the rhythm of each creak, the warmth of his hand in hers.

At one point Andrew murmured, "If I could stop time, it would be now. This moment."

Melanie pressed closer, her throat too tight for words.

The hours dwindled too quickly. Soon Melanie was driving him toward the airport, the highway unfurling ahead with a cruel inevitability. Conversation wove between them, lighter than they felt, both clinging to humor to hold off the ache.

"Remember when I thought hot dogs were suspicious?" Andrew said, smiling faintly.

Melanie chuckled, though her heart ached. "And now you're practically an expert marshmallow roaster."

"Practically," he echoed softly, turning the sea glass heart in his pocket with his fingers. *If I hold it tight enough, maybe I won't feel like I'm breaking.*

Traffic slowed near the city. Melanie gripped the wheel, wishing the road would stretch on forever.

***

The terminal was bright and bursting with a flurry of people everywhere, indifferent to their quiet heartbreak. Melanie walked with him to the security line, her arm linked tightly through his. Neither wanted to let go.

At the end of the rope barrier, Andrew stopped. He turned to her, his expression raw.

"I hate this part," he whispered. "More than I can say."

Melanie's eyes stung as she tried to smile. "So do I."

He cupped her face in his hands, his voice breaking. "Melanie, I love you. That won't end here. Not tonight. Not ever."

She nodded, tears slipping free. "I love you too. Always."

He kissed her then, not caring about the crowd, deep and lingering, as though to leave a piece of himself with her. When at last he drew back, his hands lingered against her cheeks, wiping her tears.

Then the inevitable came. He kissed her once again and then turned, shoulders squared and walked toward the gate.

Melanie stood rooted, tears still flowing down her cheeks and her hand pressed to her mouth, watching until he was lost in the crowd. The sight of his back retreating nearly undid her. *How do you let go of someone who's become your heart?*

Andrew

Every step away from her felt like a betrayal. He forced himself onward, swallowing hard, his hand clenched around the sea glass heart in his pocket. *Walk, Collins. Just walk. Don't look back, or you'll never leave.*

Marion

On the drive home, Melanie kept one hand pressed to her lips, the echo of his kiss still burning there. Tears blurred the highway, but beneath them was a fierce certainty: *He loves me. We'll find a way.*

CHAPTER 50

Andrew

The flat was quiet in the evenings. Too quiet. Andrew kept to his routines, tea at seven, a walk along the river when the weather held, his journal open on the desk and writing each night, but without Melanie, everything felt muted. He still smiled when he remembered her laugh, but the smile never quite reached his eyes.

Every email from her was a balm and every phone or video call a lifeline. He would linger over her words, reading them again in the morning, then once more before bed. And yet, the space beside him on the sofa, the silence at the breakfast table, the empty hooks by the door, and the walks by himself, all reminded him that she was not here.

You gave me back my smile, he wrote one evening, *and I find I don't know how to keep it without you near.*

Melanie

Melanie's days were full of activity. Volunteering at the library, tea with Emily, afternoons spent chasing Jack and Sophie through the yard, and baking pies...she loved it all. But in the evenings, when the house went still and she curled up with a book, her thoughts always drifted back to Andrew.

She felt his absence the most in the little things: no dry remark over her choice of novel, no gentle hand reaching for hers during the news, no quiet voice reading a poem aloud to her...and the big things, like the feel of his lips on hers. The phone and video calls and emails helped. But none of it filled the emptiness of the empty seat beside her.

One night, as she folded laundry, she stopped mid-motion, holding a soft cotton shirt against her chest. "What am I waiting for?" she murmured aloud. Her heart answered at once: *I want to go back.*

She set the shirt down, her decision blooming solid and certain. She wouldn't wait for a later date. She'd book the flight and she'd go.

The next evening, as they spoke on a video call, Andrew looked especially weary, his smile brave but thin.

"I miss you," he admitted quietly, glancing away from the camera. "Emails and video calls are not the same as seeing your face in the morning light."

She took a breath, steadying herself. "Then what if... what if I came sooner? Not months from now. Next month. I could fly into Manchester this time and spend a week with you."

Andrew blinked, his expression shifting from surprise to hope to something dangerously close to joy. "You'd come sooner?"

"Yes," she said firmly, her eyes soft. "I don't want to wait. I'd rather have one more week with you now than circle dates on a calendar and ache for them."

He pressed a hand to his face, laughing shakily. "Melanie, if I could reach through this screen, I'd kiss you senseless."

"Then you'd better let me get the ticket," she teased, her voice trembling with happiness.

His eyes shone. "Manchester. I'll be there, waiting."

And for the first time in weeks, they both smiled without effort, as though the distance had just shortened by half.

CHAPTER 51

elanie stepped off the plane and felt the difference immediately. Heathrow had been a vast, humming hive, full of endless corridors, restaurants, duty-free shops and voices from a dozen languages echoing off high glass ceilings. Manchester, by comparison, felt smaller and much easier to navigate. The signage was clearer, the pace less frantic, though she still felt the tug of weariness from the long flight.

After customs, she followed the signs toward where she knew Andrew would be waiting on the other side of the barrier with a familiar mix of anticipation and joy. No nerves this time, only the ache of wanting to see him again.

And there he was. Standing just beyond the barrier, cap in hand, his face searching the crowd.

"Andrew!" Her voice lifted over the crowd, and his eyes found her at once.

The hug was immediate, solid and warm with no hesitation now. He held her as though the weeks between them had never existed, and she pressed her cheek against his shoulder, sighing into the fabric of his jacket.

"You're really here," he murmured. "At Manchester, of all places. I've never been so glad to see this airport."

She laughed, drawing back just enough to see his face. "It feels different than Heathrow. It was a lot less overwhelming. I managed to find my way without feeling like I needed breadcrumbs."

"See?" he teased gently. "You're becoming quite the seasoned traveler."

"Not without incentive," she said, her eyes soft on his.

The motorway unfurled before them, signs marked in bold blue: Leeds, York, The North. Melanie watched the countryside open up gradually, with the tangle of airport hotels and retail parks giving way to fields dotted with sheep, and hedgerows greening with spring.

"It's funny," she said, leaning back against the seat. "Flying into Heathrow felt like stepping into a city that swallowed me whole. Flying into Manchester feels... closer somehow, more human scale."

Andrew glanced at her, his smile warm. "That's a fair way to put it. Manchester's a bit scruffier at the edges, perhaps, but friendlier for it. And the drive home is kinder too, less sprawl and more hills."

Melanie pointed to a patchwork of stone walls dividing fields. "Those! I love those walls. They look like someone laid a quilt across the land."

He chuckled. "That's a poet's description if I've ever heard one. I just think of them as awkward when I'm out walking."

"Well, awkward or not, they're beautiful," she said.

For a while they rode in companionable silence, his hand clasping hers from where it rested on the seat between them.

"You know," Andrew said after a pause, "this feels

different than last time. When I met you at York Station, I wasn't sure if you'd still want to see me once the train doors opened. This time... I didn't doubt."

Melanie's throat tightened. "I didn't doubt either. Not for a moment."

He gave her a quick, sideways smile. "We're getting braver, Melanie."

"Or maybe just truer," she said softly. "I think we've always been brave. It just took time to trust it."

He reached across and squeezed her hand, his thumb brushing her knuckles. "Well, either way, I'd take this car ride with you over any train station nerves in the world."

She laughed, squeezing back. "So would I, and I feel quite spoiled not having to take the train."

"Good," he said simply, eyes on the road. "You deserve it."

The flat smelled faintly of books and polish, with a warmth Melanie remembered instantly. Andrew set her suitcase by the guest room door, but when she trailed back into the sitting room, she dropped into the sofa with a sigh.

"This feels..." she began, searching for the right word.

"Familiar?" he offered, easing down beside her.

"Yes," she said with a small smile. "And like I've come home."

They spent the next hour talking in the easy way that had become second nature, Melanie telling him about Emily's new recipes gone awry, Andrew recounting a small misadventure with Nigel and a flat tire. Their laughter rose and fell as the evening went on, the kind of laughter that comes only when two people are totally at ease with each other.

At some point, Melanie leaned back against him, her head resting comfortably on his shoulder. She murmured something, half a thought, half a sigh, and before long, her breathing had evened out, soft and steady.

Andrew froze, then slowly let out a breath. He dared not move, not even to shift the arm that now curved gently along the back of the sofa. He simply sat there, utterly still, feeling the weight of her head against him and the trust it carried.

Andrew

She has fallen asleep on me. On me. As though it were the most natural thing in the world.

Andrew's mind tumbled over the thought as he gazed down at her.

I've sat on this sofa hundreds of evenings. Alone. With books, with the radio, with silence. And now, with her. Leaning against me, trusting me enough to drift into sleep. I didn't know how empty these walls were until she filled them, and I dread the silence that will return when she leaves.

I have never been anyone's home. Yet here she is, breathing quietly against my shoulder, and I find myself believing it might be true. That I am hers, and she is mine, and that this small room is enough to hold the whole of it.

Melanie stirred after some time, blinking awake and lifting her head with a sheepish smile. "Oh dear. Did I fall asleep on you?"

Andrew's smile was soft. "You did. And I didn't mind in the slightest."

"I must have been more tired than I thought," she said, rubbing her eyes. "But it felt... safe."

He swallowed, his chest aching at the word. "I'm glad."

She shifted, stretching her shoulders. "Tea?"

He nodded, rising. "Yes. Let me."

Soon they sat side by side at the small table, cups of tea steaming between them. Their conversation grew quieter now, words giving way to comfortable silence, glances carrying as much as sentences.

At one point, Melanie reached over and covered his hand with hers. "I'm so glad I came."

He turned his hand over, catching hers. "So am I."

And as the night drew on, it felt less like a reunion and more like a continuation. It was as though she had never left, and he had been waiting only for the sound of her laughter to return.

When the last of the tea had gone cold, Andrew rose reluctantly. "I suppose I should let you get some rest."

Melanie followed him into the dimly lit hallway. There was a moment, the pause that always seemed to hang between parting and longing, and then Melanie stepped closer.

"Andrew," she whispered, her voice softer than the hush of the flat.

He bent his head before he could think, and their lips met. The kiss was unhurried, warm, threaded with weeks of absence and the joy of return. Melanie's hand came up to rest against his chest, and he cupped her cheek, the brush of her hair against his fingers achingly familiar.

When they finally drew back, both were smiling, breathless but steadied by the certainty between them.

"Goodnight," she said, her voice trembling with something more than fatigue.

"Melanie," he murmured, his forehead resting lightly against hers for a moment longer.

He took her hand, his voice quiet but certain. "You can stay."

Melanie nodded, stepping with him into the room.

What followed was private—unhurried, tender and filled with the kind of closeness that needed no explanation.

Reflections—Andrew

Tonight felt... settled.

Andrew paused after writing the word, considering it.

Not dramatic or overwhelming, but just right.

He thought of the ease between them, the absence of fear and the quiet understanding that had guided every moment. He had not needed to explain himself. Melanie had not needed reassurance.

They had met each other exactly where they were.

I didn't feel the need to retreat, he wrote. *That is new.*

What surprised him most was the calm that followed. No second-guessing. No sense of having crossed something too quickly. Only the steady awareness that closeness, when chosen with care, could feel safe.

Andrew closed the journal and rested his hand briefly against the page.

This is what I was afraid of wanting, and I was wrong to be, he realized.

Reflections—Melanie

The flat was quiet in a way that felt newly familiar.

Melanie lay awake for a few moments, listening. Andrew's breathing beside her was slow and even, and the sound settled something deep in her chest.

There had been no rush, no performance. Only warmth, laughter, and the simple relief of not having to hold herself apart anymore. She had stepped toward this, not out of loneliness, but out of trust and love.

Melanie smiled faintly into the pillow.

For so long, she had believed that wanting something for herself required apology. Tonight, she understood, finally, that love could be chosen gently, without guilt.

She turned slightly, careful not to wake him, and let herself rest in the quiet certainty of it.

She smiled again to herself, shaking her head at the wonder of it all. *How did I get here? How did I, a woman who thought her chances long behind her, find this man who makes me feel seen and cherished?*

I think I could fall asleep like this every night, she admitted silently. *And if I'm honest... I want to.*

With that truth warming her heart, she drifted back into sleep.

CHAPTER 52

The morning light shone through Andrew's kitchen window, across the table where Melanie sat with her coffee. She watched as Andrew fussed with the kettle, muttering under his breath about water temperatures and proper steeping times.

"You know," she teased, "most people just dunk the bag and call it a day."

He turned, pretending to be offended. "Most people, Melanie, are barbarians. Tea deserves respect."

She laughed, leaning her chin on her hand. "I love the way you get so serious about it. It's endearing."

He blinked, then smiled faintly, the corners of his mouth tugging upward in that way that still made her chest ache. "You're making fun of me."

"Not at all," she said softly. "I mean it."

Later that morning, they wandered through York's open-air market, the stalls alive with color and sound. Melanie admired the pyramids of apples, the wheels of cheese, the baskets of fresh bread and the smells from the street food vendors. Andrew carried the bag, slowly filling it with her chosen items of strawberries, a loaf still warm from the oven, and wedge of Wensleydale.

At one stall, Melanie picked up a jar of jam, holding it to the light. "Blackcurrant. I've never tried it."

Andrew leaned closer, their shoulders brushing. "You'll like it. Tart, but sweet underneath."

"Like someone I know?" she teased, giving him a side-long glance.

He chuckled, the sound low and warm. "Careful, or I'll buy the whole stall just to prove a point."

She laughed, and for a moment the world narrowed as she felt the warmth of his hand clasping hers after he took the jar and tucked it into the bag. The small touch sent a shiver up her arm, so simple, so ordinary, and yet so full of meaning.

They had just stepped out of a small gallery near the Shambles, Melanie still smiling about a watercolor she had loved, when Andrew stopped short.

His hand, which had been resting lightly against Melanie's back, went still.

"Andrew?" she asked, turning.

He was looking across the street. A woman stood there, elegant, sharp-featured, dressed in a fitted coat that looked just a little too polished for the narrow, crooked lane. She was speaking to someone on her phone, her posture brisk, confident.

Andrew felt something cold slip through him. *Victoria.* He hadn't seen her in years.

The woman turned, her eyes falling on him, and then flickered with recognition.

"Well," she said, crossing the street toward them. "I thought that was you."

Andrew swallowed. "Hello, Victoria."

Her gaze slid to Melanie, assessing in a way that was far from subtle. "And you must be…?"

"Melanie," she said, smiling as she offered her hand.

"Victoria," the woman replied, not taking Melanie's hand. "Andrew and I used to work together." Used to be much more than that, her tone suggested.

"Are you visiting?" Victoria asked Melanie, her voice coldly polite.

"Yes," Melanie said. "I'm from the States."

"Oh?" Victoria's brow lifted. "How… adventurous."

Andrew felt his jaw tighten.

Victoria looked him over with a faint smile. "I heard you never did marry after… well." She waved a hand lightly. "Everything."

"I didn't," Andrew said.

Her gaze flicked back to Melanie. "And you?"

Melanie hesitated, then said calmly, "I'm divorced."

Victoria smiled, but it was not kind. "Of course."

The words landed like a pinprick.

"Well," Victoria said lightly, already turning away, "it was… interesting seeing you again, Andrew. Do enjoy your stay."

And with that, she was gone, heels clicking down the narrow street.

Andrew felt suddenly exposed. Smaller. As if some old, unwelcome version of himself had just been dragged back into the light.

Melanie watched him carefully. "Are you all right?"

"Yes," he said, too quickly.

But something had shifted again...not away from Melanie, but inward.

Fear, long buried, had stirred.

They walked in quiet for a few minutes after leaving the gallery, the narrow streets slowly widening into more familiar ground.

Andrew was still with her; Melanie could feel that. His hand still held hers, his steps matched her own. But something in him had drawn inward, like a tide slipping back from shore.

Melanie tried not to read too much into it.

Still, the woman's voice echoed faintly in her mind. *Of course.* The word had been small, almost careless, but it had carried weight. *Of course you're divorced.*

Melanie swallowed hard, feeling a tightness in her throat. Not because of the woman herself, but because, suddenly, Melanie felt keenly aware of everything she might be in someone else's eyes—not enough.

She glanced at Andrew's face, the familiar kindness there, the quiet gravity. He hadn't looked tempted, only shaken.

Which was somehow worse. *Did she make him doubt? Did she remind him of something painful?*

Melanie folded her hands together, steadying herself. She had learned, in her long marriage, how easy it was to disappear when you began measuring yourself against other people's expectations. She refused to do that again.

And yet...a faint vulnerability lingered.

They walked to Andrew's flat and unpacked their market bags to prepare a small lunch. Melanie made them both some tea. *Something seems wrong. He's so quiet.*

Andrew sat at the table, fingers drumming lightly on the wood, the look on his face half-thoughtful, half-troubled.

Melanie slid his cup across to him, then sat opposite, tilting her head. "Something's on your mind."

He gave a faint smile, but it didn't quite reach his eyes. "You do see straight through me, don't you?"

"Not hard," she said gently. "Not with you sitting there looking like the world's about to end over a cup of tea."

Andrew cleared his throat. "I'm sorry I've been a bit... off since earlier."

Melanie turned to him. "You don't have to apologize."

"I do," he said. "I don't like not being fully here with you."

He exhaled slowly, staring down at the steam curling from his cup. "There's something I've never told you. Something I suppose I should, if only so you understand me better."

Her heart gave a small lurch. "All right."

She studied him, then said gently, "That woman... she unsettled you."

"Yes," he admitted. Then hesitated. "Not because of her. Because of what she represents."

Melanie waited.

Andrew looked down at his hands, his voice quieter now. "There are things I've never quite told you about... about why I stopped smiling for a while."

Something in Melanie softened, a door opening in her chest.

"Andrew," she said, quietly, "you don't have to carry it alone."

And in the hush that followed, the weight of years finally began to loosen, leading naturally into the story he had never meant to tell, but needed to.

"There was a woman, a colleague, years ago," he began, his voice low. "It was Victoria. I cared for her, more than I admitted, even to myself. She laughed at my jokes, sought me out, walked home with me once or twice. I thought perhaps..." He trailed off, swallowing. "But I never said it. Not properly. I hesitated, as I always do. She wanted certainty, boldness, deJulietions. I offered silence and caution. And before I could find courage, she was married to another."

Melanie's breath caught, her chest aching for him.

Andrew's gaze stayed fixed on his tea. "I told myself it was for the best. That she deserved someone better. But the truth was, I felt small. Not enough. Not worth waiting for. After that, I suppose I stopped believing anyone could want what I had to give. I stopped smiling. For years."

Silence stretched. Melanie reached across the table, covering his hand with hers. "Andrew," she said softly, "it wasn't that you weren't enough. It was that she didn't see what you had to give. She didn't have the patience or the heart to wait for it. That's not on you. That's on her."

He looked up then, eyes bright with something raw. "You really believe that?"

"I do," she said firmly. "Because I see you. Exactly as you are. And what you have to give... it's more than enough. It's everything."

His throat tightened. He turned his hand over to clasp hers, his grip strong. "You've given me back my smile, Melanie. I thought I'd lost it forever."

Her eyes shimmered, but her smile was steady. "Then keep smiling, Andrew. Because I'm not going anywhere."

They started to prepare their lunch again and moved easily around the kitchen, Melanie sliced strawberries while Andrew buttered bread, the radio murmuring in the background. At one point, their hands collided as they reached for the same knife, and they both stilled, their eyes meeting.

"After you," Andrew murmured, though he didn't move his hand away.

"Maybe together," she said softly, and guided the blade through the loaf with him.

When the bread split cleanly, they both laughed, the tension breaking, but as he leaned close to brush the crumbs from her cheek with his thumb, the laughter faded into a quiet that hummed with possibility.

Without thinking, Melanie tilted her head, and he kissed her, a brief, soft kiss, tasting of strawberries and sunlight.

"Stolen moment," she whispered against his lips.

He smiled, brushing his nose lightly against hers. "Keep stealing them, Melanie. I won't complain."

That evening, they strolled hand in hand along the city walls, the stones glowing with the pink and orange colors of sunset. From the height, Melanie pointed out the patchwork of rooftops, the spire of the Minster rising above it all.

"I still can't believe I was here before," she murmured. "But this feels different now. Not just sightseeing. It feels like…"

"Life," Andrew supplied gently.

She nodded. "Yes. Life. With you."

He squeezed her hand, lifting it briefly to his lips as they walked. "You make it feel that way for me, too."

They paused at a quiet stretch, the city hushed below, and Andrew turned to her. This kiss was slower, deeper than the one in the kitchen, a kiss that spoke of everything unspoken between them, the distance already overcome, and the distance yet to bridge.

When they parted, Melanie rested her forehead against his chest, listening to the steady beat of his heart. "I don't want this to end," she whispered.

He tightened his arms around her, his voice low and certain. "It won't. Not anymore.

CHAPTER 54

Reflections—Andrew

Andrew sat at the desk by the window, York quiet below him, pen moving slowly across the page.

I didn't expect to see Victoria today, he wrote.

I didn't expect the old doubts to come rushing back either.

He paused, then continued.

Melanie saw it. I couldn't hide it from her, and perhaps that's a good thing.

He exhaled softly.

I told her the truth. About the way I loved someone once and lost my nerve. About how that loss made me afraid that I am... easily left.

He stared at the page.

And yet here is Melanie. Gentle. Steady. Real.

After a moment, he added:

I love her.

The words felt both terrifying and right.

What I fear most is not losing her, it is believing I might be worthy of being chosen.

It astonishes me, how easily she fits into my life. Shopping in the market, cooking in my kitchen, walking the walls at sunset. None of it was grand or unusual, and yet every moment carried weight. Perhaps that is what love is, the transformation of the ordinary into something extraordinary.

She teased me about my tea again, and instead of feeling foolish, I felt... seen. Cherished, even, for my quirks. When her hand clasped mine at the jam stall, it was as though the world narrowed to that small touch. How can something so simple leave me reeling?

And the kisses. God help me, I could write a book on the way she kisses. Light as laughter in the kitchen, deep as the sunset on the walls. Each one felt stolen, but not forbidden, more like gifts exchanged without ceremony. And I find myself greedy for more.

Melanie sees me. She doesn't want louder or braver or more dazzling. She wants me, exactly as I am. I cannot describe what that does to a man who has carried the weight of being "less" for half his life. It feels like having a stone lifted from my chest, like air filling my lungs for the first time in years.

I told her she has given me back my smile. It was the truest thing I've ever said. Tonight, I believe, perhaps for the first time in years, that this is not fleeting. That she truly means to stay.

Reflections—Melanie

The room was dark except for the small lamp by the bed. Melanie sat against the pillows, hands folded loosely in her lap, staring at nothing in particular.

Andrew's voice still echoed in her heart, not the details

of what he'd said, but the way he'd said it. Carefully. As if afraid of breaking something precious.

So that's why, she thought softly. Not because he hadn't loved before…but because loving had cost him something and he'd lost hope. She pressed a hand to her chest. The ache she felt wasn't jealousy. It was something far gentler, compassion.

Victoria hadn't made her feel small after all. She had made her understand.

Andrew wasn't holding back because Melanie wasn't enough. He was holding back because he was afraid to hope.

Melanie closed her eyes. *I won't compete with his past,* she thought. *I'll simply be here in his present.* And for the first time since that unsettling encounter, her heart felt steady again.

Melanie curled beneath the quilt and thought back over the day. The market stalls bursting with color, the brush of his thumb against her cheek, the taste of strawberries lingering when he kissed her.

She could still see Andrew across the kitchen table, his hands folded around his teacup, the way his voice caught when he spoke of the woman who had married another.

Her heart ached for him. Not because of the lost chance, no, she thought fiercely, he dodged that bullet, but because of how deeply it had wounded him. To think of Andrew, dear, steady Andrew, carrying that belief that he wasn't enough… it almost broke her.

She replayed his words in her mind: *"I suppose I stopped believing anyone could want what I had to give."*

She turned onto her side, blinking back the sting in her eyes. *Oh, Andrew. If only you could see yourself the way I do. If only you knew how rare it is to find someone who listens as you do, who steadies a room simply by being in it. Someone who makes the ordinary feel precious.*

She smiled into the dark. *I love him. I never thought I'd have this again. Not at my age, not with my history. But here I am, cooking bread and jam with a man who makes me laugh until my eyes water and holding hands on ancient walls like a girl in love for the first time.*

The memory of his words echoed: *"You make it feel that way for me, too."*

Her heart swelled, the ache of missing him already beginning even though he was just in the next room. "I don't want this to end," she whispered into the stillness. And she meant it with every fiber of her being.

For the first time in years, she fell asleep not worrying about tomorrow but dreaming of it.

CHAPTER 55

The little pub Margaret had chosen sat on a quiet side street, its sign swinging gently in the breeze: The Black Swan. Inside, the air smelled of roast chicken and herbs, and the low murmur of voices gave the place an easy warmth.

Margaret was already at a corner table when they arrived, her scarf looped neatly around her neck, her shopping bag tucked at her side. She stood, kissed Andrew's cheek, then turned to Melanie with a smile that was both welcoming and sharp.

"Melanie," she said warmly, taking her hand. "So glad you could join us. I thought it was high time we had a proper chat again."

Melanie laughed softly. "So did I."

As they settled in, menus between them, Margaret wasted no time. "Now, Andrew here has been keeping you all to himself, and I think that's quite selfish. Don't you agree?"

Melanie's eyes sparkled as she glanced at Andrew, who

rolled his eyes with an air of long-suffering patience. "I can see you're very good at keeping him in line."

"Oh, someone has to," Margaret said briskly. "He's been far too serious all his life. Always with his books, his students, his journals. It's good to see him smiling again." She gave Melanie a pointed look.

Andrew muttered, "Here we go," but Melanie only squeezed his hand under the table.

The food arrived: roast chicken for Andrew, a hearty stew for Melanie, and a salad for Margaret. Conversation flowed easily, moving from the weather to stories of Andrew as a boy.

"Did he tell you about the time he tried to build a raft in the garden pond?" Margaret asked with a grin.

"I was ten," Andrew protested. "And it floated, for your information."

"For five seconds," Margaret said dryly. "Then you were waist-deep in mud, furious as a hornet."

Melanie laughed, picturing it. "I wish I'd known you then," she said softly, and Andrew's eyes warmed at the words.

Just then, a familiar voice boomed from the bar. "Andrew! I might have known you'd be here, hiding from me in broad daylight."

Andrew groaned, half-smiling as Nigel appeared, pint in hand. "Nigel, honestly..."

Nigel pulled up a chair with his usual easy grin, but something shifted when his eyes met Margaret's. It was brief, no more than a pause, a fraction of a second where his smile tightened and her expression sharpened in response, but it was there. He greeted her politely enough, even warmly, yet the warmth didn't quite reach his eyes.

Margaret inclined her head, cool and composed, her reply measured in a way that felt deliberate.

Conversation moved on quickly with Andrew saying something dry and Melanie laughing, but beneath the table, the air felt faintly altered, as though an old current had stirred and then been carefully smoothed back into place.

Melanie noticed it only because she was paying attention—the brief stillness between them, the way Nigel's smile didn't quite land and Margaret's reply came back carefully neutral. *What was that?* she wondered, just for a moment, before the clink of cutlery and the sound of Andrew and Nigel's voices drew her attention away again.

Nigel chuckled. "Look at you, Collins. Surrounded by two women who actually tolerate you. Never thought I'd see the day."

Melanie laughed, while Andrew rubbed his forehead, muttering, "Why do I put up with you?"

"Because you'd be boring without me," Nigel shot back. Then he leaned toward Melanie. "He's happier now, you know. Don't let him fool you. I've known him for decades, and this is the best I've seen him. So don't you dare leave him sulking back into his books."

Melanie reached for Andrew's hand again, her smile gentle. "Don't worry. I don't intend to."

For a moment, silence settled, warm and sure. Margaret's eyes softened, Nigel nodded in satisfaction, and Andrew's cheeks looked a little red, but his smile was steady.

After lunch, they walked back out into the sunshine, Andrew shook his head. "Well. That was... an ordeal."

Melanie slipped her arm through his, laughing. "It was

wonderful. They adore you, Andrew. And they're happy for you."

He glanced at her, his voice low. "They're happy for us."

And in that moment, Melanie felt like she had truly stepped into his world, not just beside him, but with him.

CHAPTER 56

That afternoon, the sunshine drew them back into the winding streets of York. Melanie slipped her arm through Andrew's as they strolled, her head turning this way and that to take in the crooked buildings and shop signs.

"What did you call these little alleys again?" Melanie asked, peering down a narrow passage between two timbered houses.

"Snickelways," Andrew said, his voice touched with amusement.

She stopped, laughing aloud. "Snickelways? That sounds like something out of a children's book! Like a path where fairies sneak about."

"Well," Andrew said, eyes twinkling, "it's not far off. They're little passageways, there's a tangle of them all across York. The name itself is a combination of snicket, ginnel, and alleyway. People have been ducking through them for centuries."

"Snickelways," Melanie repeated, savoring the word. "I

love it. Lead me through one, Andrew. I want to feel like I'm sneaking back in time."

He obliged, guiding her into one narrow lane where the buildings leaned so close together she could almost touch both sides with her hands. The stones beneath their feet were worn smooth, and the air carried the faint scent of baking from a nearby kitchen.

"It feels secret," she whispered, her voice hushed in the quiet.

Andrew nodded. "During the Middle Ages, these paths were shortcuts between streets and markets. Some of them haven't changed much since then. They're a bit of living history, hiding in plain sight."

Melanie tilted her head, her eyes soft. "I love how you know things like this. You make me notice the details I'd miss."

He glanced at her, touched. "And you remind me not to take them for granted."

At one particularly narrow turn, she stumbled slightly, her shoulder hitting against his chest. He caught her with a steadying hand, his arm slipping around her waist.

"Careful," he murmured.

"I think you just wanted an excuse to hold me," she teased, though her pulse quickened at his nearness.

His lips curved. "And if I did?"

She smiled, leaning in just enough to brush a quick kiss on his lips before pulling away with a laugh. "Then I'd say you're learning."

―――――

The rain had begun as a fine mist, so when Andrew

suggested they duck into York's Chocolate Story, Melanie brightened immediately.

"Ohhh," she said, her voice lilting with delight as she read the sign. "Now this is my kind of history."

Andrew's mouth quirked. "History you can eat."

Inside, the air was warm and rich, filled with the scent of cocoa and sugar. Display cases gleamed with wrappers and molds from centuries past, and guides in cheerful voices told the story of Rowntree's and Terry's, of how chocolate became York's legacy.

Melanie leaned closer to one of the displays. "Imagine, making entire fortunes out of sweets. If only my sweet tooth had known, it might have felt more justified."

Andrew chuckled. "I suspect your sweet tooth would have been their most loyal customer."

As the tour wound on, they sampled small pieces of chocolate. Melanie's eyes lit up at the first taste, dark and smooth on her tongue.

"Oh Andrew," she whispered, eyes half-closed. "That's heavenly."

He laughed softly, though his gaze lingered on her face more than on the chocolate. "I can't decide if you're enjoying the confection or torturing me."

She opened one eye and grinned. "Why not both?"

When the guide encouraged them to try blind-tasting different chocolates, Andrew looked skeptical but agreed. Melanie covered his eyes with her hand, her laughter bubbling as she fed him a piece.

"Well?" she prompted.

He chewed, thoughtful, then said, "High-quality milk chocolate, perhaps with a hint of caramel."

"Correct," Melanie said, impressed. "You really are a serious taster."

He arched an eyebrow. "Your turn."

She closed her eyes, and when he placed a piece carefully against her lips, she let it melt on her tongue. "Mmm... dark chocolate, orange zest?"

Andrew smiled, his voice softer now. "Exactly right."

The warmth between them seemed to deepen, sweet as the chocolate itself.

At the end, they lingered in the gift shop. Melanie picked up a small box of truffles, turning it in her hands. "I should bring these home for Emily and the children," she mused. Then she glanced up at him, her eyes dancing. "And perhaps another box... just for us."

Andrew slipped the second box into their basket without hesitation. "I'll consider it our Viking spoils," he teased.

She laughed, leaning into him. "The sweetest spoils of all."

Later, back at Andrew's flat, the world felt quieter again. They cooked together, a simple meal of pasta and vegetables, then settled at the small table with candles flickering softly between them as they ate their meal.

"Oh! Don't forget, we have chocolate," she said, holding up the small bag.

Andrew raised an eyebrow. "And tea. A combination unmatched in history."

He brewed a pot while she set the truffles out in their little gold foil cups, arranging them neatly on a plate.

Melanie bit into the first truffle with a soft sigh. "Oh, Andrew. This may be the best decision I've ever made."

He smirked, settling beside her on the sofa with his teacup. "Kissing me will rank a close second?"

She laughed, nudging him with her shoulder. "Cheeky." Then, quieter, she added, "But yes. Very close."

They ate slowly, savoring both the chocolates and the moment. At one point, Melanie held a piece toward him, her fingers brushing his lips as he took it. His gaze lingered on her hand, then on her eyes, the intimacy of the gesture settling warmly between them. She turned to him and kissed him, tasting the chocolate on his lips.

"You do realize," he murmured, "that I shall never again be able to eat chocolate without thinking of you."

She smiled, her voice soft. "Good. That's exactly how I want it."

When the truffles were gone, they moved to the sofa. Melanie curled against his side, her head resting easily against his shoulder. He kissed the top of her hair, and she closed her eyes, smiling. They sat back with their tea, her hand resting comfortably in his.

"This is what I want," she murmured.

"What is?" he asked softly.

She lifted her head just enough to meet his gaze. "Simple evenings like this with you."

He tightened his arm around her, his own voice quiet but steady. "Then they're yours. For as long as you'll have me."

The evening ended but continued, lingering and sweet, tasting faintly of chocolate and promise as they slept in each other's arms.

Reflections—Andrew

Day Three. Today was a collision of worlds, and I am surprised at how well it all fit together. Lunch with Margaret and Nigel, with the two of them ganging up on me was inevitable, and Melanie sitting there smiling, laughing, not the least bit put off. She slipped into the rhythm of it as if she'd always been part of the circle.

The Snickelways in the afternoon were... magical, in their way. She said the word sounded like fairies sneaking about, and I thought, of course she would hear it that way. I've walked those paths for years, but through her eyes they felt new again. She kissed my cheek in one narrow passage, quick as a spark. It astonishes me how something so fleeting can light me up inside as though it were a firework.

Tonight, at the table, she said this was what she wanted: simple evenings with me. I wanted to give her every evening I have left.

Reflections—Melanie

Melanie lay in bed, feeling the warmth of Andrew's arms around her, with the faint light from the streetlight slipping through the curtains. She thought of the day: Margaret's warm scrutiny, Nigel's boisterous teasing, Andrew's patience through it all. She had worried, just a little, about stepping into his world beyond the two of them. But what she found was acceptance. They could see how he smiled at her, how she smiled at him, and they welcomed her into it.

She had meant that quick kiss in the Snickelways playfully, but the look in his eyes afterward, steady and tender, as though it mattered more than she knew, had stayed with her all evening.

And then his words tonight, "Then they're yours. For as long as you'll have me."

She pressed a hand to her chest, her heart swelling. *For as long as I'll have you? Andrew, I'll want you always.*

With that truth circling warmly inside her, she drifted into sleep, smiling at the thought of tomorrow.

CHAPTER 57

They set out early, the car humming along the motorway as the morning sun lifted a soft haze from the hills. Melanie leaned against the window, watching the countryside unfold, fields stitched with stone walls, sheep grazing as though they'd been painted there centuries ago.

"It looks like a postcard," she said, her voice hushed with wonder.

Andrew chuckled, glancing at her. "The sheep or the walls?"

"All of it," she replied. "Though the sheep do seem very... English."

"They'd say the same about you," he teased.

She laughed, nudging his arm lightly. "I imagine they'd be quite confused. 'What's this American woman doing in our field?'"

"Probably wondering if you've brought snacks," Andrew said dryly.

As the road curved into the Lake District proper, the landscape shifted, the hills grew taller, the green deeper, dotted with wildflowers. Melanie gasped as they crested a rise and a stretch of water appeared below, gleaming silver in the sun.

"Andrew! Look at that."

He slowed slightly, his eyes softening at her excitement. "Windermere. England's largest natural lake."

"It's beautiful," she whispered. "Like something out of a storybook."

He smiled. "Poets thought so too. Wordsworth, Coleridge... half of English Romanticism came wandering these hills."

Melanie turned to him, eyes dancing. "And now me."

"And now you," he echoed, his voice carrying something deeper than jest.

They parked in a small village and walked down toward the water, the air cool and carrying the scent of damp earth and pine. Boats bobbed gently against wooden piers, and ducks waddled near the shoreline.

Melanie slipped her hand into Andrew's, her gaze sweeping the horizon. "It's so peaceful here. Like the world has slowed down just for us."

"Maybe it has," he murmured.

They wandered along the shore, stopping now and then to watch the water ripple or to laugh at a pair of ducks squabbling over crumbs.

At one point, Melanie bent to pick up a smooth pebble, pressing it into Andrew's palm. "A little souvenir. Put it in your pocket with the sea glass, two pieces of us, one from each shore."

Andrew closed his hand around it, his throat tight. "I'll keep it safe."

They followed a path up a small rise, where the view opened wide over the lake and the hills beyond. Melanie stood still, her eyes shining. "I wish I could paint. I'd never want to forget this."

Andrew studied her, the wind lifting strands of her hair. "You don't need paint. It's already in your face, the way you're looking at it."

She turned to him, surprised, and he flushed faintly, shrugging. "That's what I'll remember. You, looking at this. That will be enough for me."

The inn was low-ceilinged and warm, its beams dark with age, a fire crackling merrily in the hearth. They took a small table close to the flames, the smell of roasting meat and fresh bread making Melanie's stomach growl despite the late hour.

"This is exactly what I pictured an English inn would feel like," she said, running her hand along the polished table.

Andrew smiled. "You should try something hearty, then. Proper northern fare."

When the waitress arrived, Andrew ordered steak-and-ale pie for himself. Melanie scanned the menu and then, on impulse, looked up with a grin. "I'll try the Cumberland sausage. It sounds... adventurous."

Andrew chuckled. "Adventurous? It's just sausage, Melanie."

"Well, it sounds grander than the ones I grew up with,"

she teased. "Besides, it comes with mash and onion gravy. How could I resist?"

When the food arrived, Melanie's eyes widened at the size of the sausage curled on her plate. "Good heavens! Andrew, this is bigger than the skillet at home."

He laughed, the sound echoing warmly. "I did warn you before about hearty northern portions."

She took her first bite, then paused, her eyes brightening. "Oh. Oh, that's wonderful."

Andrew leaned back, pleased. "Consider yourself properly initiated."

The road unwound slowly out of the Lakes, rolling hills giving way to open stretches of green stitched together by stone walls and grazing sheep. Melanie watched it all like someone afraid to blink and miss a moment.

"It's like the countryside never ends. I don't think I'll ever tire of seeing stone walls and sheep." she murmured.

Andrew smiled. "This is still Yorkshire. We take our scenery seriously."

When the car dipped into Helmsley, Melanie leaned forward in her seat. The village seemed to appear out of a painting with warm stone buildings clustered around a small square, flower boxes bursting with color, narrow shopfronts tucked side by side.

"Oh, Andrew," she breathed. "It's lovely."

"Thought you might like it," he said casually, though he had clearly chosen it on purpose.

They wandered slowly through the square. Melanie paused at nearly every window—a bakery, a tiny stationery shop and a sweet shop that looked as though it hadn't changed in decades.

Andrew watched her more than the shops. There was something about the way she delighted in small things, not loud or exaggerated, just quietly enchanted, that tugged at him.

At the edge of the square, the ruins of Helmsley Castle rose behind an iron gate, worn stone against the pale afternoon sky.

Melanie stood still for a moment. "I can't believe places like this just... exist."

Andrew stepped closer beside her. "History everywhere here. It sneaks up on you."

She glanced at him, smiling. "I think that's why you belong here."

They walked on, stopping to share a small paper bag of warm scones from the bakery. Melanie laughed when crumbs dusted Andrew's coat sleeve, brushing them away.

They found a bench near the green and sat for a moment, the village humming quietly around them.

"I love how England feels," Melanie said softly. "It's slower. Gentler. Like people still notice things."

Andrew turned to her, heart tightening. "You notice things."

She smiled. "I'm glad you do too.

Then Andrew cleared his throat lightly. "Best head back before we lose the daylight."

Melanie nodded, rising with a lingering look around the square.

CHAPTER 58

Instead of fussing with dinner at the flat, Andrew pulled into a small shop with a sign reading Traditional Fish & Chips.

"A chippy," he explained as they stepped inside, the smell of fried batter and salt thick in the air.

"Chippy," Melanie repeated, wrinkling her nose with a smile. "Not chippie?"

"Depends on who you ask," Andrew said. "But either way, you're about to have the proper experience."

They carried the steaming paper-wrapped parcels back to his flat, unwrapping them on the table. Melanie's eyes widened at the golden slab of fish and the pile of thick-cut chips.

"This is for one person?" she asked, laughing.

"Consider it tradition to share," he said, spearing a chip with his fork and offering it to her.

She leaned forward, taking it with a grin. "Delicious. Greasy and perfect."

They ate side by side, fingers brushing as they reached for chips, laughter mingling with the clink of forks.

When the meal was nearly done, Melanie set her fork down and looked at him. "Andrew… what happens next?"

He stilled, then set his own fork aside, meeting her eyes. "You mean when you go back."

She nodded. "We can keep writing, calling. But the visits, how often? What about your life here, and mine there? I don't want to pretend this is easy."

He leaned back, thoughtful. "It isn't easy. But I know this much: I don't want to stop. I'd rather face the difficulty than go back to the silence before you."

Her throat tightened. "I feel the same. I want more days like this. More evenings like this."

He reached for her hand across the table, his voice steady. "Then we'll find a way. Whatever it takes."

Melanie smiled, squeezing his hand. "Whatever it takes."

<hr>

The table was cleared of their fish-and-chip papers, the lamps turned low. Andrew rummaged through a drawer in the sideboard and returned with a small leather-bound album. He sat beside Melanie on the sofa, their shoulders touching as he opened it.

"These," he said with a wry smile, "are the embarrassing years."

Melanie leaned closer, peering at the faded photographs: a boy with tousled dark hair, missing teeth, holding a fishing pole; another of him squinting in the sun beside a girl with the same sharp eyes.

"That's Margaret," Andrew said. "She bossed me from the time I could walk. Still does, really."

Melanie laughed softly. "You look so serious in this one."

"I was trying to look dignified," he said, mock solemn. "I believe I was seven."

"You look like you're about to lecture the photographer on grammar."

Andrew groaned, but his eyes twinkled. "I suppose some things never change."

They turned the pages slowly, Andrew offering stories of climbing trees, falling into the river, sneaking biscuits from the tin when he thought no one noticed. Melanie added her own tales, summers chasing fireflies in her grandmother's yard, the smell of lilacs through her bedroom window, the way her cousins teased her for always carrying a book. She'd not had any siblings, but her cousins Tom and Oliver had almost seemed like brothers.

Their laughter softened into silences, the kind that felt safe. At one point, Andrew moved a lock of hair from her face, his fingers lingering against her temple. She leaned in, kissing him softly, their lips lingering longer than before.

"I love hearing your stories," she whispered. "It makes me feel like I've always known you."

He swallowed, his voice low. "Perhaps you have. Maybe I was just here waiting for you all these years."

They kissed again, deeper this time, before she rested her head against his shoulder, the photo album still open across their laps.

When the clock chimed softly, Melanie rose, reluctant. "It's late."

They kissed once more, slow, sweet, lingering just long enough to make want become a feeling, before heading to bed.

Later, wrapped in the quiet of the flat, they found their way back to each other without words, not as a question but as something already understood, they loved each other.

Reflections—Andrew

Tonight we looked at photographs, the faded sort where the corners are bent and the colors are soft. She laughed at my missing teeth, teased me for my solemn seven-year-old frown, and listened to every story as though they mattered. And somehow, with her beside me, they did. My childhood has always felt like a collection of memories, nothing more. Tonight, telling them to her, it felt like a story worth keeping.

She told me of fireflies and lilacs, of summer evenings across the ocean, and I could picture it, her, small and bright, already carrying books in her arms. It makes me ache that I did not know her then. But perhaps we were meant to meet now, with all our histories behind us, ready to be shared.

When she said it felt as if she'd always known me... I believed her. And for the first time, I allowed myself to wonder if love, even now, can stitch two lives into one story. God help me, I think it can.

Reflections—Melanie

Melanie sat brushing her hair slowly, her heart full. The images of Andrew as a boy lingered in her mind, serious, mischievous, so unmistakably him. She had seen him as a man, steady and kind. Tonight, she saw the child he had once been, and it only deepened the tenderness she felt.

She thought of her own stories, how his eyes lit when she spoke of lilacs and fireflies. He hadn't laughed at her memories; he had treasured them. As though every piece of her life mattered because it was hers.

How did I find this, so late in life? And yet, how right it feels. As if we were only waiting for the right time, the right place, to find each other.

CHAPTER 59

The morning sun slanted through the blinds, casting pale stripes across the kitchen table. Melanie sat with her coffee, watching Andrew deftly move about the stove. The smell of sizzling bacon and toast filled the small space.

When he set the plates down, she blinked, amused. "This is your bacon?"

Andrew raised an eyebrow. "What's wrong with it?"

She picked up a piece, holding it between two fingers. "It's... wider. Floppier. In the States it's all thin and crisp. This looks more like ham."

"It's back bacon," Andrew explained. "Perfectly proper. None of your brittle shards."

Melanie laughed, taking a bite. She chewed thoughtfully, then grinned. "Okay. I'll admit, it's delicious. But I still think it looks like ham."

"Barbarian," he muttered into his tea, though the corners of his mouth curved upward.

She reached across the table, touching his hand lightly. "Don't worry, I'll adapt. For you."

His smile softened at that, his thumb brushing hers. "Then I suppose I can forgive your bacon heresy."

They lingered long after the plates were cleared, talking idly, about films they both loved, memories of schooldays and childhood summers. Andrew listened, chin propped on his hand, utterly absorbed in the way Melanie's face lit when she described running barefoot across wet grass after a thunderstorm.

"You have a gift for making ordinary things sound extraordinary," he said quietly.

"Or maybe I just know they are extraordinary," she replied. "Sometimes we only realize it when we look back."

He nodded, his expression thoughtful. "Perhaps that's why I've written so much over the years. To catch the ordinary before it slips away."

"Like this," Melanie said softly, gesturing to the table between them. "This is ordinary. And yet it feels like everything."

Andrew's gaze held hers, steady and full of meaning. "It does."

After breakfast, they moved to the sitting room. Melanie curled into the sofa with a book while Andrew settled beside her with his journal. From time to time, he'd reach absentmindedly to touch her hand. At one point she leaned her head against his shoulder, and he kissed the top of her head without a word.

It was quiet, but the kind of quiet that brimmed with peace, the rhythm of two people living not as guests in each other's company, but as if they belonged.

CHAPTER 60

The bell over the door of Hartland's Book & Brew gave a gentle chime as they stepped inside, and Melanie paused just long enough to take it in.

The shop was narrow and deep, shelves rising almost to the ceiling, their spines worn and loved. There were hand-written cards tucked between books — *Staff Favorite, Slow and Thoughtful, For Rainy Afternoons* and *When You Need a Laugh.* Somewhere deeper inside, the unmistakable scent of tea drifted out, warm and comforting.

"Oh," Melanie murmured, smiling. "This is dangerous."

Andrew chuckled. "I thought you might like it."

"I already do."

Behind the counter, a woman, her hair, henna-dyed brown shot through with copper, looked up from a stack of newly arrived paperbacks. She wore a scarf in shades of teal and rust, and her smile was immediate and genuine.

"Andrew," she said. "Back again? I was beginning to wonder."

"Impossible," he replied lightly. "I've brought someone I'd like you to meet. This is Melanie Brooks."

Eleanor's eyes warmed as she stepped forward, extending her hand. "Eleanor Hartland. Welcome."

"Melanie," she said, returning the handshake. "This place is absolutely lovely."

Eleanor laughed softly. "It grew that way on its own. I just keep the kettle on."

Melanie glanced around again, already drawn toward a shelf labelled *Letters, Lives, & Longings*. "Do you mind if I browse?"

"Please," Eleanor said. "That shelf is for people who linger."

Andrew smiled at them both. "I'll be over here pretending I'm not buying anything."

As Melanie traced her fingers along the spines, Eleanor joined her, gesturing toward a slim novel. "That one's been quietly brilliant. About starting over later than expected."

Melanie picked it up, reading the back. "I think we might have similar reading habits."

"I had a feeling," Eleanor said, amused. "Tea drinker?"

"Always."

"Dog-ear pages or bookmarks?"

"Bookmarks," Melanie replied. "Pressed flowers, if I can manage it."

Eleanor's smile widened. "Then we are definitely of the same tribe."

They shared a small laugh, easy and immediate.

"I run a book club here," Eleanor said after a moment. "Every other Thursday afternoon. Four or five of us usually, sometimes six if someone brings a friend. We talk books, drink too much tea, and wander off topic entirely."

"That sounds wonderful," Melanie said, and she meant it.

"You're welcome anytime," Eleanor added. "Even if

you're only in York for a little while. We meet today in about an hour, if you'd like to check us out."

Melanie hesitated, then smiled. "I'd love that. I'm not sure what we are doing next today, but I would love to."

Andrew looked up from the book he was examining. "I can drop you off here after our ice cream and I'll just do a few errands close by while you are here."

They left the bookshop with a small bag; Andrew insisted on buying her a poetry book, and wandered toward the park, where an ice cream cart stood near the gates.

"Now," Melanie said, studying the flavors painted on the board, "this is serious business."

Andrew smiled. "I'm a vanilla man myself. Reliable. Steady."

She gave him a mock look of scandal. "Vanilla? Andrew Collins, you surprise me. I would have pegged you for something bold. Rum raisin, perhaps."

"I'll have you know vanilla is classic," he said firmly, handing over coins for his cone. "Besides, it doesn't distract from the important bit, the ice cream itself."

Melanie considered, then chose mint chocolate chip. When she took her first bite, she closed her eyes with a sigh. "Perfect. Sweet and sharp all at once."

Andrew eyed her with a smile. "Just like you."

She laughed, nudging his arm as they strolled through the park, cones in hand. "You're learning flattery, Mr. Vanilla."

"Not flattery," he corrected gently. "Observation."

They found a bench beneath a spreading oak tree and sat side by side, watching children run across the grass.

Melanie reached over and swiped a bit of ice cream from his cone, licking it off her finger with a grin.

"Cheeky," he muttered, but his eyes were dancing.

Consider it a tax," she teased.

"Then I should have chosen chocolate," he said dryly, earning a laugh that made her lean into his shoulder as they ate.

The tearoom at the back of the shop felt like a small, carefully kept secret.

Melanie paused just inside the doorway, taking in the round wooden table, the mismatched chairs, the soft murmur of conversation. Afternoon light slanted in through the window, warming the china cups and the stack of books piled in the centre.

"There you are," Eleanor said, rising with a welcoming smile. "Come in...we're never terribly formal."

"That's a relief," Melanie said lightly. "I don't do formal very well."

Introductions followed with first names, kind smiles, the easy rhythm of women who enjoyed time together. Someone slid a chair back for her; another passed a plate of shortbread without ceremony.

They were talking about books that lingered long after the last page.

"The ones that feel like companions," one woman said. "You don't quite know how to let them go."

Melanie wrapped her hands around her teacup, listening for a moment before speaking. "I think the best ones make you feel braver," she said thoughtfully. "They remind you that starting over doesn't belong only to the young."

There were nods around the table. A soft murmur of agreement.

"Well said," Eleanor said, meeting her eye.

The conversation drifted gently, books, travel, quiet changes made later in life. Melanie found herself speaking more than she expected, laughing softly and listening closely. It felt comfortable.

At one point, someone mentioned a novel about a professor living in Boston, and Melanie smiled. "Sounds like my cousin Tom," she said. "He's a professor, lives in Boston and is very...well, very particular about books."

Eleanor glanced up, curious. "Oh?"

"He pretends not to like most of them," Melanie said with affection. "But the ones he does like, he *really* likes. He just doesn't advertise it."

A few of the women laughed.

"That sounds familiar," someone said.

Eleanor smiled too, but said nothing more, only tucked the name away, the way one does with interesting details that might matter later.

When Melanie eventually rose to leave, Eleanor walked her to the door.

"You're welcome anytime," she said warmly. "Even if you're only here for a short while."

Melanie hesitated, then smiled. "I hope it won't always be."

Eleanor held her gaze for a moment, thoughtful. "York has a way of keeping people," she said gently. "Especially the ones who notice it."

Melanie stepped out onto the street and lingered a moment there, adjusting the strap of her bag, feeling pleasantly full, of tea, of conversation and of the quiet sense of having belonged somewhere unexpected.

She spotted Andrew almost at once.

He stood a little apart from the flow of people, hands in his coat pockets, watching the street with patient familiarity. When he saw her, his face eased into a smile that felt private, as though the rest of York had gently blurred at the edges.

"There you are," he said as she reached him.

"There you are," she echoed, smiling back.

"Good timing," he added. "I've just finished what I needed to do."

She tilted her head. "Did you? All your very important errands?"

He huffed a quiet laugh. "Very important. Collected a parcel, posted a letter, and was reminded by the man at the counter that I look like someone who loses track of time."

"I can see that," Melanie said fondly. "I hope it wasn't too dull."

"Not at all," Andrew replied. "It felt... useful. And it gave me something to do while you were busy."

She fell into step beside him, the rhythm between them easy. "I'm glad," she said. "The book club was lovely. Warm. The kind of place you don't realize you're missing until you find it."

"I had a feeling you'd enjoy it," he said. "Eleanor has a knack for creating that sort of space."

"She really does," Melanie agreed. Then, after a beat, "I think I'd like to come back again sometime."

Andrew glanced at her, something quietly pleased in his expression. "I'd hoped you might say that."

They walked on together, holding hands again, the afternoon drawing gently toward evening.

CHAPTER 61

The table was simple, a board spread with slices of Wensleydale, sharp Cheddar, and that soft blue Andrew had insisted Melanie try during her first visit, alongside bunches of grapes, crisp apples, a loaf of bread, and thin savory crackers.

"It's beautiful," Melanie said as she settled into her chair. "Almost too pretty to eat."

"Then let's ruin it properly," Andrew said with a wry smile, cutting into the Cheddar.

They ate slowly, sipping tea, tasting and comparing. Melanie wrinkled her nose at the blue cheese but admitted it was better with fruit. Andrew teased her for piling strawberries on everything, which only made her laugh harder.

When the plates were half-cleared, Andrew grew quiet, his eyes softening. "I have something for you."

He reached into the drawer of the sideboard and returned with a small bottle of ink, Midnight Rose. He placed it gently into her hands.

"Remember this? You looked at it in the market on your first visit, and I went back for it.

Melanie blinked, her throat tight. She held the bottle and looked at the ink shimmering inside. "Andrew... I can't wait to write with it. Thank you."

Then she rose and fetched the small bag she had hidden in her suitcase. Returning to the table, she handed him a worn book.

"One of my favorites. I've read it more times than I can count. I thought you should have it. And..." She opened the cover, where a pressed lilac bloom lay flat against the page, tied with a ribbon. "This is from my garden at home. Lilacs always remind me of childhood, of safety, of beginnings. I wanted you to have a piece of my world."

Andrew's breath caught. He closed the book gently, as though it were fragile. "Melanie... I'll treasure this. Always."

They leaned across the table, their kiss slow, tender, full of unspoken promises.

"I love you," Melanie whispered.

"I love you, too," Andrew said, his voice steady and sure.

Later, as they sat together on the sofa, the weight of tomorrow pressed in, not as dread, but as necessity.

"What happens now?" Melanie asked softly. "When I go home again."

Andrew hesitated, his hands twining with hers. "We keep writing, calling, visiting. But Melanie... I don't want visits forever. I want more than weeks here and there. I want a life with you."

Her eyes filled, her chest aching. "I want that too. But how do we do it? Your life is here. Mine is there. I can't leave Emily and the children forever. And you shouldn't have to leave York."

He swallowed, his jaw tightening. "I thought... I thought perhaps we could make both places ours. Keep your home, keep my flat. Travel back and forth. Maybe four months at a time or something like that. A life that belongs to us in two places."

Melanie smiled through her tears, her heart soaring. "That sounds like us. Rooted, but free. Not either/or, but both."

Andrew leaned closer, his voice trembling just a little. "And perhaps, one day, we could make it official. Melanie... I've never asked this before, not of anyone. But with you, I want to. I want to marry you. I just don't know how to ask in a way that's worthy of what you mean to me."

She pressed her hands to his, her voice breaking with joy. "You just did, Andrew. And the answer is yes. Yes... thousand times yes."

Their kiss this time was longer, deeper, sealing not just love but the promise of a shared future.

Reflections—Andrew

Tonight I gave her a bottle of ink that I knew she wanted. She gave me a book she has loved until the pages nearly turned transparent, with a lilac pressed between them.

And then I said it, not polished, not grand, just the truth that had been waiting in my chest. That I wanted to marry her. I thought I was clumsy, but she answered before I had finished. Yes, she said. Yes, yes, yes. The sound of it is still ringing in me, like church bells after a wedding.

I am fifty-nine years old, and for the first time, I am beginning a life. Not half a life, not the life of a man folded in on himself. A life full and bright and shared. A life with Melanie.

Reflections—Melanie

Melanie sat in bed, the lilac scent lingering in her imagination, her fingers still tingling from Andrew's touch. She had kissed him goodnight softly, reluctantly, her heart so full it felt almost too much to bear.

He wanted to marry her. He had asked, not on bended knee, not with jewels or speeches, but with the truth of his heart. And she had said yes, because how could she not? Everything in her knew it already.

She thought of the bottle of ink resting on her nightstand, a gift from the man who had written his whole life into journals. Now, he was writing her into his future. And she thought of the look in his eyes when she gave him her book and her lilac, as if she had just given him the world.

She pressed a hand to her chest, whispering into the quiet: "Yes. Yes. Always yes."

And she fell asleep smiling, dreaming two homes, one in Boston and one in York with Andrew waiting at both doors.

CHAPTER 62

Andrew

The first thought in Andrew's mind when he woke was, *she said yes.* He lay still, staring at the ceiling, scarcely daring to move in case it all dissolved into dream. But no, the quiet hum of the flat was real, and so was the faint sound of Melanie in the next room. *She was here. She was his. His fiancée.*

He chuckled softly at the word, rolling it around in his mind like a secret jewel. He had never imagined using it. And yet, now that it belonged to him, to them, it felt inevitable.

He rose, pulling on a jumper, already smiling at the thought of seeing her at the table again, her hair tousled from sleep, her smile the brightest part of the room.

Melanie

She woke and lay there for a long moment, listening to the stillness, her heart full. She had said yes to Andrew, to the man who had restored her joy, who made her laugh over bacon and books and walks through crooked alley and to the man who kissed her as if he were writing a vow with his lips.

She stretched, smiling to herself. *Engaged. Me. At fifty-eight. Who would have thought? And yet it felt more right than anything she'd ever said yes to in her life.*

She rose, humming softly, to ready herself for the day.

Andrew was already at the table when she padded in, the kettle steaming. He looked up, his smile immediate. "Good morning, fiancée."

Melanie laughed, her cheeks warming. "Good morning, fiancé."

They both lingered over the words, as though trying them on for the first time.

Breakfast was simple, toast, jam, and the tea Andrew fussed over, but it stretched long with quiet conversation, shared smiles, and small touches. Melanie reached across now and then, covering his hand with hers, and Andrew kissed her knuckles without a thought.

Afterward, they moved about the flat in comfortable rhythm. Melanie folded the blanket on the sofa while Andrew watered the plants on the sill. At one point they found themselves side by side at the sink, washing and drying dishes.

"This feels… ordinary," Melanie said softly, handing him a plate.

"Do you mind?" Andrew asked.

"Not at all," she replied with a smile. "I think it's perfect."

They settled back in the sitting room, tea in hand, the clock ticking softly. For a while they simply enjoyed the quiet, but eventually Melanie looked at him with a half-smile.

"So…lunch. What do you suggest for our last full day?"

Andrew set down his cup, considering. "We could keep it simple. Something here. Or…" He hesitated, his eyes thoughtful. "We could go out. Somewhere nice. To mark the day."

She reached over, covering his hand with hers. "What do you want, Andrew?"

He smiled faintly. "Honestly? I just want to sit across from you one more time and commit every detail to memory. It doesn't matter where."

Her eyes softened. "Then let's choose somewhere that feels like us. Comfortable. Warm. Nothing fussy."

"Agreed," he murmured.

They chose a small café just off Stonegate, the kind of place where locals lingered over tea and scones. A corner table gave them a measure of privacy, though Melanie suspected Andrew would have spoken just as openly in the middle of the room.

Their food came quickly, soup and sandwiches, nothing grand, but they hardly noticed, too caught up in the conversation spilling between them.

"We'll have to tell everyone." Melanie said, stirring her soup absentmindedly. "Emily, Daniel and the children, and Margaret? And, of course, Nigel!"

Andrew smiled faintly. "My sister will pretend she's shocked, but she'll be secretly delighted. As for Nigel, God help us both when he hears. He'll insist on giving a toast immediately, probably with the nearest pint."

Melanie laughed. "Emily will cry. Happy tears, but she'll scold me for not telling her first. And the grandchildren...oh, Andrew, they'll be so excited. Jack will probably want to be best man."

"Then Nigel can be his assistant," Andrew quipped, eyes dancing.

They laughed together, then fell into softer talk about visas, travel, holidays spent in both York and Massachusetts. The practicalities were tangled, but instead of daunting them, it felt almost like planning an adventure.

"We'll keep both homes," Melanie said with quiet certainty. "Your flat. My house. We'll go back and forth, like the tides."

Andrew reached across the table, threading his fingers through hers. "Like the tides. That feels right."

After lunch, they strolled through the city, ducking into quiet lanes, their hands never parting. They spoke of seasons, Christmas in York with its markets and lights, spring in Massachusetts with the lilacs blooming. Melanie described Jack's baseball games; Andrew painted the picture of York's Minster bells ringing on a frosty morning.

It wasn't a blueprint. It was a weaving of their lives, their families, their futures laced together with laughter and promise.

At one point, Melanie stopped, her eyes brimming. "I thought I was done with all this...with dreaming...and now look at us."

Andrew squeezed her hand, his voice steady but thick with feeling. "We're just beginning, Melanie."

That evening, Andrew insisted on keeping things simple but special. He laid out a supper of roasted chicken, fresh bread, with a bottle of wine, and candles flickered on the table.

They lingered over the meal, toasting with quiet laughter, stealing kisses between bites. By the time the plates were cleared, Melanie was glowing from more than the wine.

Later, they settled on the sofa. Andrew drew her close, and she curled against him, their hands clasped, their laughter quieter now.

"I still can't believe it," Melanie whispered. "We're engaged."

Andrew kissed her hair. "Believe it. I've never been surer of anything in my life."

Their kisses grew longer, deeper, each one a promise sealed. There was no rush, no fear, only the joy of knowing they were each other's future.

That night was softer than the others—less about discovery and more about holding on, with love.

Reflections—Andrew

We spent the afternoon planning, if you can call it that. Not blueprints or timetables, but dreams woven together, Massachusetts in spring, York at Christmas, holidays split across oceans, children and grandchildren folded into both. It felt less like logistics and more like writing a new story, the two of us side by side, turning pages together.

Tonight, at supper, she laughed and teased me, and I

thought: this is my life now. When she called me "my love" at the door, I thought my heart might burst. My love. At my age, with all my doubts, to hear those words from her lips...

Tomorrow, she leaves.

Andrew let the sentence sit alone on the page.

And yet, this does not feel like loss.

He thought of the quiet of the evening, the way they had held each other without urgency, as though neither of them needed to prove anything now.

What we have is not fragile, he wrote. *It is simply not finished yet.*

That knowledge surprised him with its strength.

He had once believed that loving someone meant bracing for departure. That closeness inevitably led to absence.

Tonight, he understood something different. Love, he realized, could stretch.

Andrew closed the journal and turned off the light.

Tomorrow would be hard. But it would not be the end.

Reflections—Melanie

Melanie lay awake a little longer that night listening to him breath. She pressed a hand over her heart, smiling at the memory of Andrew's words, the way his eyes softened whenever he looked at her.

Engaged. The word seemed almost too big, too impossible, and yet it fit, as natural as breathing.

She remembered the way they had dreamed aloud in the café, his Minster bells, her lilacs, his Yorkshire winters, her Massachusetts springs. Not either/or, but both. Together. Always together.

Tomorrow would be hard. Saying goodbye always was. But tonight, she let herself hold only joy: Andrew's laughter over blue cheese, his hand closing firmly around hers, his whisper, *"Believe it. I've never been surer of anything in my life."*

CHAPTER 63

The flat was hushed that morning, the scent of tea and toast mingling with the sharpness of goodbyes waiting at the edges. Melanie sat across from Andrew at the kitchen table; her fingers wrapped around her cup.

"I don't want to keep doing this," she said softly. "The visits, the goodbyes. It hurts too much."

Andrew set down his toast, meeting her gaze. "I don't want it either. Last night, I lay awake thinking of you walking through that gate today. And I thought, why should we wait? Why not begin the rest now?"

Melanie's heart gave a leap. "You mean…"

"I mean let's marry sooner, not later," he said steadily. "Sort the paperwork, the visas, everything we need. Travel together, not apart."

For a moment, her throat tightened too much to answer. Then she reached across the table, taking his hand firmly. "Yes. Let's do it. I don't care about all the logistics. I care about being with you."

His fingers tightened around hers. "Then that's settled.

No more circling dates on calendars and counting the days apart. Next time, we'll face it together."

Tears shimmered in her eyes, but she was smiling. "Together."

The motorway unfurled beneath them, signs for Leeds, Manchester, Departures flashing past. Melanie leaned into the seat, her hand clasped tightly in Andrew's on the gearshift.

She tried to memorize it all: the countryside sliding past, the hum of the car, the warmth of his hand. He glanced at her now and then, his smile bittersweet.

"I hate that I'm driving you away," he murmured.

"You're not," she said, squeezing his hand. "You're driving me forward. To us."

The terminal buzzed with travelers, the hum of rolling luggage and the calls of departures over the loudspeaker. They stood close, their luggage a quiet sentinel at their sides.

Andrew smoothed a tear from her cheek, his thumb lingering. "This isn't the end, Melanie. It's the last time we'll say goodbye like this."

She nodded, her heart aching and soaring all at once. "The next time, it will be together."

He leaned down, kissing her deeply, heedless of the crowd. It wasn't a kiss of farewell, but of promise, steady and unshakable.

When they drew apart, her eyes shone. "I love you, Andrew."

"And I love you," he whispered. "Safe flight, my heart."

She turned toward the gate, glancing back only once, to see him standing tall, watching her walk away.

As she walked on, she thought, *This is not a goodbye. This is the beginning.*

And Andrew, watching her disappear into the crowd, thought the same.

Reflections—Andrew

The flat is quiet again. Her suitcase no longer by the door, her laughter no longer bouncing off the walls. But the silence does not feel the same as before. It feels like a pause, not an ending.

This morning, she said yes again, not only to me, but to the life we will build together. We will not circle dates forever. We will not live in the ache of partings. We will begin the rest now. Marriage, papers, visas and whatever else is required. She is mine, and I am hers, and the world will just have to rearrange itself around that truth.

At the airport, when she kissed me, it felt less like a goodbye and more like a promise written across my lips. The last farewell. The next time I stand in a terminal, it will be to travel with her, not to watch her walk away. That thought will keep me until she is back in my arms.

He opened her book—her book, now his, and began to read, the lilac bloom tucked inside as his reminder.

Reflections—Melanie

Melanie sat by the window, the clouds spread like cotton fields beneath her. Her hand still tingled where Andrew had held it, her lips still burned softly with his last kiss.

She closed her eyes, breathing deeply, holding on to every detail: the warmth of his flat, the smell of tea steeping, the way his hand had tightened around hers in the car.

It hurt, oh, how it hurt, to fly away from him. And yet for the first time, she did not feel as though she was leaving him behind. Instead, she carried him with her: in the fountain pen tucked into her bag, in the memory of his eyes when he asked her to marry him, in the certainty of a shared plan.

She smiled through her tears. *This is not the end. It's the last time it will be this way. Next time, I won't be flying back alone. Next time, Andrew will be beside me.*

Her heart steadied with that truth, the ache gentled by hope.

And as the plane carried her home, she whispered to herself, "Soon. We will be back together soon."

CHAPTER 64

Andrew

Andrew spotted her before he reached the end of the corridor. Melanie stood near the railing just beyond arrivals, hands clasped in front of her as if to steady her excitement. The overhead lights caught the silver in her hair, softening it into a quiet halo. When her eyes found him, her face lit in that warm, unmistakable way that had carried him across an ocean.

For a moment, he simply stopped.

All the noise of Logan airport faded behind the rush of his heart.

She stepped forward first, smiling through tears she didn't bother to hide.

"You're here," she whispered.

"I'm here," he replied, and gathered her into his arms.

The embrace was not tentative this time. It was full and certain, the kind that comes after distance has already proven love stronger than fear.

When they finally pulled back, Melanie laughed softly, still holding his hands.

"Welcome home."

Andrew looked at her, at the woman who had changed the course of his life simply by being brave enough to step toward him first. Home, he realized, was no longer a place on a map. It was wherever she stood.

Outside, Boston waited, her world, now theirs. In a few short days they would stand before family and friends and promise aloud what their hearts had already chosen.

But the truth was already settled between them, steady and unshakable.

Distance had ended and love had begun.

EPILOGUE

Andrew

*A*ndrew stood just inside the small side room of the chapel, fingers loosely clasped, heart thudding with a steadiness that surprised him. He had imagined nerves, but what he felt instead was an immense, grounding calm.

He could hear voices outside, and the soft scrape of chairs being adjusted. Nigel hovered nearby, straightening his tie for the third time.

"You're smiling," Nigel said, eyeing him. "Are you nervous?"

Andrew smiled wider. "Strangely enough, I don't feel like I am."

Nigel huffed. "Fair enough." He paused, glancing toward the doorway. "Your sister's arrived."

Andrew sighed with relief. "I'm glad she's here. I was afraid she wouldn't make it in time. Her flight was delayed."

"Oh, she's here. Magnificent, composed, and watching me like a hawk to see if I make a mistake," Nigel replied dryly. "So, yes. Entirely herself."

Andrew chuckled softly. He had noticed the tension in the past, the distance between them, and the way Margaret's eyes lingered on Nigel before flicking away. Something unresolved lived there, sharp as an old paper cut. Not today's concern, he reminded himself, though he suspected it would be someday.

Today was Melanie. He thought of her laugh, the way she tilted her head when she listened, and the quiet bravery it had taken for her to step onto a plane and change both their lives.

Nigel cleared his throat. "You ready?"

Andrew nodded. "I've never been more ready for anything."

Melanie

Melanie stood in the small side room with Emily, smoothing her hands over the simple ivory dress she had chosen. It wasn't elaborate, just... her.

"You look beautiful," Emily said, eyes shining. "Radiant, actually."

Melanie laughed softly. "I don't feel radiant. I feel... grounded."

Emily smiled. "That's even better."

Jack darted past the doorway, Sophie close behind. "Grandma!" Sophie whispered loudly. "You're getting married!"

"Yes," Melanie whispered back, laughing. "That is generally how this works."

Emily leaned closer. "He's good for you. You know that, right?"

Melanie met her daughter's eyes, emotion tightening her throat. "I do. And thank you... for letting me have this."

Emily shook her head. "You don't need permission anymore, Mom."

The music began and Melanie drew a breath.

This is my life, she thought. *And I am choosing it.*

Andrew

When she appeared at the end of the aisle, Andrew forgot how to breathe.

Melanie's gaze found his immediately, and the world narrowed to the space between them. She walked steadily, chin lifted, eyes bright with joy and certainty.

She chose me, he thought, wonder flooding him anew. *She chose this life with me.*

Nigel nudged him gently. "Close your mouth," he murmured. "You'll catch flies."

Andrew barely heard him.

Melanie

Andrew's eyes were damp when she reached him, and something in her chest loosened completely. This man, this quiet, thoughtful soul, had crossed an ocean for her.

She took his hands. "They're cold," she whispered.

"I'm terrified," he whispered back.

She smiled. "Good."

Andrew

Their vows were simple and honest.

"I promise to keep choosing you," Melanie said, voice steady. "Not out of obligation, but out of joy."

Andrew swallowed hard.

"I promise to be brave enough to stay," he replied. "To speak when fear tells me to be silent, and to love you without reservation."

When the officiant smiled and said, "You may kiss your bride," Andrew didn't hesitate, and applause rose around them.

Andrew caught sight of Margaret in the second row, dabbing at her eyes, and a few seats away, Nigel, standing straighter than usual, expression unreadable.

Melanie

The reception was held in a sunlit room just off the chapel, flowers on simple tables, and laughter spilling freely. Tom and Oliver were already arguing amiably about the quality of the cake.

"This is lemon," Oliver announced. "You hate lemon."

"I don't hate lemon," Tom protested. "I merely distrust it."

Margaret stood near the window, listening.

Melanie walked over to her, "Have you met my cousins Tom and Oliver yet? Tom will be spending time in York soon on an academic sabbatical."

Margaret turned, appraising him with calm intelligence. "York is the perfect place for that."

As she spoke politely with Tom, and then Oliver, Nigel

stood a few feet away, clearly listening but also avoiding conversation that included her.

Melanie noticed and leaned toward Andrew. "Something is going on there between those two."

Andrew sighed softly. "Yes. I've noticed that but haven't wanted to interfere."

Melanie smiled. "Wise for the moment."

Emily clinked a glass, drawing their attention back to the reception. "A toast!"

As the evening wound down, Andrew pulled her into a slow dance, just swaying, her head resting against his shoulder.

"I never thought I'd get this," she murmured.

"Nor I," he replied. "But I'm very glad we didn't stop believing."

Melanie kicked off her shoes by the door and laughed softly.

"Well," she said. "That happened."

Andrew smiled, loosening his tie. "It did."

They stood for a moment, just looking at each other, as if neither quite wanted to break the spell by moving too quickly.

Melanie reached out first, resting her hands on his chest. "Are you all right?"

He covered her hands with his own. "I've never been better."

They moved to the small sitting room and sat together on the sofa.

"I keep thinking," Melanie said quietly, "about that first email you sent me...about pudding."

Andrew laughed. "An inspired opening, I thought."

"It was," she said. "I almost didn't reply."

His smile faded just slightly. "I'm very glad you did."

She studied his face. "So am I."

Andrew leaned his forehead against hers. "You crossed an ocean for me."

She shook her head gently. "We crossed it together."

After a moment, Andrew said softly, "You know... I spent a long time thinking love was something you missed your chance at...like a train you don't board in time."

"And now?" Melanie asked.

"And now," he said, kissing her temple, "I think it waits for you to be ready."

She smiled, eyes shining. "Good. Because I'm very ready."

As they sat there, wrapped in the certainty of what they had chosen, and the quiet promise of what came next, just two people who had finally stopped holding back, Melanie knew that this was not the end of a story. It was the beginning of a life.

Some journeys don't begin with a plan...but with a single decision to go. As Tom Laurent leaves Boston for York, England, he has no way of knowing that this is where his story will truly begin.

Discover what happens in my full-length novel:

Where the Light Lingers

Book Two of The Lives We Choose series.

For details, visit my website:

www.lizbrownbooks.com

ABOUT THE AUTHOR

Liz Brown writes cozy, heartwarming romance about second chances, meaningful journeys, and love that grows stronger with time. Her stories often celebrate later-in-life romance, exploring connection across distance, the comfort of home, and the courage it takes to begin again.

Inspired by travel, small towns, and the quiet moments that shape a life, Liz creates character-driven novels filled with warmth, humor, and hope.

She lives in Maine, where she writes with a favorite fountain pen nearby and far too many books within reach. When she isn't writing, she enjoys visiting England, collecting story ideas, and imagining the next chapter for her characters.

www.lizbrownbooks.com

instagram.com/lizbrownauthor
facebook.com/lizbrownauthor
tiktok.com/@lizbrownauthor